Praise for Elizabe...

The Queen's Head

"Humor and suspense are cleverly interplayed, but the novel's best feature is the reality with which the people and the period are brought to life."

—*Booklist*

The Merry Devils

"A believable, satisfying mystery, colorfully costumed and staged, with a bawdy, raffish, and utterly amiable cast."

—*Publishers Weekly*

The Trip to Jerusalem

"The plot moves briskly as a mystery, [and] the detail gives the book a fascinating array of colors."

—*Chicago Tribune*

The Nine Giants

"Rich in background color, language, and vivid characters . . . Marston has another winner here."

—*Kirkus Reviews*

The Mad Courtesan

"Riotous . . . The tragedies being performed onstage pale in comparison to all the blood and thunder offstage."

—*The Washington Post Book World*

Also by Edward Marston
Published by Ballantine Books:

THE QUEEN'S HEAD
THE MERRY DEVILS
THE TRIP TO JERUSALEM
THE NINE GIANTS
THE MAD COURTESAN

THE WOLVES OF SAVERNAKE

Edward Marston

FAWCETT CREST • NEW YORK

A Fawcett Crest Book
Published by Ballantine Books
Copyright © 1993 by Edward Marston

Library of Congress Catalog Card Number: 93-25419

ISBN 0-449-22310-8

This edition published by arrangement with St. Martin's Press, Inc.

Manufactured in the United States of America

First Ballantine Books Edition: May 1995

10 9 8 7 6 5 4 3 2 1

To
Brother George Witte
of the
Abbey of Saint Martin
MISERICORDIAS DOMINI

This is the twentieth year of William, King of the English. At his orders a description of all England was made this year in the fields of the various provinces, in the holdings of the various lords, in their fields, in houses, in men both bond and free, both in those living only in cottages and in those having houses and fields, in ploughs, in horses and other beasts, in the service and rent of the land of all. . . . The country was troubled with many disasters arising from the collection of royal finances.

Robert Losinga
Bishop of Hereford
1086

"Beware of false prophets, which come to you in sheep's clothing, but inwardly they are ravening wolves. . . ."

The Gospel According to St. Matthew

WILTSHIRE IN 1086

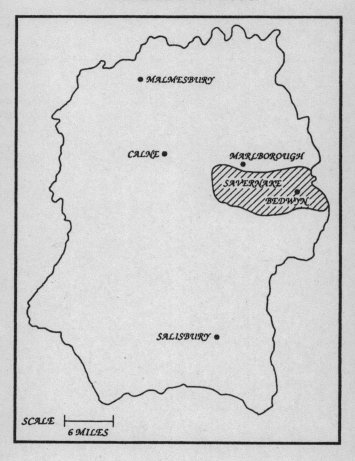

MALMESBURY

CALNE

MARLBOROUGH

SAVERNAKE

BEDWYN

SALISBURY

SCALE

6 MILES

Prologue

SAVERNAKE FOREST TREMBLED IN THE FADING LIGHT. A cool breeze came out of nowhere to whistle through its undergrowth, to rustle its leaves, and to make its boughs genuflect fearfully towards the heavens. The sun was falling slowly into the seductive embrace of the horizon and only a few last rays were left to probe through the fretwork of branches and to conjure shapes out of the gathering gloom. When the breeze stiffened, the whole forest shivered with a pale fear. On a warm summer evening with its trees in full leaf, its grass thrusting forth in unchecked profusion, and its shrubs at their most riotous, it stood silhouetted against the watchful quietness of the sky and felt the icy touch of premonition.

The crouching figure who moved quickly and furtively along the river-bank paid no heed when birch and oak and ash came to life to bend and whisper all around him. He was a creature of the forest and knew its whims and wilfulness of old. When a weeping willow dived angrily downwards to sweep the ground then thresh it with violent malice, the man did not even lift his eyes. Alric Longdon was a miller, one of eight in the area, a low, squat, round-shouldered man of forty or more with a compact strength in his hunched frame and a face as big, white, and plain as a sack of his own flour. He was carrying something in his hand and scurried along with a stealth born of long acquaintance with Savernake. Tied to the river for his livelihood, married indissolubly to the swift current of this

1

tributary of the Kennet, he listened to the restless surge and followed water to his destination.

A noise made him halt in his tracks. It was the resounding hiss of bracken being trampled by heavy feet. Longdon froze. Savernake was a royal forest and subject to forest law. King William protected his hunting grounds with a savagery such as the miller had never known under Saxon rule. Longdon was already trespassing. If he was caught by a keeper or a verderer, he would be beaten or fined or both. If the court decided he was poaching, Longdon could be blinded or castrated. His free hand went to his eyes to guard them against the unthinkable, then it travelled down to his groin to cover it against the unbearable. The miller had a young and beautiful wife who satisfied his lust without complaint and who lay beneath his sweating nakedness with gentle obedience. He would not surrender his manhood for a walk in the forest. Better to kill than to be cut down to such humiliation. His hand tightened on the dagger in his belt.

But his alarm was unnecessary. There was a wild flurry of movement in the bracken, then hooves pummelled the earth. Whatever had been approaching him, it was no forest official with a warrant to enforce the law. The animal was even more frightened than he and took flight as soon as it caught his scent. Alric Longdon continued on his way. He then turned off the river, following to its source a rippling stream that fed into it. As he climbed steadily upwards, he saw the water cut deep into the chalk. It vanished briefly below ground and became a gurgling echo. It surfaced once more and twisted back down towards him through its narrowing banks with playful urgency.

Savernake was not continuous forest. It was a vast acreage to the north of the county, a series of straggling woods and coppices, linked by areas of heath and gorse and downland which might themselves be dappled with timber or criss-crossed with hedgerow. Red and fallow deer were the favoured prey of the king and the herds needed trees in which to hide and open spaces in which to forage. Hunters

2

required paths along which they could gallop, glades where they could rest, and fields where they could run down their quarry. Savernake was a great, rich, rambling, and largely uncultivated wilderness that was teeming with animal life to provide royal sport for the royal personage.

Alric Longdon was now in light woodland, tracing the serpentine writhing of the stream and blending happily with the foliage in the half-darkness. He was safe. No keeper would find him here in his secret territory. He knew his way by instinct. The water swirled capriciously in a semi-circle, then it took him farther up the hill before it disappeared below ground again. Longdon stopped, felt the leather pouch he was holding, then knelt beside a withered yew. Blasted with age and split by lightning, it stooped over the stream at the point where it issued forth from its subterranean cavern. The tree was skirted by moss and swathed in so much bindweed that it looked as if its huge, gaping wound had been bandaged to stop the crevice from widening. The miller stroked the yew as if welcoming an old friend.

Another sound disturbed him and caused him to look up. But it was only a bird, startled by his presence and taking to the air through the branches with a vigorous flapping of its wings. Alric Longdon laughed silently. He thought of his mill, his wife, his welcoming bed. He thought of his cunning scheme and his hopes of good fortune. He thought of Savernake and its eternal mysteries. He thought of his most favourite place in the whole forest. His lips were still curled in a smile when the bushes nearby parted abruptly.

Black eyes glared at him, teeth glinted, and a low growl set his hair on end. Longdon tried to scramble up, but he was far too slow. Before the first scream of horror could reach his mouth, he was knocked over backwards and his throat was eaten away in one vicious, all-consuming bite. His head, his shoulders, and his leather bag were submerged in the stream that had led him to his death. Blood gushed out of him and darkened the water, forming a long red slick that was carried along with increasing force through the woodland. As it joined the river and met the main current, it was borne along on the surface like a stain on nature itself. Alric Longdon lay dead beside a yew tree in Savernake Forest while a part of his being raced towards the biggest mill in the valley.

His soft-eyed young wife was sitting patiently in her kitchen, awaiting the return of her husband. There was food on the table for him and submission in her heart. The mill was a clamorous homestead. As the massive wooden wheel went on its ear-splitting round over and over again, dipping and rising endlessly through the foaming water, it never occurred to her that the man she had married was helping to turn it with his life-blood.

Chapter One

THEY HAD TRAVELLED WELL OVER TEN MILES BEFORE THE
madness seized him. One minute, he was riding at the
head of the little cavalcade, talking amiably with his companions and enjoying the unhurried progress across Salisbury Plain; the next, he went completely berserk. Letting
out a blood-curdling cry, he dug his heels into the flank of
his mount and rode hell-for-leather up the grassy incline
ahead. Mantle streaming behind him and one hand aloft
with a sword in its grasp, he charged at an invisible enemy
and terrified them into immobility with the fury of his attack. Ralph Delchard was half a mile away before he reined
in his horse on the crest of the rise. He gazed at something
in the distance and waved his sword in salute. A Norman
lord with position and age that should bring dignity was be-
having like an impetuous young soldier in his first battle.
As the others trotted slowly in his wake, they could hear his
ripe laughter echoing across the plain. Was this drunken-
ness or sheer lunacy?

Gervase Bret was the first to catch him up. His honest
face was crumpled with apprehension. Ralph was a friend,
a mentor, almost a father to him. A son does not expect
such wild abandon in a revered parent. Perhaps it was the
fault of the animal. It had taken its master unawares and
bolted. One glance at the grinning Ralph Delchard disposed
of this theory. He was one of the supreme horsemen in the
service of the Conqueror. Not for him the small, sturdy,
compliant English mounts that most of them rode. Certainly
not the braying donkey that Canon Hubert sat astride.

Ralph was in the saddle of his destrier, a Norman steed with a high Norman temper, a big, fiery war-horse which had been trained for action in the field and which would gallop on command through the mouth of hell itself without losing its stride.

"What ails you, Ralph?" asked Gervase.

"I wanted to feel the blood race in my veins."

"You frightened us."

"We needed some exercise," said Ralph, slapping the neck of his stallion with an affectionate palm. "And we wanted to see it first."

"See what?"

"Wait for the others, Gervase."

"But what did you see?"

"Wait, wait . . ."

Canon Hubert coaxed a final spurt out of the donkey with his chubby legs and joined the two men. Like Gervase, he was some yards short of the summit and his view ahead was blocked by the ample frame of Ralph Delchard. Righteous indignation turned the prelate's fat cheeks to the colour of plums. He waved an admonitory finger and put severe reproach into his voice.

"Have you run mad?" he demanded.

"Only with joy," said Ralph.

"You are here to guide and protect me, not to desert me in open country where thieves might lurk."

"No man would dare to lift a hand against you, Canon Hubert," said Ralph with amusement. "Seated upon that fine beast, you look like Christ Himself riding into Jerusalem."

"That is blasphemy!"

"It is a compliment."

"Beware of a wicked tongue."

"I speak but as I find. Besides," added Ralph, "you had no need to fear. With one man gone, you still had six left to throw a ring of steel around you." He indicated the other riders, who had now reached them. "Seven of you in all,

Canon Hubert. That is a good, round, comforting biblical number."

The prelate blustered, the donkey brayed, Ralph chuckled. Gervase Bret found smooth words once more to calm the upset. It was not the first time that Ralph Delchard had teased the short, plump, pompous canon, and it fell to the youngest member of the group to reconcile them. A sense of duty was finally restored to the expedition. An uneasy companionship was resumed.

They were eight in number. Ralph Delchard was leader of the commission, a proud, sometimes arrogant, and always strong-willed character with the rough handsomeness of a man of action. The adipose Canon Hubert of Winchester, a solemn soul with an acute mind, gave the company its spiritual weight, and his emaciated assistant, Brother Simon, a white wraith in a black cowl, lent his own spectral religiosity. Gervase Bret was the real force in the party, a shrewd and brilliant lawyer of little more than five and twenty who had risen to a high position as a Chancery clerk and who had been selected for this assignment by the king himself. Slight of build and of medium height, Gervase had a studious air that belied his capacity to defend himself against physical attack. His short dark hair framed a face that had a boyish appeal behind its keen intelligence. Four men-at-arms accompanied the commissioners, picked by Ralph from his own retinue to provide good humour on the journey as well as to enforce its purpose. Two pack-horses were towed in the rear. Ralph Delchard wore mantle, tunic, and cap of a cut and quality which marked his status, but his soldiers were in matching helm and hauberk. All of them were skilled with a sword and two of them proficient with the bows that were slung across their backs. Safety had been ensured on the journey. Any robbers would be deterred by the sight of so much expertise.

Canon Hubert had recovered his composure.

"Have you taken leave of your senses?" he enquired.

Ralph shook his head. "My senses bid me ride off."

"But why?"

7

"He wanted to see something," explained Gervase.

"See what? See where?"

Ralph Delchard tugged on his reins to pull his horse out of their line of vision. He flung out an arm to gesture at the landscape ahead and drank in its marvel anew.

"Come forward," he beckoned. "And behold!"

They nudged their animals the last few yards up the incline so that they were able to survey the prospect below. Then they gaped. Gervase Bret was frankly astonished. Canon Hubert was just as frankly horrified. Brother Simon blanched with apprehension and began to mumble a prayer. The soldiers had seen it before, but they were still impressed and bemused afresh. Even the donkey was cowed into silence.

What they saw was so stirring and remarkable that it shook them to the core. They were in the presence of sheer magic. Salisbury Plain stretched away before them in its crushing enormity, but it was no flat and featureless expanse of land. It rose and fell like the waves of the sea, surging and retreating, billowing and dying, forever changing shape and colour as the clouds scudded across the sky to obscure the sun before allowing it to filter through again and paint its vivid hues upon the earth once more. As a gust of wind set the grass and the scrub in motion, it seemed as if the waves were dancing with crazed delight.

But there in the middle, unmoved and majestic, awesome in its scope and unnerving in its certainty, was an island of defiance. Concentric circles of gigantic stones were enclosed within a much wider circle of chalk rubble which was banked up to a height of six feet or more and fronted by a deep ditch. The earthwork was broken by a broad gap on the north-east side and there were smaller gashes elsewhere. A hundred feet inside this rampart was the first circle of stones, some thirty in total, massive uprights which were topped by an almost continuous line of lintels. A few had been displaced and had crashed to the ground, gouging out a new home for their troublesome bulk. The huge blocks were carved from natural sandstone and all dressed to shape.

Within this imposing circle was a smaller, tighter bluestone circle, incomplete and largely in ruin. Uprights lay at curious angles. Discarded lintels burrowed into the ground. Some of the rock looked as if it had just been hewn from its source and not yet cut to shape. There was also a horseshoe of even bigger sandstone blocks, inside which a bluestone horseshoe had been erected with uprights that increased in height towards the centre. It was a sight so unexpected in such a setting, a sign of life in a seeming void, a mysterious order in a place of chaos. Time had attacked it viciously, but its primitive power remained. What hit the onlookers most was this sense of hideous permanence.

Canon Hubert could bear to view it no longer.

"Let us ride on," he insisted.

"But I had to show you Stonehenge," said Ralph.

"It is the work of the Devil."

"So is our king," reminded the other mischievously. "His father, the duke, was of that name: Robert the Devil. If we serve William, we serve the Devil through him."

"Take us away from here," said Hubert querulously. "It is a place of damnation."

"No," said Gervase, still excited, still absorbed, still running an eye to count the stones and trace their patterns. "Truly, it is a place of worship."

"Worship!"

"Yes, Canon Hubert. Worship of what and by whom I may not tell. But there is purpose down there on the plain. There is homage. There is sacrifice."

"To Satan himself!"

The prelate now took refuge in prayer and the donkey shifted restlessly beneath his holy burden. Brother Simon was torn between fear and fascination, joining his master in appealing to heaven while sneaking an occasional glance back at this miracle in stone. The soldiers were intrigued but warily so, as if sensing a hostility in the weird formations below them. When Ralph and Gervase elected to take

9

a closer look at the phenomenon, none of the men was keen to go with them. Ignoring the loud protests of Canon Hubert and the feeble bleating of Brother Simon, the two friends set off at a canter across almost a mile of undulating plain.

Stonehenge was even more daunting at close quarters, but the couple rode right into the heart of it. They noted the pits in the ground at regular intervals and the small white circles on its surface where the chalk had been exposed. But it was the stones themselves which intrigued them. Ralph Delchard and Gervase Bret felt like insects walking through a range of mountains. Solid rock dwarfed them to insignificance. When they had set out from Winchester, they had seen masons swarming over the half-built cathedral and hoisting up their stone with strong ropes. At Salisbury, too, they had witnessed much activity on the castle walls as they were extended and strengthened with Norman thoroughness. Nothing seen then could compare with this. The largest blocks used in cathedral or castle were only a fraction of the size and weight of the colossal uprights.

Gervase Bret still felt it was consecrated ground.

"We are in a temple," he said simply. "An ancient temple. But who built it, Ralph? And *why*?"

"That is not my question, Gervase. I ask only—*how*?"

"How?"

"These sarsens are sandstone," said Ralph, pointing to the uprights. "They come from the Marlborough Downs some twenty miles north at least. What hands could lift such boulders? What beasts could drag them all the way here?"

"And that bluestone," observed Gervase. "It varies in colour. I have seen nothing like it before."

"They say there are mountains of that hue in Wales. And how far distant is that? It would take a week to bring back a bag of pebbles from that wilderness. To drag just one of these bluestones would take a lifetime." He turned to look up at the six figures on the distant ridge and picked out the one on the donkey. "Canon Hubert may be right. The Devil may have been the stonemason here."

"No," said his friend. "I feel a power here, but it is not unfriendly. It carries a blessing."

"Then let it wish us God-speed!" Ralph's mood changed abruptly. "There is no more time to linger. We must collect the others and ride north towards Bedwyn. They expect us."

Expectation did not put a smile on the face of the town. Rather did it spread doubt, suspicion, and quiet panic. The commissioners had already visited Bedwyn once and subjected it to such a rigorous examination that its citizens felt they were facing the Last Judgement itself. Here, as throughout the whole realm, the investigation which had been decreed by King William probed so remorselessly into what everyone owned, for how long they had owned it, and from whom they had first acquired it, that it took on the character of the final reckoning. The Conqueror himself might call it a description of all England, but the name which was muttered with cold irony in the shires was the Domesday Book.

Bedwyn was a prosperous community with well over seven hundred inhabitants living in or close to the town. Its verdant meadow was strung along the water-fed valley floor and its crops usually flourished even in periods of drought. Trades thrived and commerce was developing. Situated close to the northern border of the old kingdom of Wessex, it had been sufficiently important in Saxon times to be chosen as the site for a royal mint. Savernake Forest enveloped it on three sides, but that brought advantage as well as setback. Bedwyn was an attractive town in which to live until the dark shadow of the Domesday Book fell across it.

"When will they arrive?"

"This evening, Father Abbot."

"How long will they stay?"

"Until they have concluded their business."

"What is its nature?"

"We do not know."

11

"Why did they choose Bedwyn?"

"We can but guess, Father Abbot."

"Where else have they visited?"

"This town is the sole object of their journey."

Abbot Serlo sighed. He did not like this disturbing news. A man who heard angels sing whenever he knelt to pray did not want the sound of discord in his ears. Advanced in years and destined for sainthood, Abbot Serlo and his life of piety would so soon be recorded in the celestial ledger and they needed no overzealous clerk to set them down once more in its earthly counterpart. Serlo was a big man of generous proportions with an unforced holiness. He had a kind, round face and a high forehead, but his most arresting feature was a pair of eyes that seemed to start out of their sockets like two eggs about to leave matching ovipositors. Whatever he had seen on the road to his personal Damascus, it had clearly made a deep and lasting impression.

"Prior Baldwin . . ."

"Yes, Father Abbot?"

"I have need of your help."

"It is always at your disposal."

"Meet with the commissioners."

"I will know their purpose as soon as I may."

"Inform them that I have important duties here in the abbey and not much time left in which to fulfil them. I hope to survive for another year—*Deo volente*—and there is much that will be left unattempted."

"You have been a beacon to us all, Father Abbot."

"I think that I have done my duty."

"It has been a mission, accomplished with Christian love and dedication. Bedwyn Abbey will forever be in your debt. Such service can never be repaid in human coinage. Your reward awaits you in heaven."

Prior Baldwin bowed gently. A tall, spare, ascetic man, he was ten years younger than Abbot Serlo and several stone lighter. Both of them had been plucked from the Abbey of Caen at the express wish of the Conqueror. The Battle of Hastings had not just replaced a Saxon king with a Duke of Normandy. It had given England a new nobility and a new church. In 1066, there had been thirty-five independent Benedictine houses in the country, all with Saxon abbots and Saxon monks. William steadily supplanted the higher reaches of the monastic and the secular clergy with Norman prelates. Abbot Serlo was amongst the first to be translated to his new ministry because his predecessor, Abbot Godric, always an impulsive man, had rashly answered King Harold's call to arms and been cut down at Hastings in the first charge.

Serlo was a wise choice for Bedwyn Abbey. His high learning and his administrative skills soon won the respect of his house. He not only rebuilt the abbey church, he kindled a new spirit of devotion among his obedientiaries. Other foundations were less fortunate in their new abbots. Turold from Fécamp was a combative soldier of God who subjected the monks at Malmesbury, then at Peterborough, to a regime of military harshness. Abbot Thurstan of Glastonbury had been a contemporary of Serlo at Caen, but he brought nothing like the same moral probity to bear on his actions. So cruelly and tyrannically did Thurstan treat his poor monks that he provoked a scandal. The community over which Serlo presided could make no such complaint. Their abbot was universally honoured and loved.

"I have had my victories, modest though they be," said Abbot Serlo, "but I know my limitations. My work is God's work. I would be spared interruption."

"And so you shall, Father Abbot."

"You know how to be politic, Prior Baldwin. Tell them what has to be told. Show them what has to be shown."

"I will represent you in this matter."

"My faith in you is unquestioning."

"You flatter my poor abilities."

"I have appreciated them these thirty years," said Abbot Serlo, leaning forward to turn the full beam of his protruding eyes upon the prior. "Give them only what they ask.

Send them quickly on their way. We want no more taxes to cripple our house and its good offices."

Prior Baldwin bowed again and turned to leave the abbot's lodging. The audience was over and he had been given the instructions he sought. His shrewd and agile mind had dealt with the first commissioners. A second visitation posed no problems for someone so well versed in his duties and so well informed about every aspect of the monastic income. He remembered a last question and turned once more to face the startling blue eyes, but the words never even formed in his mouth. Before he could even begin to raise the matter of the cellarer's accounts, there was a thunderous knocking on the door and it was flung wide open without invitation. A young novice came hurtling into the room and slid to a halt before his abbot. The boy's anxious face was positively glistening with sweat and his breathing was laboured. Evidently, he had run very far and very fast and his bare ankles were spattered with mud.

"Brother Luke!" scolded the prior.

"I beg . . . apology," gulped the novice.

"This is most unseemly conduct."

"It must have a reason," said Abbot Serlo indulgently. "Do not rush, my son. Catch your breath and tell me what that reason is when you are able to recall it."

The novice wrestled with his exhaustion and put enough air into his lungs to gabble out his news.

"Alric Longdon has been found in the forest. They are bringing him back now."

Serlo was alarmed. "Is the miller injured?"

"How stands it, Brother Luke?" asked the prior eagerly.

The boy burst into tears at the misery of his tale.

"Alric Longdon is dead. He was killed by a wolf."

They arrived in Bedwyn as the sky was beginning to darken. The long ride had been tiring, but it offered beauties of nature at every stage. They ascended the pleasant river valley of the Avon until they reached the small town of Pewsey, where they broke for refreshment. Climbing up

14

onto a plateau that was marked by chalk hills which rose to a height of a thousand feet, they proceeded on their way until they came down into another fertile river valley. Villagers along the route were not pleased to see them. The sight of Norman soldiers always produced hatred and resentment. After twenty years of rule, King William and his men were still regarded by native Saxons as usurping foreigners.

There was another reason why the embassy was despised.

"God has punished them hard already," explained Gervase Bret in tones of sympathy. "They are afraid that we have come to tax them even more."

"We have," said Ralph Delchard crisply.

"Last year, the harvest was ruined. This year, there have been famine and starvation. Wiltshire has not fared as badly as some shires, but there are still many empty bellies here." Gervase glanced over his shoulder at the portly Canon Hubert and lowered his voice. "A well-fed Norman prelate with soldiers at his back will not win friends among the hungry."

"Hubert will not win friends anywhere!" said Ralph with a hearty laugh, then he leaned across to clap his friend on the back. "You talk like a Saxon. Remember your station and how you came to reach it, Gervase. If you are paid to crack the whip, do not feel sorry for the horse. His pain is not yours. Serve the king and earn his money honestly."

"Why, so I do, Ralph."

None of the Chancery clerks was more diligent in his work than Gervase Bret, but there were times when he was forcibly reminded of the fact that he was not a true-born Norman. His father had been a Breton mercenary who came to England to fight for King Edward against the Danes. His mother had been a Saxon girl from a village near London. When the future of England was at stake, the mercenary put money before natural inclination and chose to serve in the invading army. He fought well at Hastings but was so badly wounded that he died soon after. Brought up by his mother but cherishing the memory of his father, Gervase thus had complex loyalties and they caused him many pangs of regret. Norman scholars had educated and elevated him, but he still shared a fellow-feeling for Saxons under the yoke.

"So this is Bedwyn!" said Ralph as they entered the town and searched for their lodging. "A goodly place."

"The Lord be thanked!" said Canon Hubert, sighing. "We would have been here an hour ago if you had not taken us to that hellish pile of stones."

"Know your enemy, Canon," said Ralph jovially. "If that was the Devil back there on Salisbury Plain, stout Christians should have the courage to stare him in the face."

"Do not mock the Church," warned the other.

"Then do not invite mockery."

They were into the main street now, a short but broad thoroughfare that climbed up the hill towards Savernake Forest. Rows of low, shapeless, half-timbered houses ran down either side of them, with glimpses of more dwellings, some of them mere hovels, in the occasional side-street. The cobbles were strewn with filth and the country smells were just as pungent here. Accommodation for the party had been prepared at the hunting lodge that was used by the king and his entourage, but Canon Hubert refused to stay under its roof. He insisted on being taken to the abbey so that his reverend bones could lie on a more suitable and sacred bed. Abbot and monks had already retired for the night, but the Hospitaller was there to receive both Canon Hubert and Brother Simon and to conduct them to their quarters.

Having bestowed their cargo within the enclave, the others were free to leave, but Ralph Delchard first took the opportunity to chat with the porter at the gate. Such men saw everyone who came and went and knew all the gossip of the establishment. The death of the miller was the main item of news and the porter talked freely about it. He described how the man's wife had raised the alarm when he failed to return at nightfall and how a search party had gone out at daybreak to comb the forest. It took hours to find the corpse in its watery grave. A novice from the abbey had first seen it. When he had summoned his fellows, he used his young legs to bring the sad tidings back to the abbot.

Ralph listened to it all with growing curiosity, but Gervase seemed not to be engaged by the story. As soon as the two of them left the gatehouse, however, the latter showed that he had heard every word and noted a significance that had escaped his colleague.

"Did you catch his name?" asked Gervase.

"Brother Porter?"

"The miller who was savaged by the wolf."

"Why, yes," said Ralph. "It was Alric Longdon."

"Does that name not sound familiar to you?"

"No."

"Think again."

Ralph bridled slightly. "I do not consort with millers."

"We should both have consorted with this one."

"What say you?"

"Alric Longdon is the man who has drawn us to Bedwyn. He wrote letters to Winchester and made protest against the earlier survey. This miller was a testy lawyer with claims that will cause a flutter in both abbey and town."

"Longdon was a principal witness?"

"Witness and informer. His death is very convenient."

Ralph considered the matter, then reached a decision.

"Even dead men can talk if you know how to listen," he said. "We will converse with this miller tomorrow."

Chapter Two

I T WAS NOW OVER FIVE AND A HALF CENTURIES SINCE BENE-dict had founded the first of his monasteries in his native Italy and set down its rules in his own fair hand. His memory burned bright within Abbot Serlo, who saw to it that his own abbey lived a life of prayer, hard work, self-discipline, and good deeds, as enjoined by the father of their order. He liked to believe that St. Benedict—deigning to visit one of the houses that bore his name—would not be disappointed by what he saw in the community at Bedwyn. Abbot Serlo scoffed at those who argued that rules which were devised for the monks of Monte Cassino in the sixth century were based on assumptions of a warmer climate than existed in more northerly latitudes. He saw no reason to soften or adapt the strictness of the daily routine. Living together in this way, he was convinced, produced a more spiritual being than any which could emerge from the secular clergy. An abbey embodied the very perfection of Christian worship.

Nor was he excused by virtue of his eminence from the round of ceaseless self-denial and prayer. When the bell rang at two in the morning for Matins, he rose from his slumbers and went down to the church to join the shuffling obedientiaries. He remained in his place until Lauds and Prime had come and gone, then he watched the monks file out for a period of reading or meditation in the cloisters. Abbot Serlo would not see them again until Terce, the first service after daybreak, followed by Mass, during which lay people were admitted into the nave of the church.

18

It was in the space between Prime and Terce that the prior liked to insinuate himself if he had anything of special importance to discuss with the abbot. Decisions taken privately at this time between the two most senior prelates could be relayed in public during Chapter. This was the daily meeting of the monks after Terce, when the temporal business of the house would be reviewed.

When Prior Baldwin called on Abbot Serlo after Prime that morning, he had one major issue to raise. It was not a matter in which he felt his word was sufficient without some reinforcement from above. Brought into the abbot's quarters to stand beneath the bulbous eyes, he explained his quandary.

"The commissioners have called upon us, Father Abbot."

"But my understanding was that they passed the night as our guests. Brother Hospitaller admitted them."

"You speak of Canon Hubert and Brother Simon," said the prior deferentially. "They are not only in the abbey but of it. Both attended Matins, Lauds, and Prime and took their place among us." He gave a thin smile. "I speak of their two companions. They are here at the gatehouse even now with their odd request."

"Wherein lies the oddity?"

"They wish to view the body of Alric Longdon."

"Our dear departed miller?"

"They seek your permission, Father Abbot."

"But why? What reason did they give?"

"It bears upon their enquiry."

Abbot Serlo blinked dramatically. "A dead body must appear before the commission? It is not right, it is not just, it is not holy. Alric Longdon gives his evidence in heaven above. He is now beyond earthly jurisdiction."

"They pressed the matter, Father Abbot."

"Pressed?"

"They are here on king's business."

"What business has the king with a poor wretch who was killed by a wolf in the forest? There is something here

I do not discern, Prior Baldwin. Some motive too subtle for my old brain. Can you enlighten me?"

"Refuse their request and the matter is closed."

"How if they press it even harder?"

"I will dissuade them," said the other firmly. "What motive they have, I do not know. But I felt mistrust. Alric Longdon has suffered enough, Father Abbot. We should not subject his corpse to prying eyes. Spare him that final indignity and let him rest in peace. This is the only answer that they deserve."

Abbot Serlo perambulated around the room, his hands clasped together and held up to his chin. Though he had distanced himself from the commissioners and their work, he could not ignore this appeal to his person. An answer had to be given and it needed thought. Acquiescence would allow laymen to prowl and poke into a hallowed place. While looking at a dead body, they might take the opportunity to see more. Refusal, on the other hand, might promote contention and antagonise the visitors. Bedwyn Abbey was already under investigation by the commissioners and it might be unwise to suggest that it had anything to hide.

"What manner of men are they?" said Serlo.

"The older is a Norman lord, a soldier who fought at Hastings and earned the gratitude of the king. Ralph Delchard is his name, from good family in Lisieux, a bold fellow who will stand his ground in argument and one who will be a stern commissioner." Baldwin sounded a note of mild complacence. "Though I have no qualms about my ability to meet his every enquiry. The other is a young man of comely appearance, a Chancery clerk with a softer tongue and a more respectful manner. Gervase Bret is his name, learned beyond his calling. He speaks Latin, Italian, and every dialect of France. English is his native tongue, but he can hold a conversation with Dane or Viking." Baldwin wrinkled his nose in disgust. "He even has a smattering of Welsh. I take this young commissioner to supply the intelligence that is lacking in his blunt companion."

"You know them well on such brief acquaintance."

"I walked with Brother Simon as we left Prime," said the prior with muted self-congratulation. "I drew him out. He was ready in his answers about his fellows, though I did not expect to meet them quite so soon."

"A lord and a Chancery clerk," mused Serlo.

"A brave soldier and a shrewd lawyer."

The abbot clapped his hands lightly and pronounced.

"Let them view the body."

"But they have no right, Father Abbot."

"I give it to them. Alric Longdon has left us and his soul has gone to heaven. What they see is no more than a whole search party found and saw in Savernake. Brother Luke beheld it and I fancy it brought the boy a step or two nearer full commitment to his Maker. Perhaps it will do the same for this pair at the gatehouse." The eyes vanished behind huge lids and a dismissive hand sent Prior Baldwin on his way. "Admit them to the mortuary forthwith. But have them accompanied each second they are within the abbey."

Prior Baldwin hid his displeasure behind a nod of obedience and left the abbot's quarters. He had hoped for the command to send the two visitors on their way, but he had been overruled. It made him smart. In his personal joust with the commissioners, he had just taken the first fall because Abbot Serlo had inconsiderately deprived him of his lance. He intended to be fully armed for the next encounter.

In the dark, dank mortuary chapel, Alric Longdon lay on a stone bier with flickering candles at his head and feet. His body had been washed and prepared for burial, but there was no way to disguise the gruesome nature of his death. Throat and neck and Adam's apple had been eaten away, leaving the head to loll at an unnatural angle to the body. A rectangular strip of cloth covered the lumpen torso. Herbs and rushes had been scattered to sweeten the atmosphere, but the prevailing stench of decay could not be subdued.

Brother Peter had been given the task of bringing the visitors into the mortuary. He was a tall, slim man in his thirties whose hunched shoulders and clear intelligence suggested long hours spent in patient study over books and manuscripts. Brother Peter was the sacristan at the abbey and he had proved himself a competent and affable holder of that office. Ralph Delchard and Gervase Bret liked him at once. He had none of the portentousness of a Canon Hubert and none of the cloying mildness of a Brother Simon. Nor was he inclined to the waspishness of a Prior Baldwin. He was there to guide them and he did so with polite confidence. His long, kind face clouded when he saw the corpse and his mouth tightened. Brother Peter had seen the hapless miller when he was first carried into the abbey, but he could still be moved and shaken. He turned away for a second and offered up a silent prayer.

Gervase recoiled from the sight of the ugly wound, but Ralph stepped in closer to pore over it. At Hastings and at subsequent battles, he had seen far too much death and disfigurement to be appalled any longer. He knew from bitter experience what lance, spear, sword, arrow, and dagger could do to a human body and he had watched that most fearsome weapon of all, the Viking ax, strike off the head of an oncoming horse. Wolves were vicious, but their weaponry was limited. It was, however, all on display before him.

"The teeth took out his neck," said Brother Peter quietly. "And the claws left their mark upon him."

He pulled back the cloth to expose the upper chest of the corpse. Two long red sets of parallel lines had been gouged into the flesh. Gervase was able to look without too much revulsion this time, and Ralph bent even closer to scrutinise the scars.

"Where is the novice who found him?" said Ralph.

"On his knees in prayer," said the sacristan. "Brother Luke did not get a wink of sleep last night for thinking upon it, nor will he easily forget this horror."

"May we speak with him?"

"Is that needful?"

"I would like to hear his side of the tale."

"It lies before you."

"Brother Luke came upon the body after the wolf had left it. Only he will know exactly what state it was in at that moment of discovery. It would interest me to hear his opinion."

"Then I will seek permission for you to do so."

"Thank you, Brother Peter."

"We are glad to assist in every way," said the other, then he shot a last compassionate glance at the tortured creature on the bier. "Have you seen enough here?"

"One moment longer," said Gervase.

He was now accustomed to the grotesque sight of the wound and had transferred his attention to the face. Alric Longdon's pallid complexion had anticipated death. Its sudden whiteness was the same as it had always been. A night in the river had done less damage to his features than might have been supposed, and Gervase was able to read something of the man's character in that twisted mouth, that square jaw, that hooked nose, and those eyes that were set at different levels. The forehead was low and sharply lined, the cheekbones high and prominent. Gervase could almost hear the gruff voice that came from the nonexistent throat. The miller was a sly and secretive man, quick to accuse another but truculent in the face of accusation himself. There was a hard, unyielding, and unlovely side to this man. He deserved sympathy, but he was no paragon of virtues.

"We have seen enough," said Gervase.

"So be it."

Brother Peter led them out of the mortuary and back up into the clean air of a summer morning. They inhaled deeply to get Alric Longdon out of their nostrils. Ralph Delchard probed for more details.

"Has the sheriff been informed?"

"It was not felt necessary."

"There was violent death here."

"He is not the only victim of the forest," said Brother Peter sadly. "Edward of Salisbury is a busy man. He would not thank us if we dragged him here to examine every dead

23

body that is brought out of Savernake. Last month, one of the foresters was killed by a wild boar. In May of this year, a woodman was crushed beneath a tree that he was felling. At Easter last, two boys were drowned in the stretch of river within the forest boundary." Brother Peter shrugged. "Our sheriff will ride hard to spy on murder, but we do not disturb him for every accident that occurs in Savernake."

"What of the dead man's family?" asked Gervase.

"His young wife, the lovely Hilda, is distraught. There is a son by his first wife, a boy of nine. This tragedy bonded them together in grief and desperation."

"They are cared for?"

"Here in the abbey. They were received into the guest-house by Brother Hospitaller and offered private quarters." Brother Peter gave a wan smile. "We are used to mourning within these walls. Abbot Serlo has taught us how to medicine the troubled mind. Hilda and the boy will be well looked after here. They deserve no less."

Ralph and Gervase found plenty more to ask and were satisfied with the candid helpfulness of the replies which they got. They learned all that they could from the amenable Brother Peter without divulging anything themselves. When the sacristan had gone off to seek permission for them to speak with Brother Luke, the two friends were able to compare their reactions to all that they had witnessed.

"Prior Baldwin is our stumbling-block," said Ralph with a grimace. "We shall hear more of that awkward gentleman when we sit in commission."

"Abbot Serlo makes all the decisions. Everyone looks up to him. You heard the reverence in Brother Peter's voice when he talked of Father Abbot."

"The sheriff may have to be called in good time."

"Why, Ralph?"

"This is a case that merits his attention."

"Edward will not stir from Salisbury for a careless miller who wandered by mistake too far into the forest."

"There was nothing careless about this man," said Ralph thoughtfully. "I read his letters before we set out this morn-

24

ing. The man can write and write well, albeit in that crude language you call English. How many millers can do that? It is an angry letter and one that is spiced with malice, but I judge it to be the work of a careful man. He was careful in his wording and very careful to urge his own part in this business."

"You are right," conceded Gervase. "That is the face of a man who could pen such strong letters. But this takes us no further. Will you summon a sheriff to arrest a wolf?"

Ralph looked around the cloister garth to make sure that they were not overheard, then he dropped his voice to a whisper to make doubly sure of privacy.

"Alric Longdon was born and bred next to Savernake. He has run his mill for twenty years at least and made more profit than all his rivals in the trade."

"What are you saying?"

"He would not prosper by carelessness. I believe he went into the forest for a purpose and we can only guess at that purpose when we view the spot where he was killed. There is much more to this miller than his letters reveal."

"He summoned us here; he dies."

Ralph was grim. "We must find out how—and *why*."

Bedwyn throbbed with unhappiness and dread. News of the wolf attack in Savernake Forest raced through the town and the surrounding countryside. Shepherds tended their flocks with more concern, swine-herds became more alert, worried parents issued dire warnings to children, and eager lovers, who had hitherto used the forest for their clandestine sport, now took their search for wanton pleasure into barn and stable and shed. One wolf could alter the habits of a whole community.

Richard Esturmy had come to England in 1066 to fight for Duke William. When the latter became King of England, the former was made Warden of Savernake and took over several holdings in the area. He reacted to the situation with commendable speed and decision, sending out his foresters to hunt the wolf and follow it to its pack. Wolves had been a menace for generations and Esturmy's house in the parish of Grafton bore testimony to this. It was called Wolf Hall. The royal forest was the preserve of royal deer, shy and retiring creatures who needed ranges that were undisturbed. Any animals which might be harmful to the deer were thus kept down and Esturmy had granted rights of warren to local men to kill foxes, hares, wildcats, and even squirrels. Wolves and boars were controlled by organised hunts with spear and net and mastiff.

The unkind death of Alric Longdon made people highly superstitious. Few outside the miller's family spared more than a passing sigh for him and there were several who were content to hear of the demise of such an unpopular man, but the link between an arrival and a sudden departure could not be neglected. As the commissioners fell on Bedwyn, a harsher judgement fell on Alric Longdon. As the Norman wolves came to threaten the town, a lone animal seized its prey in the forest. To the impressionable townsfolk, the two events seemed to be inextricably connected. The miller was simply the first victim of the royal commissioners. Who—they wondered aloud—would be the next?

"Rex tenuit Bedvinde. Rex Edward tenuit. Nunc geldavit. Nec hidata fuit. . . ."

Canon Hubert was in good voice, declaiming the Latin phrases from the inventory made by the first commissioners who visited the area. Seated beside him, Gervase Bret took it upon himself to provide a translation in English for his listeners.

"The king holds Bedwyn. King Edward held it. It never paid tax and was not assessed by hide. There is land for eighty ploughs less one. In the lordship there are twelve ploughs and eighteen slaves. There are eighty villagers, sixty cottagers and fourteen freemen with sixty-seven ploughs. There are eight mills paying one hundred shillings. . . ."

There was a communal intake of breath. Only seven of those mill wheels now turned. The largest had been robbed

26

of its master in the forest. Gervase had a pleasant voice that could be heard distinctly by everyone in the building.

"Two woodlands," he continued, "which are two leagues long by one league wide. There are two hundred acres of woodland, and pasture twelve furlongs long by six furlongs wide. To this manor belong twenty-five burgesses. This town pays one night's revenue with all the customary dues. In this manor in the reign of King Edward, there was a wood one-half league long and three furlongs wide; it was in the king's lordship. Now it is held by Henry de Ferrers. . . ."

"I hear no mention of good King Harold," challenged a Saxon voice at the rear. "Why do you have no place for him and his worth in your calculation?"

"Peace, Wulfgeat," advised a neighbour.

"I asked the question of the other commissioners and they gave me no worthy answer." Wulfgeat stood up from his bench to stare at the quartet behind the table one by one. "I ask again. Where is King Harold of blessed memory?"

"He was no king," said Canon Hubert briskly, "and no blessing attaches to his person or his memory. We recognise only King Edward, he that was called the Confessor."

Wulfgeat was unappeased. "The noble Edward, as holy a man as any that may be found in church or abbey, bequeathed the crown to Harold on his deathbed. Will you gainsay the sacred word of the Confessor? And that same King Harold made grants of land in Bedwyn that need to be acknowledged and restored. Write down the name of Harold in—"

"Sit down and be silent," interrupted Ralph brusquely.

"I have just cause."

"You will be heard at a time of our choosing."

"King Harold was a—"

"Usurper," snapped Ralph irritably. "The crown of England was promised to Duke William of Normandy by that same Confessor that you talk about. We'll have no more discussion of the matter."

He snapped his fingers and the four men-at-arms, who had been standing near the back wall, took a meaningful pace forward. Wulfgeat's neighbour pulled him quickly back down on to his bench and hissed a warning. The incident was closed and Canon Hubert took up his recitation once more.

It was afternoon and the commissioners were opening their investigation in the shire hall, a long, low structure with sagging beams and an uneven floor. Bright sunlight was beating a way in through the small windows to take its share in the proceedings and to gild the tonsures in the assembly. The visitors began by explaining to the tenants, burgesses, and other interested parties the nature of their assignment. Prior Baldwin sat in a chair in the front row with Brother Matthew, the melancholic subprior, at his elbow to represent the abbey with a show of spiritual force. Ralph Delchard presided over the meeting, Canon Hubert and Gervase Bret dealt with documents and charters, and the meek Brother Simon used a skeletal hand to act as clerk to the whole business.

As the canon's voice rolled monotonously on, Ralph took time off to study the man who had dared to raise the name of a disgraced Saxon king. Such an interruption was foolhardy, but it took courage, and Ralph would always admire that. The bearing and attire of the man showed him to be a burgess of some wealth and standing. Approaching middle age, his beard was flecked with grey but there was no hint of declining years in the fierce eyes and the burly frame. Here was a proud, fearless, virile fellow, headstrong maybe, but that was a fault that Ralph himself shared. He was called Wulfgeat and he deserved a grudging respect.

"Thus concludes the enquiry," said Canon Hubert, lifting his heavy jowls from the parchment in front of him and gazing around with smug self-importance. "All matters that pertain to Bedwyn and the land adjoining have now been read to you as is right and proper. As you will agree, those first commissioners who traversed the county of Wiltshire were conscientious men who set about their task with meticulous care." Audible groans emerged from the body of the hall. "They were charged," said Hubert, riding over the sound, "to record all information concerning the lands thrice. To wit, as it was in the time of King Edward; as it was when King William gave the estate; and as it is now." He produced a flabby smile, then jabbed with a knife at their purses. "And it was also noted whether more could be taken from the estate than is now taken."

The groans were much louder this time, swelled by verbal protest and given real edge by the contemptuous laughter of Wulfgeat. So this was why Bedwyn had been singled out for a second visit. The commissioners had been empowered to impose more onerous taxes. When the first returns were searched by greedy eyes in the Treasury at Winchester, they were seen as ripe for further exploitation. Far too much was already squeezed out of Bedwyn in rent and tax. Additional burdens would break the back of some of its inhabitants. The disaffection built into a roar until Ralph quelled it by banging the table with his fist.

"Cease this noise!" he ordered. "We are commissioners by royal warrant and have the right to call whom we wish and when we wish to face interrogation." His gaze shifted to Prior Baldwin, who was sitting serenely in front of him and remaining aloof from the general hubbub. "Tomorrow morning at ten o'clock, we begin our enquiry into the land of the Abbey of Bedwyn. Witnesses will appear to give evidence as directed." Having discomfited the prior comprehensively, he beamed around the hall. "Our business is ended for the day. We thank you for your help and your indulgence."

Benches grated as the gathering rose to disperse. Abbey lands were rich and extensive. It might take days to peruse all the relevant charters again. That gave other people a breathing space, and their discontent was tempered with relief as they muttered their way out of the hall. A cluster formed around Wulfgeat, who was clearly a spokesman for many in the town. His voice was still booming away mutinously as he led them out into the street.

Prior Baldwin waited for a modicum of calm to return before he directed his question at Ralph Delchard.

"Why must the abbey be called to account?" he said.

"That will become apparent tomorrow."

"Am I to have no warning of what lies ahead?"

"It has been given."

"The fact of your enquiry has been announced," argued the prior pedantically, "but not its inherent nature. Is our land to be subject to new taxation?"

"Be patient until tomorrow."

"What am I to tell Abbot Serlo?"

Ralph grinned. "The truth."

Prior Baldwin fumed quietly and looked to Gervase for some elucidation. When none came, the prelate turned to the Church, but Canon Hubert was not ready to divulge anything further. The prior was put at a distinct disadvantage and that was not a position in which he often found himself. Brother Simon was his only hope. If he could catch him at an unguarded moment in the abbey, he might be able to worm some intelligence out of that wasted body. Summoning all of his dignity, he rose from his chair, with a sharp nudge, compelled Brother Matthew to join him, then delivered a parting boast.

"The abbey has nothing to hide."

"Then it is not like any abbey that I have ever known!" said Ralph with a chortle. "They usually have secrets as dark as their black cowls."

But Prior Baldwin and Subprior Matthew were already marching side by side down the hall to return to their home. All the papers had now been gathered up from the table and put back into their satchels. Brother Simon bore the largest, but Gervase kept a substantial number of documents himself. He needed to study them again before confronting the abbey delegation on the morrow. It was his knowledge of legalities that would be crucial in what promised to be a ferocious debate.

Ralph Delchard was about to lead the others out when he noticed a figure hovering inside the far door. He was a stout man of middle height, close to Ralph's own age but with none of the latter's vigour. Washing his hands nervously, he was trying to compose his features into a state somewhere between gravity and ingratiation. Clearly a person of some consequence, his rich tunic was covered by a mantle that was held at the shoulder by a gold brooch. His belt, too, was that of an affluent man and his cap was trimmed with fur. Ralph despised the gartered trousers of the old Saxons almost as much as their fondness for beards. The stranger had neither of these defects of his nation.

Seeing his opportunity, the man moved in to intercept Ralph. There was authority in his tone, but it was weakened by his over-eagerness to please.

"I am Saewold, the town reeve," he said. "I was delayed with business or I would have been here to bid you a proper welcome to Bedwyn and to offer what help I may."

Ralph introduced the others, then took the newcomer aside to weigh him up in private conference. Saewold had the fussiness of a man who likes to draw attention to the importance of his office and he used the name of the lord sheriff, Edward of Salisbury, with oily familiarity. Ralph did not warm to this over-helpful reeve but saw that he was a useful source of information. He therefore asked after Wulfgeat and his earlier impression of the man was confirmed. Wulfgeat was indeed a leading burgess and one with much influence in the town. The commissioners could look for trouble and dissension from that quarter. Though he praised the man's many fine qualities, Saewold could not conceal his patent dislike of Wulfgeat. If any new taxes were levied, it would be the job of the reeve to collect them, and he knew that Wulfgeat would offer the most vociferous resistance.

About Alric Longdon he was also informative, mixing fact with anecdote to draw a portrait that was anything but attractive. The miller was widely disliked. Hard-working and successful at his trade, he was also mean-spirited and highly unsociable. He liked to browbeat people in argument and only the quality and low price of his flour saved him from losing his customers. When Saewold was into his stride, scattering local gossip like handfuls of seed, there was no holding him.

"Yet Alric could surprise us," he said. "When his first poor wife died, we felt that no other woman would ever dare to share his bed, and yet he wed Hilda—as gentle a creature as you could wish to meet—within the year. What goodness did she see in such an ogre? What love could he inspire in such an angel?"

"You say he had few friends," noted Ralph, "but did the miller have any real enemies?"

"Dozens. I tell you this," said Saewold confidingly, "if that wolf had not killed Alric Longdon then, sooner or later someone else would have done so."

Ralph terminated the conversation by turning to join his companions, but the reeve would not be shaken off so easily. He stood in front of all four of them and opened his arms in a gesture of welcome.

"It would please me greatly if you would consent to dine with me tomorrow. My wife and I would be delighted to offer you the hospitality of our humble abode."

Ralph thanked him on behalf of the others and was about to frame an excuse that would liberate them from a meal at the table of this garrulous official when he became aware of another figure entering the hall. She was a woman of such luminous beauty that even Canon Hubert was taken aback. She was no longer young, a few years beyond thirty perhaps, but she had a mature loveliness that made her oval face shine. Moving with the grace of a dancer, she came to stand beside Saewold with a quiet dignity that identified her at once as his wife. Ralph was mesmerized. She wore a blue kirtle of some fine material beneath a short-sleeved gunna of a darker shade of blue. A gold-braided belt encircled a slim waist, then hung down to one side of her hips. Her long fair hair was held by a gold fillet and cascaded down from her wimple to rest on her right shoulder and brush a full breast. Her shoes were buckled at the ankles.

The wife of the town reeve of Bedwyn was dressed like the lady of a Saxon earl.

Saewold presented her to the four commissioners.

"This is my wife, Ediva," he said proudly.

She acknowledged each of them in turn with a soft and confident smile, but she held Ralph's gaze marginally longer and all barriers of language, custom, and degree between them dissolved in an instant. In her brilliant green eyes, he saw something which his colleagues would never dare to look for and which her husband would never recognise for what it was. When Ralph's interest quickened, she let him see that she was pleased.

He countermanded his original decision.

"Dear lady," he said with a gallant half-bow, "your husband has kindly invited us to dine with you tomorrow. We are delighted to accept that invitation."

"Thank you, my lord," she replied. "I wait upon you."

Ralph Delchard felt that a bargain had been sealed.

Chapter Three

BROTHER LUKE WAS A FRESH-FACED YOUTH WHOSE RELI-
gious ardour was at last beginning to hear the vague
whispers of doubt as he approached the end of his year-
long novitiate. He was tall and angular, with a gawkiness
that had not yet been cured by the sombre pace of monastic
life. Though he wore the cowl willingly, it still looked like
a garment he had just tried on that minute rather than a
home in which he had taken up permanent and unquestioning residence. He was alert and well educated but reticent
in the presence of strangers. Ralph Delchard left it to
Gervase Bret to set up a dialogue with their guide.

"How long have you been a novice, Brother Luke?"

"Ten months, master."

"It was your own choice to enter the abbey?"

"Mine and that of my parents," said Luke. "They entered
me as a postulant and look to see me a brother of the order
soon. I hope I will not disappoint them."

"There is surely no chance of that?"

The youth shook his head without conviction and lapsed
back into silence. All three of them were entering
Savernake Forest, tracing the same path along the river that
Alric Longdon had taken on that fateful evening. Abbot
Serlo had given Brother Luke permission to take the two
commissioners to the scene of the miller's death, and the
novice obeyed without demur. Gervase tried to reach the
youth with other subjects of conversation, but his replies
were laconic and the exchanges soon dried up. Ralph

Delchard threw in a piece of information that jolted Luke out of his reserve.

"Gervase almost took the cowl," he said jovially. "The monks thought they had won his heart and mind for God, but he learned that there is more to life than prayer and fasting."

"Is this so?" asked the novice with interest.

"It is only part of the truth, Luke," said Gervase.

"You entered a Benedictine house?"

"The Abbey of St Peter, at Eltham. It was founded by King William himself not long after Battle Abbey was raised. Both abbot and monks were from Normandy, but they soon mastered our tongue."

Luke was surprised. "You are a Saxon?"

"Half Saxon, half Breton," explained Ralph. "But we rescued him from misery by turning him into a Norman."

Gervase enlarged on the jocular comment. "My father was killed at Hastings; my mother and her family had limited means. The abbey was very close and the monks were very friendly. At eight, I was being schooled by them. At ten, I was allowed to spend whole days within the enclave. At twelve, I became a kind of servant and got my learning in place of wages."

"An abbey is an education for life," said Luke solemnly as he quoted the master of the novices. "All that there is to know may be gleaned from within the cloister."

Ralph's mocking laugh disagreed, but he said nothing.

Luke was intrigued. "But how did you come to rise so high in the king's service?"

"By listening and learning," said Gervase. "Eltham is close to London. Travellers of all types and all nations sought our hospitality. I helped to prepare their beds. They all had tales to tell, sometimes in languages that were so strange on the ear that I barely understood a word at first. But I was a patient student. If you know Latin, you may pick up Italian without too much confusion. If you speak Breton—and my father had instructed me in his tongue when I was a tiny child—you will be able to master Nor-

35

man French and even stray close to Welsh, for there are Celtic echoes in Breton."

"Did you become a novice at the abbey?"

"In the fullness of time."

"For how long did you stay?"

"Six months or more."

"What made you leave?" asked Luke with keen interest.

"Gervase must tell you another time, lad," intervened Ralph as they came to a fork in the river. "You spoke of a stream to the left. Is this the place?"

"Yes, my lord."

"Lead on. We follow hard on your heels."

Luke began the uphill climb, with the others behind him. Ralph winked knowingly to Gervase. They had not only made a friend inside the abbey, they had chosen one untutored in the arts of debate and prevarication of which monks like Prior Baldwin were so patently masters. The novice was a useful ally. By the same token, he would not lose at all by their acquaintance. He had evidently been drawn to Gervase when the latter's history was recounted, and there was clear affinity between them. Brother Luke was experiencing the kinds of anxieties and misgivings that had afflicted Gervase himself in a similar position. There would be more talk between the two of them in private.

"It is not far now," said the pathfinder.

"You are a true forester," praised Ralph.

"The stream goes below ground here, but we will find it again a little higher up."

It was early evening and the sun was still slanting its rays down through the trees. Birdsong surrounded them and the cheerful buzz of insects swelled the effortless music of the forest. There were other, louder, unexplained noises in the middle distance, but they did not delay the little trio. At length, they reached the ruined yew and looked upon the bank where Brother Luke had first found the dead body of the miller.

"It was here," he said, pointing an index finger.

"Be more precise, lad," said Ralph. "Which way did he lie? Where were his body, his feet, his head?"

"He was on his back, my lord, and his head was in the stream. I will show you if you wish."

"I do, Luke."

The youth needed no more encouragement. He lay on the ground beside the stream and adjusted himself so that he was hanging over it. Stretching out too far, he lost his balance and fell backwards, submerging head and shoulders in the water. Ralph gave a hearty laugh, but Gervase dived forward to grab the novice by the folds of his cowl and pull him back up onto the bank. Sodden and spluttering, Brother Luke was not distressed by the mishap.

"*That* was how I found him, sirs," he explained. "Even as I was then. On this bank and in that stream."

Ralph became serious and moved him aside. Taking up the same position, he looked all around him and saw the bushes to the side of the yew. A wolf concealed in those could launch a surprise attack, but its coat might leave some memory of its passage through the brambles. Ralph instituted a careful search and quickly found what he expected.

"Fur," he said triumphantly. "Our wolf lurked here and leapt upon the miller to push him backwards. This much seems certain. But there are still two larger questions."

"What are they?" asked Gervase.

"Wolves kill for food or when they are threatened. That heavy body in the mortuary chapel would have made a good meal for a hungry wolf and its family. Why did it take only one bite of its supper?"

"Perhaps it was disturbed," suggested Gervase.

"In as quiet and lonely a spot as this?"

"Another wolf may have disputed the carcass. They may have chased each other away. Foresters may have been on patrol. Their scent would be caught well before they came to this exact place."

Ralph was back among the brambles again, finding another piece of fur and holding it to his nose to sniff. He located a third tuft and repeated the process.

"It smells like a wolf," he said, "and, then again, it does not. I wonder if we are naming the wrong animal as the murderer. A mad dog would kill for the sake of it and leave a victim to bleed to death." He crouched behind the bushes, then jumped up by way of demonstration. "If it sprang up high enough and hard enough, it could knock him flat, then sink its fangs into him."

"You forget something, my lord," said Luke diffidently.

"What is that?"

"Those marks upon his chest."

"Front paws would leave such grim reminders."

"Not in Savernake," continued the novice. "Forest law is strict. All dogs in and around Bedwyn are lawed. They must have three claws removed from each of their front paws so that they may not bring down game."

"Even hunting dogs?" said Ralph.

"Only a few escape the rigour of this law."

"And who would own such mastiffs, excepting the Warden of Savernake himself? This is a royal forest, but the king cannot ride here often. Who else has hunting privileges?"

"None but the lord of Chisbury."

Gervase was curious. "Hugh de Brionne?"

"The same. He keeps a pack of hounds."

Ralph and Gervase exchanged a meaningful glance. When the problem of the abbey lands came before them on the next day, Hugh de Brionne would be called as a principal witness. They had so far liked nothing that they had heard of the domineering lord, and the fact that one of his mastiffs might possibly have killed an innocent man did not endear him to them any the more. Ralph put his first question aside and turned to the other, but he did not wish to ask it in the presence of Brother Luke. When the novice got back to the abbey, he would be catechised by the prior about his walk in Savernake Forest. Ralph did not wish the abbey to be party to all his researches.

"Walk further on, Gervase," he said casually. "If wolf or dog came down this way, find the route by which it left. It would seek cover in its flight. See if you can choose its direction."

Gervase understood that he was being asked to get Luke out of the way and did so with such natural ease that the youth did not suspect for a moment why he was being taken farther up the hill by way of a ruse. To help in the search for clues gave the novice a sense of excitement, but it paled beside the chance of being able to question Gervase further about his release from his vows in Eltham Abbey.

As soon as they were out of sight, Ralph took out his sword and used its point to describe the shape of Alric Longdon as he lay on the bank beside the stream. Why had the miller come to such a place alone? It was not an area of the forest into which anyone could stray accidentally. He stood on the chest of the dead man and looked around with utmost care, but not even the ghost of an answer flitted across his path. He turned to gaze down into the stream. Gushing out of its underground passage, it was no more than six or nine inches deep, but he was unable to see the bottom of its channel. The foliage above formed such a complete covering that the stream was in shadow even on the brightest day.

He used his sword point to prod through the water and test its chalk base. Ralph jabbed the weapon in a dozen different places, as if he were trying to spear fish, and his enterprise was eventually rewarded. The sword met resistance and he jiggled the point around before thrusting hard to penetrate the object. He brought his hand up slowly to see what he had caught. It was no fish but a far more valuable catch. What was impaled on the end of his sword was a dripping leather pouch. Its draw-string was loosened and it was empty, but Ralph's mind was racing now. If the miller had been tumbled into the stream with the pouch in his hand, its contents might even now be still resting on the bottom.

Putting sword aside, he knelt down and thrust an arm

into the stream. Groping fingers soon located a prize and he brought it out. It was a coin of high value, much more than would normally be paid for a sack of flour. When he dipped in his hand again, he came up with three coins of the same kind. Two minutes of stretching and feeling about beneath water earned him a substantial amount of money and one more item which helped to explain the hoard. Ralph Delchard found a key. Alric Longdon finally spoke to him.

The miller had brought his treasure to a hiding place in the forest. He was about to stow it away when he was attacked and killed. If he was kneeling when the animal lunged at him, then his position in relation to the stream would be more easily accounted for, since a standing man would have been knocked much farther back. Exhilaration made him smile. His instincts had been right all along. Alric Longdon did have a purpose. When he knelt where the man must have knelt, all became clear. The yew tree was the object of the secret visit at dusk.

Ralph leaned forward to look into its hollow shell, but it was far too dark within. Once again his sword was used to reconnoitre and it met with something hard and solid deep inside the yew. He had to stretch both arms to reach the heavy lump that his fingers now encountered. Alric Longdon had chosen his hiding place well. It was safe and dark and well protected from the elements. No human being could stumble upon it and no animal could do it any harm. It was wedged so tightly in place that he had to apply some strength to heave it loose. Out it came with a shower of moss and wood lice dropping from it.

He was holding what felt like a large wooden box. It was wrapped up snugly in a sack whose floured whiteness proclaimed its origin. The man had gone to some lengths to protect his treasure chest. What was in the pouch was a generous haul for any miller. How much more would Ralph find when he inserted the key into the lock of the chest?

"God's blood!"

The oath came out through gritted teeth. When the sack

came off, the box he had felt turned out to be no more than a block of wood. There was no chest, no money, no hoard of any kind. Had Alric Longdon put his life at risk to inspect a piece of timber from the forest? It did not make sense. The sound of approaching voices made him start. Gervase was giving him warning of their return. Ralph moved swiftly. The key and a few coins were slipped into the pouch at his own belt. The block of wood and the leather pouch were quickly rolled up in the sack and stuffed back into the tree. When Gervase and Brother Luke rejoined him, he was pretending to poke around in the bushes with his sword.

"Did you find anything?" asked Gervase.

"No," said Ralph with mock annoyance. "It was a waste of our time. This has been a wild goose chase."

The abbot was the father of an abbey and the monks vowed obedience to him, staying in the same place for their whole lives as members of a Christian family. Love and tolerance of each other was an article of faith, and Abbot Serlo saw to it that his house evinced a spirit of mutual co-operation. All men were equal before God and all of his brothers were equal before Abbot Serlo. Close friendships nevertheless grew up between members of his community, and Prior Baldwin made a point of watching them carefully so that he was in a position to make use of them if the occasion arose or to pounce on them if the special relationship threatened to take on an intimate dimension. The prior always knew where to go and to whom to speak. It was the reason that his steps took him into the sacristy that evening.

"What else did he say, Brother Peter?"

"Very little beyond that, Prior Baldwin. The boy's head was so turned by this remarkable Gervase Bret that he could talk of nothing else. I am not sure that it was wise to let him converse so freely with a layman, especially one who was a novice himself until he succumbed to the temptations of life outside the cloister. This Gervase Bret is a fine model for the benefits of a sound education, but he is hardly a fit subject of study for a callow youth who is wavering."

"Is he still so?"

"I fear me that he is."

They were in the sacristy, where all the valuables of the abbey were stored. In addition to the vestments, linen, and banners, there were gold and silver plate, vessels of the altar, precious ornaments and other gifts from benefactors, together with a collection of holy relics that was envied far and wide. The bones from the right hand of St. Mary the Virgin brought in pilgrims from great distances, who also came to view the strands of hair from the beard of her beloved son, Jesus Christ, and a splinter of wood from the cross on which He perished at Calvary.

When the prior called on him, Brother Peter was happy at work, polishing a pair of silver candlesticks until he could see his reflection in their gleaming surfaces. He had become the confidant of Brother Luke, who found the strictures of the master of novices far too harsh to bear at times. In Brother Peter, the novice discovered a gentle and unjudging friend who gave him succour when he most needed it and warm friendship when he did not. It was the sacristan who had helped him to get through the difficult early months and to shape his mind for service to God. The prior could easily understand why Luke had gravitated towards the sacristy.

"You are the perfect example for the boy," he said. "He is tempted to go out into sinfulness and corruption, but you came to us in flight from them. Our sacristan was not born to monastic life as so many of us were. He sought us out as a refuge from the baseness and futility of common life."

Brother Peter nodded ruefully. "Base and futile, indeed! And perfidious, too, in its workings. A man's soul is greatly imperilled in such a world. Only here can it truly be lifted up unto the Lord."

"Impress that point upon Brother Luke."

"I have done so daily."

"Use your persuasion with him."

"My talents lie elsewhere, Prior Baldwin," said the sacristan as he held up a candlestick. "When I made these for the abbey, I was inspired by a higher purpose. When I was a silversmith in the town, I thought only of working for gain and personal advantage." He replaced the candlestick with loving care. "The abbey has given my life a meaning."

"Implant that same meaning in Brother Luke."

"He will stay with us, I think."

"Not if he is led astray by this Gervase Bret," said the prior sharply. "I have spoken to the master of the novices to keep the boy well occupied. Do you likewise. If we turn his gaze within these walls, he will forget what idle charms may lay without."

"Is the young commissioner to be forbidden further access to Luke?" said Peter.

"If it were left to me, he would. But Abbot Serlo might take a more tolerant view of their association. I spy danger in it." The prior narrowed his lips and hissed his command. "Should Brother Luke and this fallen novice chance to meet again, I wish you to be present."

"I understand, Prior Baldwin."

"They have come to try to take some lands away from the abbey," said the other in exasperation. "I will stop them there with the help of Subprior Matthew. If they fail to steal our land, I do not wish them to walk away with one of our novices. Fight for the boy. It is our Christian duty."

Baldwin picked up another example of Peter's craftsmanship. It was a large silver box embossed with an image of Christ, and it had taken months to fashion. When Baldwin pressed the catch, the lid sprung back on its hinge, revealing the abbey's precious supply of frankincense. He inhaled the latent odour of sanctity for a moment, then reinforced his decree. "Do not let Brother Luke smell the foul stench of the outside world. Fight hard for him."

"He will be saved," said Peter. "I swear it."

"Amen!"

Prior Baldwin snapped the lid of the box shut and the gleaming figure of Christ became their silent witness.

The hunting lodge was fitting accommodation for two men who were trying to track down a wolf and an act of criminality.

"Did you tell him the whole truth, Gervase?"

"As much as I needed."

"Then you lied to the boy."

"I was prompt in my answers."

"But deceitful."

"There was no deceit practised, Ralph," said the other. "What Brother Luke required to know, he was told. And more will be added on another occasion when we talk further."

"Be honest with the lad."

"Why, so I was."

"Come to the heart of the matter."

Gervase Bret almost blushed and had to turn away. Ralph Delchard laughed, then reached for his cup and drained it of the last of the wine. They were at supper in the hunting lodge and sat either side of the long table, with food, wine, and a few candles between them. The accommodation had been put at their disposal by the Warden of Savernake, who had also provided a cook to feed them and servants to wait on them. The stabling was good, the beds comfortable, and the absence of Canon Hubert and Brother Simon a double boon. Six people sharing a lodge that had been built to house a king and his hunting retinue were given luxuries of space and attention which did not always fall their way.

Ralph returned to affectionate teasing of a friend.

"Have you written any letters?" he said.

"I have been too busy with my affairs."

"Nothing should take precedence over that."

"Nothing does," promised Gervase.

"You will be sorely missed in Winchester."

"The king's business must be discharged."

"So must a man's more private offices." Ralph refilled his cup and sipped more wine. "I'll wager that the novice hears nothing of your real desires."

"They do not concern him in the least."

"Woman is every man's concern. If Brother Luke could but see the Lady Alys, he would throw off that cowl with shouts of joy and run naked through Savernake to prove his manhood to the world." He gave a low chuckle. "*She* is the reason you broke the vow of chastity. Tell him, Gervase. Talk of Alys. Acquaint him with the meaning of true love. Release the lad from a life of toil in a house of eunuchs."

Gervase nodded to close the discussion, but he would open his heart to no man, still less to a faltering novice. Alys was his betrothed. Thoughts of her kept his mind pure and his life in a straight, clean furrow. It also made him critical of Ralph's exaggerated interest in female company. He was sensible enough to make allowances for his friend. Ralph Delchard's wife had died in childbirth trying to bring their only son into the world and the boy himself had lingered for only a week before following his mother to the grave. The experience had turned a caring husband into a suffering recluse for over a year. He had buried himself on his estates in Hampshire, stirring out only at the express summons of the king. When the fever of remorse finally broke inside him, he vowed he would never marry again and looked to forge a lesser relationship with women. The recluse became such an energetic lecher that even Gervase was forced to lecture him from time to time. Ralph Delchard was a Norman lord of great distinction until his roving lust led him astray from the path of duty and sobriety.

"Tomorrow we dine with the reeve and his sweet wife."

"Forget her, Ralph," urged Gervase.

"Have you ever seen such a comely Saxon lady?"

"She is not for you."

"That long-winded Saewold is not worthy of her."

"It is a matter between the two of them."

"When a marriage is that heavy, it sometimes takes three to bear the burden."

"We have come to Bedwyn on urgent business."

"Pleasure may help that business, Gervase," argued

Ralph with a pensive smile. "This reeve will gossip about everyone in the town, but Ediva may tell me things that even he does not know. If you wish to gain supremacy over another man, you must strike him at his weakest point. His wife, Ediva—that face, that skin, those eyes—is his weakest point."

"No, Ralph," said Gervase levelly. "She is yours."

Canon Hubert was a visible Christian. He was a devout man who liked his devotion to be made manifest in front of others. Having taken up residence in the abbey, therefore, he joined in all its services when he could and competed for the attention of his God and of those around him. Brother Simon's was an altogether more restrained and undemanding worship. He was simply waiting to inherit the earth. Hubert chose a more assertive route to heaven. Waiting was quite superfluous in his case. He did not need to inherit what he felt he already owned by right.

Abbot Serlo had received him as a courtesy and offered the comfort of his own quarters to the two guests. Hubert had refused on the grounds that an abbey was his spiritual base and that he felt happy within it only if he was on equal terms with its lowliest occupant. A hard bed would teach him the joys of self-abnegation. It is easy to play the willing martyr for a short while if you know you will be returning to your palatial quarters at Winchester Cathedral before too long. Abbot Serlo mumbled approvingly but he got the measure of this ostentatious canon. Appointing his prior to represent the abbey before the commissioners had been a sagacious move. Baldwin could outmanoeuvre Hubert.

The rivals met again at Matins and traded a faint nod. Lauds gave them a chance to lock their eyes for a second, and Prime set them next to each other on their knees. A silent battle took place, each trying to subdue the other with a show of piety and to make a deeper impression on the congregation of monks around them. Brother Simon remained indifferent to the struggle and did not realise he might become a weapon in it.

"Brother Simon . . ."

"Good day, Prior Baldwin."

"I crave a word."

"As many as you wish."

"Abbot Serlo was asking after you and Canon Hubert."

"We are indebted to his kindness."

"He is troubled in his mind, Brother Simon."

"On some matter in particular?"

"Indeed, yes," said the prior solemnly. "And it lies within your power to allay his fears and ease his troubles."

They were walking across the cloister garth with their heads down and their hands folded inside their sleeves. In the period immediately after Prime, the prior had stalked his prey until it was unprotected, then moved in for the kill.

"This dispute about the abbey lands . . ." he began.

"It is not my doing," apologised Simon.

"But you know its import?"

"In bare essentials."

"Has someone made a claim against the abbey?"

"It is not for me to say, Prior Baldwin. I am bound by my allegiance to Canon Hubert to divulge nothing that bears upon the work of the commission."

"That is not what I ask," said the other, guiding the wraith into a corner so that he could turn him and peer into his hollow eyes. "I search for reassurance for Father Abbot. Nothing more. May I tell him, then, that all the abbey lands are safe? That is what will relieve him most."

Brother Simon's mouth began to twitch. "I hope that they are safe," he said with obvious embarrassment.

"Who is this other claimant?" probed Baldwin before a show of retraction. "No, no, I withdraw that question. It is putting you in an invidious position, and that must never be. I know it cannot be Hugh de Brionne who contests that land, because that debate is over and won."

The twitching mouth was eloquent once more. Hugh de Brionne was clearly involved and that fact defined the exact land in question. Prior Baldwin was now forewarned and wished to be forearmed against any eventuality.

"Is this all that brings you back to Bedwyn?"

"This is weighty enough in its implications."

"Hardly, Brother Simon," reasoned the other. "We dealt with that stretch of land in half a day before the first commission, and you look to have able counsellors sitting beside you at the table."

"Very able."

"Then they will judge it a trifling matter."

"Two days at least have been set aside."

Simon bit his lip as the words trickled out before he could stop them. The prior's gaze intensified and bore deep into the skull in front of him. The nature and scale of the dispute had now been discovered. It remained only to find out why the process was being instituted.

"The Church has countless enemies," he intoned. "An abbey is a spiritual fortress against the wiles of the outside world. We must strengthen our defences and repel any siege. Wicked men envy our mean possessions. If an abbey loses its lands, the whole Church is the weaker for it." He inclined his head until their foreheads were almost meeting. "It is not for my benefit that I ask this, Brother Simon. I am but a humble servant of the Lord. Father Abbot rules here and he is not long for this world. Will you send him to heaven in distress? One name will content him. Nobody else but he will hear it, and I myself will forget who told it to me, so we are all absolved of guilt." The twitching mouth was his encouragement once more. He struck hard. "One name that brought you here to Bedwyn. One man who hates the Church that we both serve. One foul miscreant who could undo all of Abbot Serlo's work in this abbey and send that reverend body into a worrisome grave."

Brother Simon trembled. "I may not name him."

"Then point him out by other means. Tell me where he dwells, show me what he does, give me *something* to take with me into my prayers."

Brother Simon was helpless beneath the piercing gaze. Meekness was no defence against the prior. Nor were all the dire warnings that Canon Hubert had issued. Brother Simon clutched at a straw. The case was altered. The novel and dramatic circumstances changed everything. There was no point now in protecting a man who would never be able to testify before the commissioners. He capitulated.

"Abbot Serlo may be content," he said. "Your accuser has already met the wrath of God and lies in the mortuary chapel. He was our signpost to the town of Bedwyn."

Brother Simon closed his eyes to escape the steely glare of his persecutor. He kept them shut tightly and prayed for forgiveness. He had broken an oath in conceding such an important detail of the commissioners' work, and guilt made his face burn and colour. If Canon Hubert or any of his other colleagues found out what he had done, he would be severely chastised and might even lose his place beside them. Yet he had been helpless in the grip of his guileful inquisitor. When he lifted his lids again, he expected to see the prior towering still over him, but Baldwin was now in the quarters occupied by two of the abbey's guests.

He was comforting the miller's grieving widow.

It was market day in Bedwyn and everyone from miles around converged on the town to sell produce, buy food, search for bargains, haggle over prices, or simply catch up on the local gossip. The death of a miller and the arrival of royal commissioners had now merged into one unified disaster and it even displaced the weather as the main topic around the carts and stalls. Saxons smouldered with impotent rage as they endured yet another destructive and unwanted Norman invasion. The usual friendly bustle was replaced by a more fraught atmosphere.

The market was held in the middle of the town on the large, open triangular space at the bottom of the hill. It was a natural meeting place and allowed visitors to stream in from different directions. Had any of the angry men or the fearful women cared to walk fifty yards down the long, narrow street which followed the valley, they would have seen a more sacred transaction taking place. The man whose death was keeping the flames of debate crackling away was now having his soul offered up to heaven. In the tiny church that stood in the middle of a well-filled graveyard, Mass was being sung and prayers were being said for Alric Longdon.

It was a small funeral. Father Edgar, the ancient and hobbling priest, took the service and struggled hard in his address to find kind words to say of the deceased. Apart from the widow, her stepson, and a younger woman who consoled both of them, there were three people from the town and two monks from the abbey. The Saxon church was no more than a stone-built porch, nave, and chancel which clutched each other for support against an ungodly universe and which were further bonded together by arcading which ran entirely round the building. Windows were small and splayed, floors were paved and cold, and the chancel arch with its simple motif cut into the stone was so low and narrow that Father Edgar was partially obscured from sight when he went up to the altar.

The graveyard was sullied with the vulgar noise of the market, but the priest did his best to lend a frail dignity to the proceedings. Alric Longdon was lowered into the ground and the first handfuls of earth tossed down upon him. As the weeping Hilda almost swooned, the young woman moved in quickly to support her with a caring arm. The funeral was soon over and the mourners stood helplessly around the grave. Brother Luke had asked to attend and pay his last respects because he had been the person to find the corpse. Brother Peter had accompanied him and stayed him through the novice's own turbulent emotions. When the youth recovered enough from the harrowing occasion to take stock of those around him, he saw for the first time the sad beauty of the dark-haired young woman who sustained widow and boy with such compassion. She was soberly dressed, but the fine material of her kirtle and gunna disclosed that she was of good family.

Luke was entranced by the heart-shaped face with its silken complexion, its dark eyes, its long black eyelashes, and its full red lips. A feeling which had no place whatsoever on consecrated ground brushed against him like a cobweb.

He huddled against his companion to ask his question.

"Who is she, Brother Peter?"

"That is Leofgifu," said the sacristan.

"She is a member of the miller's family?"

"No, she is here solely out of kindness. Leofgifu is a true Christian and a rare young woman."

"Where has she come from?"

"She is the daughter of Wulfgeat." His voice hardened. "Do not stare at her, Luke. It is unseemly. Lower your eyes and pray for the soul of Alric."

The novice obeyed, but Peter ignored his own injunction. While every other head in the churchyard was bowed down with grief, his remained only slightly tilted forward so that his eyes could watch and marvel at the tenderness of Leofgifu. Here was unselfishness made manifest and real concern for those in distress. Everyone hated the miller, yet she was somehow able to offer love and sympathy to the widow and her stepson. Brother Peter gazed at Leofgifu as if he were in the presence of a saint.

The Warden of Savernake was thorough. When his huntsmen and foresters returned from a fruitless search, he sent them out again next day at first light. They scoured forest and field once more but found neither wolves nor traces of their depredations. Deer were seen in profusion, wild boar could be heard grunting in the undergrowth, and there was even a glimpse of a badger as it dived into its set, but the wolf which had killed Alric Longdon had fled. In the twelve hours since the body had been discovered, it could have run a very long way.

As the disconsolate posse headed back to report their failure, they began to wonder whether a wolf had indeed been responsible. Other animals were considered, and the balance of opinion swung behind the notion of a mastiff. They were picking their way through woodland not far from where the attack had occurred when they finally

51

sighted something. It was fifty yards away, across a clearing and half-hidden by gorse bushes, but they saw movement and sensed danger. The creature was too large to be a boar and too small to be a stag, but the brown hue of its fur could well be that of a wolf.

Hounds were released and spears held at the ready as the huntsmen goaded their horses in pursuit, beating a way through the undergrowth and fired up by the thrill of action. But it was all to no avail. The scent was lost and the trail went cold. Whatever they had been chasing in Savernake Forest had vanished into thin air. They were deeply annoyed and highly frustrated, but the news which they bore back to their master could sound at least one positive note: The animal had finally been seen.

The mysterious killer still lurked in the forest.

Chapter Four

HUGH DE BRIONNE WAS INCENSED WHEN HE RECEIVED the summons to appear before the commissioners. It arrived at short notice and gave him no details as to its true implications. He was simply ordered to appear before the tribunal like a common criminal being hauled before a court of law. His anger first simmered, then boiled over. He was the lord of the manor of Chisbury and had extensive holdings in the rest of the shire as well as in other parts of the country. A man of his standing and temperament was at the beck and call of nobody. He tore up the summons, drank himself into a stupor, and staggered off to bed with his ire still undiminished. His wife was grateful when exhaustion finally got the better of his wild imprecations. Marriage to Hugh de Brionne had many pains for the gentle Lady Matilda.

Her lord awoke next morning to recapture his spirit of rebellion and defy the command to appear. He was minded to send his sergeant-at-arms into Bedwyn to give the visitors a dusty answer, but another course of action soon commended itself. He would appear in person to have the pleasure of reviling them and letting them know the force and character of the man with whom they dealt so peremptorily. Hugh de Brionne, therefore, kept them waiting an hour before he stormed into the shire hall with a dozen armed retainers at his back. The first sight which the commissioners had of this bellicose lord was thus rather intimidating.

"I am Hugh de Brionne!" he announced, as if throwing down a gauntlet. "What have you to say to me?"

They were too busy adjusting to the suddenness of his appearance to say anything at all. Legs apart, back straight, and jaw thrust out pugnaciously, he gave them a moment to view the full temper of the witness they had dared to call. Hugh de Brionne was a man of exceptional height and powerful build, and fifty years had taken no toll on his vitality. A large and craggy face was centred around a prominent nose which kept two furious eyes apart to stop them from fighting each other. He was clean-shaven, but cheeks and chin bore scars of battle that were worn with blatant pride. The other mark of a warrior was more disturbing to behold. His right arm had been lopped off at the elbow and the stump was poking out of the sleeve of his tunic. Sheathed in leather to hide its full horror, it was nevertheless a startling deformity.

He looked along the table from one to the other and made a swift assessment of them, finally settling his gaze on Ralph Delchard as the only person worthy of conversation.

"What means this summons, sir!" he demanded.

"I will answer when you are ready to be answered, my lord," said Ralph. "And that is when your knights are sent about more lawful business. There is no place here for a show of force unless you wish to answer to the king."

Hugh de Brionne studied him until he was persuaded that Ralph was making no idle threats. The royal commissioner was as firm of voice as the glowering lord himself and possessed of just as much determination. A flick of the hand dismissed the military escort from the hall. Ralph Delchard nodded his approval and gestured to his own men, who stood against the back wall. Two of them brought a large chair for the visitor and placed it directly in front of the table. After glaring at everyone in the room once more, Hugh de Brionne consented to sit down, throwing his mantle back over his shoulder to expose his family crest on the chest of his tunic.

They were staring at the head of a large black wolf.

Hugh snorted. "Why am I brought here?" he said.

"Invited, not brought," corrected Ralph. "You were good enough to furnish information for our predecessors who came to Bedwyn earlier in the year. Our task is to check some of those findings against new claims that have emerged."

"Claims against *me*!" growled Hugh. "They are false. I can justify every acre of land with a charter, every house and manor with a lawful grant. The man who tries to rob me of anything is a liar and a thief and I will settle the argument with steel before I concede."

"There is no claim against you," said Ralph calmly. "We will take nothing and tax nothing. What we need to find out is whether or not we should *give* you more."

Hugh de Brionne was soothed but far from quiescent. He remembered the first commissioners only too well. They had kept him sitting in that same shire hall for hours while they sniffed through his documents like a pack of dogs trying to find a rat. He rid himself of a few blunt opinions about those who had subjected his wealth to such close inspection.

"Your predecessors were idiots," he said roundly. "If they had respected my position and taken my word, they would have been given a precise account of my holdings in a tenth of the time. But they argued and accused, they pushed and they prodded until I all but reached for my sword to cut the delay in two." His chest swelled and the wolf rippled. "I am too busy to waste time with lawyers' quibbles. Those who hem me in should remember my value to the Conqueror. I fought by his side and lost an arm in his service."

Ralph bristled. "I, too, bore a sword that day and with such honour that I was shown favour by William, young though I was." He indicated his neighbour at the table. "This is my dear friend and colleague Gervase Bret, whose father likewise joined the invasion of England under the duke's banner. You merely lost an arm, my lord. Gervase lost a father."

"What's past is past," said Canon Hubert irritably. "We must not spend a morning fighting a battle that happened twenty years ago. Let us address the issue at hand."

"I have never liked churchmen," said Hugh with measured contempt. "Let me deal with a soldier any day."

He turned to face Ralph once more, but it was Gervase who took the initiative. Looking up from a document, he spoke with a crisp authority that made the visitor blink.

"Our task is plain, my lord," he said. "We follow where others have led; we correct where mistakes have been made. We have power to change and a licence to punish any fraudulence or evasion." He glanced at the document. "Here in Bedwyn, we have detected a serious irregularity."

"Too many Saxons," sneered Hugh.

"I talk of land that adjoins your holding upstream towards Chisbury on the north-west side. Two hides in all."

"I know it well."

"In the description of this town, as compiled by the earlier commissioners, that land belongs to Bedwyn Abbey."

"It is mine!" snapped Hugh.

"You have disputed this case before."

"Yes!" protested the other. "Disputed and lost because those witless fools who sat behind that table just as you do now would not support my claim."

"The abbey had a charter."

"And so did I."

"Theirs countermanded yours."

"I went by custom and usage."

"Even there, they had a prior claim, my lord."

Hugh de Brionne roared. "Prior claim! That lying Prior Baldwin advanced their prior claim. He tied us all hand and foot with so much legal rope that we could not budge one inch. So part of my holding was gobbled up by the abbey."

"But they had use of that land," noted Canon Hubert.

"Word of mouth confirms it to be mine."

"It gave them rights."

"Indeed, my lord," said Gervase. "Two hides amount to well past two hundred acres. That is enough land for three farms and other small holdings. Then there are two mills which sit on the river that runs directly through that land. All those subtenants pay their rent to the abbey and not to you."

"I am owed that money by a grasping abbot."

Canon Hubert bridled. "Abbot Serlo is a saint."

"I believe it well, sir. Of him and of his prior. Serlo has a belly big enough for a dozen saints, and that scheming Baldwin is the patron saint of robbers. Give him a legal wrangle and he will talk the pizzle off a Pope and make it dance around the room and sing Te Deum."

"My lord!" exclaimed Hubert with moral outrage.

Ralph Delchard chuckled, Brother Simon hid his reddening face in some documents, and Gervase Bret afforded himself a smile of amusement. This Norman lord did not mince his words in the presence of the clergy. The black wolf was an apt symbol for Hugh de Brionne. He was a scavenger with sharp and deadly fangs. The abbey might have ousted him with argument, but it had earned itself an implacable enemy. If there was the faintest chance of revenge, he would take it.

"Restore those lands to me," he instructed. "Give me the rent that is due from the subtenants. Fine the abbey for its insolence and bury Prior Baldwin in a dung-heap so that men may know his character as they pass."

"I will not endure this!" wailed Canon Hubert.

Gervase resumed control. "The situation stands thus. You claim the land. The abbey had use of it and a charter to enforce that use. But there is now a third voice with a legitimate interest in those fertile acres. And that might disqualify both you and Prior Baldwin."

"Who is this rogue?"

"We may not say as yet," explained Gervase, "but he has a charter which may make both yours and that of the abbey as light and insubstantial as air. This is no idle claim, my lord. It is supported by Alfred of Marlborough."

Hugh de Brionne stiffened. Alfred was an important figure in the shire, with holdings even greater than his own. In wealth and reputation, he exceeded Hugh by far and the jealous lord of Chisbury could not wear this indignity. He and Alfred of Marlborough were wary rivals. If a new claim had such weight behind it, then it was threatening indeed.

"Why did this claimant not emerge before?" he asked.

"He lacked the charter to uphold his right."

"He has it now?"

"We will come to that," said Ralph Delchard, taking the reins once more. "We summoned you by way of courtesy to acquaint you with this news. Bring your charter to us again and we will set it against this new claim. And try them both once more against the abbey's right and title."

Hugh de Brionne remonstrated afresh, but it was only token bluster. The name of Alfred of Marlborough had sounded a warning note. He needed to consult with his steward and to make private enquiry of this counter-claim. Rising to his feet, he adjusted his cap and straightened his mantle. The clasp at its corner was a gold-embossed wolf that jogged a memory behind the table.

"You have, I believe," said Ralph, "hunting privileges in Savernake Forest."

"Why, so I do. Twice a month I ride." He curled a lip derisively. "I rid the forest of vermin. I may kill as many monks and novices as I can find, but only the king can hunt down a wily fox of a prior or a great fat bear of an abbot."

"Heresy!" shouted Canon Hubert.

"God made me the way I am."

"My question is this," said Ralph, unruffled. "Do you possess some mastiffs who have not been lawed?"

Hugh was evasive. "My animals are my concern."

"Do any of them have the freedom of Savernake?"

"My dogs have keepers who know their occupation."

"I have hunting dogs myself," said Ralph. "If they are

bred for the chase, they may sometimes chase of their own free will. Let such a creature off the leash and he may kill or maim as viciously as any wolf."

"That is true," admitted Hugh. "We have had such a case in our pack before now. When a dog runs amok, I order my men to put it down. There is no place for madness in the kennels of Hugh de Brionne."

He strode away to the door, then paused as he was struck by a final malignant thought. It produced a leer.

"This new claimant of yours," he said. "Tell him that I will happily cede the land to him if it will serve to spite the abbey. I'd willingly lose two further hides and half another arm to see that sheep-faced villain of a prior put in his place."

His laughter was like the howl of a wolf.

Monks were human. Though they aspired to the condition of sainthood, they could reach it only by the mundane paths of their pedestrian abilities. An abbey could not exist simply as a metaphor for God's purpose. It was a living organism. It had to be fed and watered, clothed and bedded, maintained and improved. An obedientiary might, therefore, have to till fields, cook meals, brew ale, clean plates, fetch rushes, supply hot water, shave heads, provide cowls, change bedding, ring bells, or rehearse the choir to the right sweetness of pitch. Whatever skills a man brought into the enclave were welcomed and employed. There was labour for all arms and work for all minds. No talents were wasted at Bedwyn Abbey.

Brother Peter still bent over his bench to produce fine silverware. Brother Thaddeus still handled a plough with the rough-handed zeal he had shown when he was a farmer. Brother Thomas still sewed and embroidered like the tailor he had once been. And Brother Luke, the robust young novice, still toiled in the bakehouse as his father had taught him. Even when monks were promoted within the house, they found it hard to let their old lives slip entirely away.

"We have been summoned, Matthew."

"When?" asked the lugubrious subprior.

"Tomorrow morning at ten."

"We will miss Chapter."

"That cannot be helped," said Prior Baldwin. "I have spoken with Abbot Serlo and we have leave to go and face these royal commissioners."

"Do we know their purpose, Prior Baldwin?"

Baldwin smirked. "We know it and we may refute it."

"That gladdens my heart," said Matthew, looking even more miserable than ever. "You talked with Brother Simon?"

"He talked with *me*."

The subprior came as near to smiling as he had done in the past five years, but he changed his mind at the very last moment and commuted the smile to a lick of his lips. They were in the scriptorium, the library of the abbey, where patient men with gifted hands sat at their desks to produce the beautiful illuminated manuscripts which adorned the shelves or which went to other parts of the country as cherished gifts. Subprior Baldwin was more patient and gifted than any and his work served to guide all other. If the prior wished to find his assistant, he had merely to open the door of the scriptorium.

"There is another claim," explained Baldwin.

"To which stretch of land?"

"The two hides we disputed with Hugh de Brionne."

"But that argument is over and settled."

"It is now, Matthew."

"Where is this other claimant?"

"Under six feet of earth in the parish graveyard."

"Alric Longdon?"

"He will trouble us no more."

"Then why do the commissioners still call us?"

"A mere formality," said Baldwin airily. "We may swinge them soundly for taking us away from our holy work and then send them on their way to Winchester once more."

"What of my lord, Hugh de Brionne?"

60

"The great black wolf has been chased from the forest."

"Will he contest that holding once more?"

"He may not. We have the charter to prove it is ours."

The monks nodded in unison with easy satisfaction. The subprior still wore his mask of sorrow, but it was lit around the edges like a dark cloud with a silver trim. He lifted his hand above the parchment and let it work its magic once more.

They dined at Saewold's house that afternoon. The town reeve had a comfortable dwelling on the edge of Bedwyn, with land at the front and rear to indicate his status and guarantee him privacy. They sat around a long oak table and feasted on beef, mutton, pork pies, capon, fish, cheese, pastry, blancmange, and fruit tarts. Wine and milk were also served. There were even some oysters for those with a discerning palate.

Gervase Bret was quietly impressed with the house itself, noting its size and furnishings and plate. Canon Hubert confined his admiration to the repast, at first refusing each new dish that was offered, then deigning to find just one more tiny corner in his capacious stomach. Brother Simon was still tormented by his indiscretion in the cloister garth that morning and dared not eat a thing for fear that he would bring it up again out of sheer guilt.

Ralph Delchard saw nothing but Ediva. Struck by her charms at their earlier encounter, he could now study them at his leisure. She bore herself well at table, composed yet merry, and her conversation moved from the light to the serious with no loss of fluency. Ediva was an educated woman in a country where most of her sex were kept ignorant. Ralph began to lose his heart over a plate of oysters.

"You have always lived in Bedwyn?" he asked.

"No, my lord," she said demurely, "I was born in Warminster and travelled with my father to France and Italy when I was younger."

"You look well on your voyaging."

"Would that I could journey so far afield again."

"Lady, I sense adventure in your soul."

She said nothing but conveyed a world of meaning with a gesture of her fine-skinned hands. The reeve still burbled.

"Have you concluded your deliberations for the day?" he said with an oleaginous smirk. "Is all well?"

"Yes," said Brother Simon tamely.

"No," overruled Canon Hubert.

"We have much more yet to do," said Gervase.

"And will you call my lord, Alfred of Marlborough?"

Simon winced, Hubert rumbled, and Gervase gave a non-committal shrug. Saewold knew more than they intended to let him know at this stage. A name which had only been spoken in the presence of Hugh de Brionne had now reached the ears of the town reeve. It made the commissioners treat their host with even more caution. This obliging official who was so anxious to volunteer information could garner it with equal speed. He needed to be watched.

While Saewold went on to divert them with more local gossip, Gervase appraised the man again. The reeve had done well to secure his office and to hold on to it through twenty years of Norman rule. Most Saxons who held positions of authority treated their overlords with a polite respect that masked their inevitable resentment. They obeyed and co-operated because they had no choice in the matter. Saewold dealt successfully with the Normans by doing his best to become one of them. In speech and fashion, he followed his masters and referred condescendingly to his fellow Saxons as if they were an inferior civilisation who had been delivered from their near barbarity by the arrival of a cultural elite from across the Channel. Gervase Bret took the opposite point of view, steadfastly believing, on the evidence of his own experience and observation, that the rich heritage of the Anglo-Saxons was being debased by the cruder values of the invaders. Looking at Saewold now, he saw the man as a rather depressing hybrid who embodied the worst of both cultures. In the next generation or so, Saewolds would populate the whole country like a brood of monstrous children from the forced marriage between

Saxon and Norman. Gervase was profoundly dejected. The reeve was the face of the future.

"I must tender my apologies," said their host with an open-armed gesture. "Tomorrow I must ride to Salisbury on important business and may be absent for a few days. I will not be on hand to superintend you here, but I will leave a deputy who will answer for me and render what assistance you may require."

"We are sorry to lose you," lied Ralph convincingly, "but we will manage very well without you here." His mind was on personal rather than royal affairs. "Your help and your hospitality have made our stay in Bedwyn much more pleasant and profitable than might otherwise be the case."

"Indeed, indeed," muttered Brother Simon.

"Yes," decided Canon Hubert. He weighed the excellence of the food against the nuisance of the reeve's zealous aid and came down in favour of the latter's departure. "Should we need your advice again, we may send to Salisbury. In the meantime, commend me to my lord, the sheriff."

"I will, Canon Hubert."

The meal was over and they rose to leave. Gervase had noted with dismay the blossoming relationship at the other end of the table and he sought to interpose himself between Ralph and Ediva so that no further conference might take place between them. Ralph was forced to take proper notice of his host for the first time and it sparked off another memory. From beneath his mantle, he produced the coins he had salvaged from the stream in the forest and showed them to Saewold.

"Do you recognise these, sir?" he asked.

"I do," said the reeve confidently. "Those coins were made here in Bedwyn. And recently, too, to judge by their shine. Few hands have soiled these. But they are ours."

"Can you be so certain?"

"I would know the work of our moneyer anywhere." He pointed to the markings on the face of the coin. "See here, my lord. This indicates where it was made and this is Eadmer's signature."

"Where is your mint?"

"Close by the church. It backs on to the river."

"And your moneyer? What name did you call him?"

"Eadmer. A curious fellow but skilful at his trade."

"I would meet with this Eadmer soon."

"My man will guide you to him."

"No, Husband," said Ediva with a natural poise which took all hint of impropriety from the offer. "I will conduct my lord to the place at his leisure."

Ralph Delchard smiled. He could kill two birds with one stone. It was arranged as easily as that.

"Father," she implored, "I ask this but as a favour to me."

"It may not be granted, child."

"Would you deny a heart-felt plea?"

"It falls on deaf ears."

"They are in distress and suffer dreadful pain."

"Let the abbey look to them," said Wulfgeat. "It is more suited to the relief of sorrow than my house."

"Will you not show pity to a poor widow and child?"

"I pity them, Leofgifu, but I will not take them in."

Wulfgeat was poring over his account book when his daughter came to see him, and the fact of her interruption was made more annoying by its nature. Leofgifu wished to bring the widow and son of the late Alric Longdon into their home so that she could sustain them through their mourning. Wulfgeat resisted the idea strongly. He was not unkind and was capable of an astonishing generosity at times, but he drew the line at helping the relatives of an enemy.

He was forthright. "I hated Alric," he said.

"That is no reason to hate his wife and child."

"They are tarred with his ignominy."

"What harm have they ever done to you?"

"None at all," he confessed, "but there was no need. Alric caused enough harm for all three of them. The rogue cheated me out of fifty marks and threatened to take me to court over another matter he thrust upon me."

"Why, then, did you do business with such a man?"

"His price was cheap and his sacks full of good flour. If this miller had stuck to his mill, I would have no quarrel, but he grew avaricious and wanted more than his due."

"Hilda had no part in this."

"She profited by his foul deception."

"Where is the profit in a dead husband?"

Leofgifu spoke with unexpected vehemence. She had always been a dutiful daughter who bowed herself to her father's will, but here was something which even she could not accept without protest. Her father—like so many in the town of Bedwyn—may have loathed and distrusted Alric, but she hoped that loathing would not pursue him beyond the grave. Wulfgeat's own bereavement should have taught him the value of tenderness and concern, for it was what now bonded father and daughter. Within the last year, her father had lost his wife and Leofgifu had lost both mother and husband. In returning to live at home, she found a softness and a vulnerability about Wulfgeat that she had never known before, and it had drawn them ever closer. Adversity had deepened their love and understanding. It hurt her, therefore, when he was unable to show that same love and understanding now.

"Have you so soon forgotten?" she pressed.

"Peace, child. You touch on my pain."

"It is shared by a wife and child," she argued. "They have no one else to turn to at this time. The abbey has opened its doors, but a community of monks can never offer the special solace that a family can which welcomes them into its bosom." She put her hands on his table and leaned down at him. "Let me be more plain, sir. Hilda needs the company of a woman. I can be of use in her travail."

"Then visit her at the abbey."

"Invite her here."

"I am the master of this house and I refuse."

"Then I will no longer stay beside you."

Wulfgeat was shocked. "Leofgifu!"

"I have been obedient in all else, Father, even when my heart counselled against it. But this time, I will not submit to your rule." She straightened her back and lifted her chin to show her firmness of purpose. "Hilda and the boy beg for help. If you will not give it, I will find a way on my own."

"You would *leave* your home?"

"If I find such cruelty here, I will."

"Leofgifu . . ."

"My mind is set. They need our Christian charity."

Wulfgeat was deeply troubled. He got up from his seat and came around the table to offer his arms, but she pulled away. His daughter's intensity was so uncharacteristic that it took him unawares and he was unable to cope with it. He moved about the room and fingered his beard as he searched for a compromise which would content her yet leave his feelings in the matter quite unchanged. He came to a halt.

"We will give them money," he suggested.

"They need love not alms."

"But we will pay for their lodging, Leofgifu."

"They have lodging enough," she pointed out. "If that were all their need, they could stay at the abbey or return to the mill itself. It is not just a room that they require. It is a woman who comprehends their misery and who can make that room a place of comfort."

They faced each other across a widening gap. Both feared the horror of separation, yet neither could find the way to prevent it. Wulfgeat made a last attempt at exerting his paternal authority.

"They will not come and you will not leave," he said.

"I am not at your command."

"A daughter must be subject to her father."

"I am subject to no man," she insisted, her eyes blazing. "When you gave me to my husband, you gave him the right that you now urge. I served him like a loving wife and

66

grieve for him still. But I will not give allegiance to you or any man on earth." She spun on her heel. "I will make arrangements to quit your house today."

"Stay!" he appealed. "I need you here beside me."

"Others have a stronger claim."

"Hold there, Leofgifu!"

She had opened the door, but the anguish in his voice made her stop and turn. He looked as fierce and unyielding as ever, but there were tears in his eyes. Leofgifu met his gaze without flinching. Throughout her life, she had asked so little of him that she felt entitled to make this one demand even if it tore them both apart. Imperceptibly, his coldness began to thaw.

"How long would they stay?" he murmured.

"As long as they find it necessary."

"I would not wish to see them myself."

"Nor will you," she promised. "The house is large and they will need small space. I'll keep them close by me. Your presence would distress them only the more."

"I despised that man!"

"Do not punish them for his offence."

Wulfgeat wandered around the room once more and punched a fist into the palm of the other hand. A man whose command had ruled his house for decades could not easily receive an order himself, but then he had never been challenged from such an unprecedented quarter.

"You may fetch them both here, Leofgifu."

"Thank you, Father!" She ran to him to bestow a kiss.

"They are your responsibility," he warned. "I will pay to feed them and house them, but you must supply all else."

"Indeed I shall."

"They may come here tomorrow."

"Why delay?" she said, pressing home her triumph. "I will hurry to the abbey now and secure their release. They will be here within the hour."

She flitted out of the room before he could stop her. Wulfgeat heaved a sigh. His own wife would never have stood up to him the way that his daughter had just done. He had to respect her for that. It was ironic. Wulfgeat was rightly feared by all in Bedwyn for his iron will and a fierce Saxon pride that would not even moderate itself in the presence of his Norman rulers. Few would dare to cross him in argument and fewer still live to boast that they had bested him. Yet he now lay completely routed and the person who had accomplished the feat was no fellow-burgess who could roar even louder than he. It was the mildest young woman in the town and the only thing in life that he still truly loved.

Brother Thaddeus did not spend all his time chained to one of the abbey ploughs or fetching in the harvest. His strong muscles were put to other service in Bedwyn Abbey. As he strolled into Savernake Forest that evening, it was this secondary employment that was on his mind. A brawny man of middle height, he had a big, shapeless, weather-beaten face that seemed at odds with the careful tonsure above it. As he stumped through the undergrowth on huge and undiscriminating feet, he sang snatches of the Mass to himself and looked about him. He reached a grove of birch trees but rejected them on sight. They had the soft downy twigs that were hopeless for his purpose. He snapped a branch off idly and cast it to the ground. It had too much mercy in it.

Other twigs cracked nearby and he paused to listen. He was being watched. By what or by whom, he did not know, but he sensed at once that he was under surveillance. Stopping as casually as he could, he picked up the fallen branch and pretended to examine it while trying to work out exactly where the sound had originated. When he was confident of direction, he tapped the branch gently against a tree, then turned without warning to fling it with venom at the watching creature. His aim was close enough. There was a scramble in the bushes and the sound of flight. Thaddeus pulled the sharp knife from his scrip and thundered after the noise, but all he managed to see was a flash of matted brown hair as it scuttled into oblivion.

Panting with his exertions, he stopped to recover his

breath and to wonder what it was that he had seen. He recalled the dead body he had helped to carry in from the forest and guessed at some connection with this phantom animal. His lumbering pursuit brought one consolation. He was now standing beside another birch and one more fitted to his needs. Thaddeus grinned, the knife slashed, and he gathered up a handful of the harsh, rough twigs. He took a great swipe at the trunk itself and left it scarred with the power of his arm.

Brother Thaddeus was happy. When he got back to the abbey, he would be fully equipped to administer correction to any wrongdoers. It was a pleasing way to serve God.

Gervase Bret still occasionally felt that lust for solitude which had drawn him to the monastic life in his youth, though not always from the same promptings. Time alone meant time to think of his beloved Alys back in Winchester and to rehearse the speech with which he would next greet her. He missed her more each time that they were parted, but the king's work had to be done and that meant constant travel away from the Treasury. Domesday Book was a prodigious undertaking and the commissioners who had visited the various circuits had been as rigorous in their researches as they could, but the very speed of their enquiry told against them, for their returns were full of minor errors, strange inconsistencies, deliberate lies, patent malpractices, and clear evidence of criminal behaviour. Gervase Bret and his colleagues would be months on the road before their work of detection and arrest was fully completed. Alys would have to pine for him in Winchester.

Time alone also meant time away from Ralph Delchard. The closeness of their friendship became an aggravation whenever Ralph found a new woman to court and conquer. Apart from scandalising the faithful Gervase, it drew attention to the exigencies in his own romance and increased his sense of yearning. If he could do nothing to stop Ralph's pursuit of Ediva, the wife of the town reeve, he would not encourage it by letting his friend talk interminably about his carnal ambitions. On this issue, if on no other, they neither thought nor acted as one.

Gervase mixed seclusion with curiosity. Instead of walking aimlessly near the hunting lodge, he headed for the river and strolled along its bank towards the disputed land which had brought them down on Bedwyn. It was a most pleasant walk in the warm evening air and his eyes remained alert to take in every change and beauty of the landscape. His mind, however, shifted to other things. Bidding farewell to Alys, his thoughts turned back to the bizarre experience on Salisbury Plain when he had looked on Stonehenge for the first time. It affected his whole perception of himself and the world in which he lived and he was exercised by the notion, if not the certainty, that the circle of stones on the plain was the work of an intelligence and a faith that went back thousands of years to the dawn of time. He was still trying to divine its mysteries and to pluck some meaning from its fractured magnificence when he saw the mill.

He knew that it had belonged to Alric Longdon, because its wheel had been stopped. It was a low, squat, ramshackle construction, with the cottage leaning against it for support like a child clutching the skirts of its mother. Yet it was well situated to catch the best of the current and its wheel gained further advantage from a primitive sluice-gate which had been installed a little farther upstream. In times of drought, when the river level dropped, the gate could be partially closed to restrict the channel and quicken the surge. Alric Longdon was an astute miller who knew how to exploit nature to the full. His sluice-gate was the only one in Bedwyn because his rivals were deterred from following his example by the heavy cost of the enterprise.

Gervase Bret was mesmerised. What had made a lovely young woman like Hilda share her life with an unpopular man in the deafening roar of his mill? How had the ugly creature he had seen in the mortuary chapel met and married such a wife? What did they talk about in the isolation of their home? How did they pass their days and spend their nights? These and other questions crowded into his mind, to be expelled at once and replaced by a much more immediate query: Who was *this*?

For the mill was not as neglected and uninhabited as it appeared. Someone was at the window. The figure disappeared from view, then emerged again from the door. He turned to slam it shut and lock it with a key, testing it to make sure that it was sound. The key vanished into the man's scrip and his tonsured head vanished into his hood. With swift and sandalled feet, he hurried off in the direction of the abbey and was soon blending with the shadow of the trees.

Gervase watched it all with surprised interest. There was something about the man's manner which suggested defeat and annoyance, as if he had entered the building in search of an object which he never found. While Gervase could only speculate on his purpose, he was certain of his identity. He had met this man before. Gervase was too far away to recognise the face but close enough to observe the stance and gait of the visitor. Those years spent in Eltham Abbey had taught him how to distinguish monk from monk even when they were hooded and bowed. Each man moved in a different way, knelt in a different way, and prayed in a different way. This tall and long-striding prelate declared himself as clearly as if he had yelled out his own name.

It was Prior Baldwin.

Chapter Five

COLD FEAR TIGHTENED ITS GRIP SLOWLY BUT INEXORABLY on the town of Bedwyn. A man had been savaged by a wolf, but the animal had neither been tracked nor caught. Something had been sighted in Savernake Forest by the warden's huntsmen, and one of the verders also claimed to have caught a glimpse of a peculiar creature that flitted through the trees. Rumours now came from the abbey of Brother Thaddeus's encounter with this nameless beast. Bedwyn locked its doors and slept uneasily. Something was out there in the forest which could elude all attempt at capture. It concentrated the mind of the whole community. When would it strike again?

The longer it remained at large, the more hysterical became the theories about its true identity. Some claimed it was a giant fox, quicker and more cunning than a wolf, able to deceive and outrun its pursuers with ease. Others believed it to be a bear, long thought extinct in Savernake, hiding in safety in some tall tree and descending only to search for food. More exotic animals were also numbered in the catalogue of horrific possibilities. Lions and tigers were the favoured species, even though neither were native to England. Leopards were also invented to explain the nimble feet with which the predator could so swiftly vanish. Those most in terror fled into the realms of myth and decided that Savernake was haunted by a gryphon, a dragon, or a minotaur and that it would descend upon the town at any moment to wreak its havoc.

Wulfgeat did not surrender to the general frenzy, but he

nevertheless supplied an idea which acted as its focus. An early visitor to the market that morning, he found the hubbub unabated on the subject of Alric Longdon's death. Scoffing at the wilder suggestions, he produced a much more telling one.

"The widow and the boy stay at my house," he said, and immediately set off a murmur of surprise. "Leogifu is able to bring comfort and that is our Christian duty. My daughter has talked at length with the poor woman. What she has found may kill off wolf, fox, and bear."

"Hilda can name the creature?" asked a listener.

"No," said Wulfgeat, "but she can point to a sworn enemy of her husband."

"Then she can point in any direction!" came a cynical retort. "We were all sworn enemies of that man. You as much as anyone, Wulfgeat. We bear witness to that."

"I may have wished him dead but would not do the deed myself. This other foe *would* seek his life. In her own malicious way." Wulfgeat lowered his voice. "I speak of Emma."

The name turned the expectant buzz into a torrent of abuse. They seized upon it with ferocious glee.

"Emma!"

"The Witch of Crofton!"

"A foul slut with a wild dog!"

"An evil sorceress!"

"A slimey hag!"

"Blood-sucker!"

"Devil-worshipper!"

"Poisoner!"

"Whore!"

Wulfgeat raised his hands. "Calm yourselves and hear the argument," he told them. "I do not accuse Emma, but I do avow she had both cause and means. Or so the widow claims."

"What did Hilda say?"

"That her husband fell out with Emma." Wulfgeat spoke on over the mocking laughter. "Yes, yes, everyone fell out

73

with Alric sooner or later, but not in this manner. He bought a potion from her—for what, I do not know. When it did not work, he demanded his money back. When Emma would not pay, he beat her black-and-blue."

"Serves the witch right!" sneered a voice.

"She put a curse on him," explained Wulfgeat. "Alric looked to have another son by his new wife, but Emma said her womb would henceforth be barren. When the miller beat her again, she screamed that he'd be dead within the month."

"When was this, Wulfgeat?"

"But three weeks past."

The angry listeners needed no more persuasion. Emma, the so-called Witch of Crofton, the maker of potions, the caster of spells, was promptly installed as the culprit. Out went wolf, fox, bear, and other animals and in came the big black slavering dog that Emma kept in her hovel. Bent on summary justice, they were all for riding down to Crofton there and then to slaughter both witch and dog and rid the shire of two excrescences in one swoop, but Wulfgeat exerted control.

"Silence!" he decreed. "Yesterday, you feared a pack of wolves in Savernake. Today, you are that pack of wolves yourselves. Guilty she may be, but that guilt is not proven in a court of law. This is work for the sheriff. If Emma *is* a witch and that dog is her familiar, she will be held to account. Her curse and her cur destroyed Alric Longdon."

The men laughed with brutal delight. They were content. They now had a scapegoat.

She waddled along through the bushes and gathered herbs into her basket. Somewhere in the thickets, her mangy companion nosed around for food and snuffled excitedly. Emma was a short, rotund woman who was barely into her thirties yet who looked many years older. Her pudgy face had merry eyes, a snub nose, and a full mouth, but its inherent jollity was offset by the thick, dark eyebrows and the unsightly facial hair that spread upwards to merge with her own straggly thatch and make her rather daunting to behold. Even in the heat of summer, she wore a tattered hood and cloak over her stained gunna and she had on the gartered stockings of a man. Her feet were covered in tight bundles of rags.

Emma of Crofton lived just north of the village in a tiny cottage. She was thus within easy walking distance of Savernake Forest and often penetrated its boundaries to search for herbs or to gather firewood in winter. Born and raised in Burbage, to the south-west, she had been fined for adultery with a married man, then driven out by the women of the place to seek a more isolated life. Her cottage was a huddle of stones with a leaking roof, and its stink could be picked up a hundred yards away. But Emma had come to prefer her own company and lived in mild contentment.

She could make ointments, medicines, and compounds for the cure of the sick and set a bone better than any doctor in the area. Even those afraid of her sometimes used her magic. Emma was a potent woman who had grown to be part of the landscape. Nobody bothered her unless they needed help—and even then would they keep their distance.

The man on the roan was not from the locality. As he was trotting towards Bedwyn, he came upon the figure of a fine fat wench groping in the bushes. Because she was bent double, all he could see was the shape of her buttocks and the vigour of her movement. It was enough to kindle lust. Checking that nobody was in sight, he reined in his mount, dropped from the saddle, and approached her boldly from the rear.

"Good morning, mistress!" he said.

"Go your way, sir," she advised without looking up.

"Then give me a kiss to send me on my way."

"I will give you more than that."

The hirsute face turned to confront him and he backed away with disgust. He did not get far. Hurtling out of the thickets with a loud yelp came a huge black dog which did not pause for introduction. It simply launched itself at the man and knocked him flat on his back, baring its fangs in

75

his face and keeping him prisoner for several yapping minutes until a command from his mistress drew him off. He
scrambled up and raced to his horse at full speed, unsure
whether the dog or its owner was the more frightening.
Emma cackled and the animal barked. They had put the
man to flight.

He would have a story to tell when he reached Bedwyn.

Prior Baldwin and Subprior Matthew presented themselves
at the shire hall at the appointed hour. Their daily life set
to a rigid timetable, they were slaves to punctuality. The
commissioners were seated behind the table. Ralph
Delchard rose to welcome them and gesture them forward
to the two chairs which had been set ready. Matthew moved
at his usual funereal pace, but Baldwin had a spring in his
step. He was obviously looking forward to matching his
wits against those of his examiners and seemed assured of
success. There was a tranquil confidence about him which
contrasted with the irritation he had shown the previous
evening as he left the mill. Disappointment had been put
behind him. Only victory and vindication could lie ahead.

When both men were seated, with a satchel of documents
resting on the floor between them, Ralph went through the
formalities and introduced each member of the commission.
He then left the early exchanges to Canon Hubert, who
seized his moment like one who has been waiting for it all
his life.

"Bedwyn Abbey must be put under close inspection," he
said smugly. "We are unhappy about several details of the
return that was made by our predecessors."

"The fault is with them and not with us," suggested
Baldwin tartly. "The abbey can withstand any scrutiny."

Hubert reprimanded him. "It is not your place to criticise
the royal officers. May I remind you that the first commissioners included no less a person than His Grace, the
Bishop of Durham?"

It was time to trade their credentials.

"We answer to Osmund, Bishop of Salisbury," asserted Baldwin superciliously.

Hubert replied in kind. "We answer to Walkelyn, Bishop of Winchester and my own master."

"My master is Abbot Serlo."

"He falls short of a bishopric."

"Abbot Serlo was Prior of Caen," said Baldwin with emphasis, "and I was his subprior."

"I held that office in Bec," replied Hubert, "when Lanfranc ruled the house. Archbishop Lanfranc now rules the English Church from Canterbury, while you and Abbot Serlo remain in a lowlier station."

"We are servants of the Benedictine order."

"I am the servant of God!"

Canon Hubert was wreathed in smiles. He felt that he had drawn first blood, and he turned to nod at Brother Simon. The abbey representatives maintained a hurt silence that was broken by Ralph Delchard.

"What does it matter who serves whom?" he bellowed. "Hubert struts around in Winchester Cathedral, while Abbot Serlo and his monks paddle about in this backwater. Each has found his own vocation and must be respected for that. True Christianity lies in showing tolerance."

Gervase Bret was startled to hear such an observation from so unlikely a source, and the clergy—monastic and lay alike—were quite astounded. To be lectured on Christianity by a man as brash and worldly as Ralph Delchard was too much to bear. They complained in unison, but he cowed them into silence once more and slapped the table with a firm palm.

"Let us get down to the main point of our visit."

"Very well," agreed Canon Hubert, taking the parchment that was slipped to him by Brother Simon, "it concerns two hides of land whose ownership is as yet unclear."

"To which land do you refer?" asked Baldwin, concealing his foreknowledge. "Two hides, you say? Two miserable hides? Did you really ride all the way from Winchester to quarrel over such a small parcel of land?"

"There is an issue at stake here."

"I fail to see it, Canon Hubert."

"Your capacity for failure already has been noted."

"Identify this land," said the prior through clenched teeth, "and we will answer you."

"It lies to the north-west of the town, along the river. Three farms and two mills occupy it. Hugh de Brionne had an interest in it, but the abbey set it aside."

Baldwin nodded. "I know this land well."

"Do you have proof that it belongs to the abbey?"

"We have brought a charter with us."

"That is very resourceful of you, Prior Baldwin," said Gervase. "When the abbey has so much land and so many holdings, how did you know that this was the charter that would be needed?"

"Simple guesswork, sir."

"And the power of prayer," added Matthew.

"Yes," said Ralph sharply. "You prayed that one of us would let fall a hint of today's business." His eye flicked to Brother Simon. "It appears that one of us did so."

"Abbot Serlo needs us," resumed Baldwin airily, "so we would not be detained long here. Brother Matthew will show you this document to affirm our right. You can verify our claim, put these two hides to rest, and let us return to our spiritual duties at the abbey."

The subprior had the parchment in his hand at once and unrolled it to spread it on the table. He and Baldwin then sat back with the satisfaction of men who are certain they have just won the day. They could boast about it over dinner with Abbot Serlo. Ralph Delchard gave the document a cursory glance and passed it to Gervase Bret. The latter pored over it intently as Hubert picked up his theme.

"There is another claimant to this land."

"The lord of the manor of Chisbury has been ousted."

"I speak of a third voice."

"Then let us hear it now."

"That is difficult," conceded Brother Simon.

"Be quiet, man," reproved Hubert, "you have said more than enough already. *Silentium est aurium.*"

Simon accepted the rebuke with a meek nod. There would be further castigation to face from the canon, and he was not looking forward to it. He sagged penitentially.

It was Baldwin's turn to crow. "Brother Simon touches on the truth of the matter. No claimant, no dispute. Unless you wish to dig him up from the churchyard and ask him to recite his argument. The abbey will not be dispossessed by a dead miller." He rose to go. "May we please depart?"

"No," said Ralph.

"But Alric Longdon will not appear."

"He does not need to, Prior Baldwin," said Hubert with a shrug. "He is not himself the claimant."

Complacence was wiped from the countenance opposite. "Then who is?" demanded Baldwin, sitting down.

"His wife."

"Hilda?"

"Even she."

"But she made no mention of this," whined the prior. "I spoke with her but yesterday and she talked only of her husband's charter. The poor woman was beside herself with grief, but she would know the difference between what belongs to her husband and what to her. Would she not?"

Gervase continued to peruse the document but solved a little mystery at the same time. Prior Baldwin had been to the mill to search for the charter. Having inveigled the key from the widow, he let himself into their home, intent on finding and destroying evidence of another's claim to abbey lands. Fortunately, he left empty-handed.

Matthew came to the help of his beleaguered prior.

"If the woman has a claim, why did she not make it in front of the first commission?"

"Because she did not live in Bedwyn at the time. Alric had not then married her. Hilda—or her father, to be more precise—made their sworn statements to the commissioners of the Worcestershire circuit."

"Worcestershire?" repeated Matthew.

"Hilda lived in Queenhill. You know the place?"

"No," snarled Baldwin, "and do not wish to know it."

"You will come to," promised Hubert. "Queenhill is a pretty village among several in the area. They include Berrow, Pendock, Ripple, Castlemorton, Bushley, and—"

"We need no lessons in geography," said Baldwin.

"Plainly, you do." Hubert gave the professional smile of an executioner who has just been handed his weapon to carry out a sentence. "Castlemorton, Bushley—and Longdon."

Baldwin and Matthew froze. "Longdon?" they chorused.

"It is where Alric's father was born," explained the canon. "Hence his name. Alric Longdon. He took it out of loyalty to his father, as you will hear in time."

The prior fought hard to recover. "None of this is germane if the miller is dead. What do we care about his parentage? It has no bearing here."

"But it does. It is the key to the whole affair."

"How?"

"All will be explained."

"This is most perplexing," said Baldwin, then opted for a frontal attack. "Does the widow possess a charter?"

"Yes."

"Do you have this document?"

"Not yet."

"Then you have no case."

"And we may go back to the abbey," said Matthew.

"Not so fast," warned Hubert. "We may not have the charter itself, but we have a fair copy."

"A copy is worthless," said Baldwin.

"Alfred of Marlborough did not think so. When it was shown to him, he supported every word of it. We are duty-bound to take seriously the oath of such a man as he."

Baldwin and Matthew were writhing about like two eels caught in a net. They were confounded. Hubert enjoyed the sight before prodding them with an invisible spear.

"You have been lazy," he mocked. "You are not well informed enough to carry your argument. You prepare to

80

fight against Alric, and his widow is your opponent. You think that we have come here for two hides of land, when it is the entire estate of Bedwyn Abbey that we question. If there is one act of deception, there may be a hundred more. This is not a casual enquiry that we make here. You are on trial."

"I will not suffer any more of this!" exclaimed the prior, trying to bluster his way out. "We have a charter and the other claimant does not. The law is on our side, the first commissioners are on our side, God is on our side." He stood once more and restated his case. "Dispute is irrelevant. We have the charter."

Gervase Bret looked up with a smile and nodded.

"Yes, Prior Baldwin," he said, "you have the charter. But that will not advantage you in the least."

"Why not?"

"The document is a complete forgery."

Brother Luke's doubts about his future continued to grow. It made him preoccupied and careless. He was distracted during his lessons and the master of the novices upbraided him sternly in front of his fellows. Sarcasm has a cutting edge, and it was a lacerated Brother Luke who sought out his one true friend at the abbey. Brother Peter was in his little workshop near the stables, crouched over his brazier as he heated something up and added a dry turf to bring the blaze to the right temperature. Luke knocked on the door and entered, only to be struck by the force of the heat in the confined space. Peter smiled a welcome, the perspiration glistening on his brow and turning his tonsured head into a veritable mirror.

Busy as he was, Peter sensed the greater needs of his young charge and put his work aside instantly. He sat Luke down and let him pour out his troubles at will, hearing of qualms and fears that he himself had experienced when he first entered the abbey. He told the novice how he had wrestled with them and finally overcome all reservation.

"Do you have no regrets, Peter?"

"None at all, save one."

"And what is that?"

"I wish I had been a postulant at your age."

"Truly?"

"The world coarsened me, Luke."

"But how?"

"It dragged me down; it snared me in temptation. It gave me a trade—I practice it here, as you see—but my life was empty and wasted. It had neither form nor direction until I came here. Abbot Serlo was my salvation."

Brother Luke winced. "I feel he is my gaoler."

"Our holy father is a blessed man."

"You may say that, Peter, because you have come through the torment, but I still suffer it. I still yearn for my freedom. I still toss and turn at night."

Peter shook his head. "You are wrong. There is torment here still for me and I must endure it." He glanced in the direction of the abbot's quarters. "I have an audience with Abbot Serlo soon and he will take confession."

"But you have no sins on your conscience."

"Indeed I do, Brother Luke."

"May I know what they are?"

"You see one right in front of you."

"This workshop?"

"I serve the Lord in my own way but neglect my other duties. I have missed services in church and been lax in the sacristy of late. Brother Paul, the subsacristan, has hidden my misdeeds and made excuse for my absences, but someone else has reported me to Father Abbot."

Luke was shocked. "You will be punished?"

"Severely. I deserve no less."

"But you are sacristan."

"Then I should dignify my office, not let it slip."

"No brother in the abbey labours more than you."

"It is true," agreed Peter, "but my work conflicts with my allotted tasks. I come here instead of to the sacristy. I leave the dormitory at night to find more time at my bench."

"For what reason?"

"Shall I show you?"

The boyish face lit up. "You are making something?"

"My finest piece of work."

"Let me see it. Please let me see it."

"Nobody else must know."

"I can keep a secret, Brother Peter. Trust me."

Peter closed the door in case anyone should chance to pass, then he took a key from his scrip to unlock a drawer in the workbench. Something large and heavy was lifted out with reverential care and laid down on the wooden service where it could catch the morning light through the window. The object was wrapped in an old sheet, and Peter lifted back the folds with delicate movements of his hands. When Brother Luke finally beheld it, his eyes moistened with emotion.

"A crucifix!"

"Silver-plated, with an enamel Saviour."

"It is beautiful, Peter! Such workmanship."

"Wait till it is finished."

"Abbot Serlo will not correct you for making this," said Luke earnestly. "He will fall to his knees and give thanks for your goodness."

Peter smiled soulfully. "I think not."

The silversmith put the crucifix away and locked the drawer, then he took the novice on a walk around the garden to let him voice his disquiet once more. When Luke finally left his friend, his anxieties had been stilled and his faith rekindled by what he had seen in the workshop. Brother Peter was indeed a fine example for the boy.

Abbot Serlo disagreed. When he had heard confession an hour later, he rolled his bulging eyes with disapproval at his erring sacristan. Obedience to the rule had been flouted and that could never be ignored or forgiven.

"You have sinned, Brother Peter."

"I know it, Father Abbot, and do confess it."

"Others rely on you and they were sorely let down."

"I was led astray by my work."

"You are a monk first and foremost," chided the other. "That fact must guide your every waking thought."

"And so it did," said Peter, "until this month."

"You are guilty of neglect and deception," Abbot Serlo adjudicated, "and Subsacristan Paul did you no favours by concealing your shortcomings. They were bound to be revealed in good time and bring you to my sentence."

"I accept it willingly, Father Abbot."

"Serious offences call for serious punishment."

"Pronounce upon me."

Abbot Serlo stared down at the wayward monk and took time to consider his fate. Peter's record at the abbey had been blameless until now and brought him promotion to the office that he held. To deprive him of that office would be a humiliation, and Serlo stopped short of that. What was needed was a painful shock to awake the sacristan to the pre-eminence of his duties. The abbot might be destined for sainthood, but that did not absolve him from making stern decisions while he still remained on earth. He cleared his throat noisily, his jowls vibrated, and his eyes threatened to leave their sockets entirely. Brother Peter took a deep breath and braced himself for the verdict. Abbot Serlo was succinct.

"Here is work for Brother Thaddeus. . . ."

Four hours of unremitting tussle with Prior Baldwin and with Subprior Matthew left them feeling exhilarated but tired. It had opened up all kinds of possibilities. The prelates had limped away to report to their abbot and to cover their disarray. As they left the shire hall, the commissioners were pleased with their prosecution of the case. They had won a resounding victory at the first skirmish, but the battle was far from over. Baldwin and Matthew would soon be back with other weapons and other forms of defence.

Ralph Delchard and Gervase Bret rode back alone towards the hunting lodge, choosing the route which took them along the river as it bordered Savernake. Both had been impressed by the role that Canon Hubert had taken that morning.

"He roasted the prior over a slow fire," said Ralph with a chortle. "He led him along by the nose before he struck. Our canon is no mean fighting man, Gervase."

"Brother Simon was his bait."

"That was why he left him alone with Baldwin at the abbey. Simon knew only what we wanted him to know."

"Yes," said Gervase with a grin. "When he told the prior the truth, he really believed it himself. He did not realise it was only part of the truth, fed to him on purpose so that it could be wheedled out of him."

"Innocence is a blessed thing."

"It has its uses."

The sky was overcast now and there was a hint of rain in the wind. Savernake Forest looked overgrown and surly. It was certainly in no mood to yield up the secret which still tantalised them. Ralph had given it much thought.

"Alric Longdon kept his hoard in the yew," he said, "and he was about to add to it the day he was killed. But someone else found his hiding place and took his treasure chest away."

"Before or after his death?"

"Who can say?"

"Why was it kept there and not in his mill?"

"For the sake of safety," said Ralph. "The mill had many visitors and there was a wife and son to consider. Alric concealed his bounty even from them. Besides," he continued with a grim chuckle, "had he left it in the mill, any thieving prior might find it when he let himself in to search for a missing charter. I now believe that the charter, which we all seek, is locked away in the treasure chest as well and may be worth more than all those silver coins together. The widow should have a rich inheritance."

"It is as well she has left the abbey."

"Wulfgeat's daughter tends her now."

Gervase looked across at the forest. Patches of thick woodland were interspersed with heath and scrub. Birds drew pictures in the air as they sang. Animals called out in the trees. The wind produced a thousand answering voices as it bent creaking branches and shook crisp leaves.

"You are a huntsman, Ralph," he said.

"Whenever I have the time."

"Do you think there is a wolf in Savernake?"

"Not now," said Ralph, "or it would certainly have been seen or scented or killed. Wolves are untidy guests. They leave a mess behind."

"Yes. I saw the miller at the mortuary."

"Something is in those trees, Gervase. But not a wolf."

"What sort of animal is it, then?"

"One that I will enjoy tracking down."

"We have other inquiries to make first," recalled his friend. "I must make contact with Brother Luke and see what I can learn about the abbey from the inside. And you must see Eadmer the Moneyer."

"I go to the mint this evening."

"Is it wise to take a guide?"

"Ediva offered," said Ralph artlessly. "How could I refuse such an invitation from a lady? Her husband is away in Salisbury and she has need of diversion."

"The lady is married," insisted Gervase.

"She chafes against the yoke."

"Adultery is a mortal sin."

"Then do not commit it," advised Ralph. "Think on Alys and keep yourself pure. Leave wickedness to those of us with greater urges and lesser scruples."

"Think on the *danger*!"

"That is the chief attraction."

Gervase did all he could to talk his friend around, but no headway had been made by the time they reached the lodge. He should have known better. Once Ralph Delchard committed himself to a course of action, whatever its nature, he never diverged from it. Grooms took their horses to stable them while the two commissioners went indoors. One last question remained unanswered for Ralph.

"How did you know that the charter was forged?"

"I did not," admitted Gervase. "But I do now."

The peasant woman was typical of so many who lived on the fringes of Bedwyn. Her husband was a cottar, part of a small and wretched underclass who were given a hovel and a thin slice of land in return for their labour. The man worked hard, but the good earth did not reward him well. The bad harvest of the previous year was followed by a famine that struck those at the lower end of society most keenly. When the man's sufferings were compounded by an injury to his arm while using the plough in which he had quarter share, he was unable to do his full quota of work. His wife and small children grew thin and sickly. Desperation drove him to slip into Savernake Forest one night. Two hares and some wood pigeons kept them fed for a week or more, but their good fortune was noted by envious eyes. Information was laid against the cottar and the warden's officers arrived in time to find the wife making a stew with the bones.

"He has been locked up for a month," wailed the woman.

"Forest law is cruel," said Emma with rough sympathy.

"He must wait for the shire court to sit and hear his case. If they find him guilty, he may lose his sight or worse. What condition will we be in then?"

"Think on yourself and the children," advised the visitor. "Your husband's ordeal is the worse for worrying about you. If we can make you better, we take one small load off his mind."

The woman nodded. Starvation had pushed her to extremes and she had seized on the rotting carcass of a squirrel she had found. It had filled their bellies but emptied them almost as quickly. Both she and her children were crying with such pain that Emma of Crofton had to be sent for as a last resort. While her dog sat outside the hovel, Emma reached into her bag and pulled out a tiny bottle of liquid.

"Mix three drops of this with a little water," she prescribed. "Take it morning, noon, and night. Your pains will soon abate."

"We have no money," said the patient hopelessly, "but you may look around this room and take whatever you wish."

Emma threw a glance around the mean abode and patted the woman reassuringly on the shoulder. No payment was needed. The relief of such pain and desolation was a reward in itself and her chubby face bunched itself into a kind smile. She turned to leave, but the woman clutched at her.

"Will you pray for us?" she begged.

"Not to God," said Emma sharply, "but I will offer up a plea that something will come soon to ease your distress."

The woman thanked her profusely and watched her saunter off along the road to Crofton. Witch or not, the visitor had provided the first crumbs of comfort in weeks. The woman mixed the potion as directed and gave some to the children before she drank it down herself. Relief was immediate. They felt much better but very drowsy and dropped off into a restorative sleep. Emma of Crofton had worked her wonders.

There was more welfare at hand. When the woman opened her front door that evening, something lay shining on her doorstep. It was minutes before she overcame the shock enough to bend down and pick up the six silver coins.

Abbot Serlo did not believe in the power of public disgrace. He had seen monks in other abbeys take their beatings in front of the whole house and it was an unedifying spectacle in every way. The fact of punishment was a sufficient deterrent in itself. When one brother felt the severity of his judgement, the others would take eager note and mend their ways accordingly. Brother Peter's fate would keep the abbey free from misdemeanour for several weeks. The only witness to his agony, however, would be his abbot, his fellow-monk with the mighty arm, and his God.

"Do you understand your fault, Brother Peter?"

"I understand and repent, Father Abbot."

"We must scourge the weakness out of you."

"I submit myself wholly to your will."

"Do not hold back, Brother Thaddeus," instructed Serlo.

"I will not, Father Abbot," said the eager brother as he swished the birch twigs through the air. "I will break the flesh until you tell me to cease."

They were in a room behind the chapter-house. The abbot sat in the one chair and Peter stood beside a long bench. Brother Thaddeus had been looking forward to doing his duty and his fondness for the sacristan was no bar to his patent readiness to wield the fresh birch twigs.

Abbot Serlo widened his eyes recklessly and raised his hands as if to catch them when they fell out. He sent a short prayer up to heaven and the monks bowed their heads. When he was prepared, the abbot settled back in his chair and gave a curt nod to Brother Thaddeus.

"Proceed."

"Yes, Father Abbot."

"Make yourself ready, Peter."

"I do, Father Abbot."

"Fit both mind and body to what approaches."

"I have done so."

Brother Peter crouched down to take the hem of his cowl and lift it right up to his shoulders. He then straddled the bench and lay facedown, with his naked body exposed to the view and mercy of Brother Thaddeus. The back and buttocks had already been chafed by the coarseness of the material, but its stark whiteness would now be striped indelibly with red. Brother Thaddeus took another practice swing, then stepped forward into position. The birch twigs came down with such force on the defenceless body that Brother Peter convulsed with pain. Yet he did not cry out. Buried in the folds of his cowl, he was biting on a bunched fist to stem his cries. Each time the twigs flashed through the air on their cruel journey, his teeth sank deeper and deeper until they drew blood and threatened to sever the fingers.

Brother Thaddeus might have been threshing corn. He took an uncomplicated joy in his handiwork and built up a steady rhythm with his searing strokes. The body beneath him was now inflamed with horror and streaked with blood. By shifting his feet and altering his angle, Thaddeus could spread his misery across a wider area. He was a careful ploughman who dug his furrows straight and deep. Only when the whole of the torso was thoroughly flayed did the hideous ordeal come to an end.

"Enough," said Abbot Serlo.

"Yes, Father Abbot," said Thaddeus with muted dismay.

"You have discharged your duty well." He stood up and walked across to the prostrate figure which was still heaving and twitching on the bench. "God bless you, my son."

Brother Peter was too exhausted to reply, but he felt no bitterness at his punishment. If abbot or monk could have seen his face at that moment, they would have been amazed, because it was covered with a beatific smile. With aching slowness, Peter stretched his arms wide so that he resembled the enamel figure of Christ on his own crucifix. An imaginary crown of thorns encircled his throbbing head. He was wounded beyond endurance and yet he was strangely content.

His sins had now been expiated.

Chapter Six

RALPH DELCHARD KNEW THE VALUE OF LETTING A RO-
mance find its own pace. Hasty wooing could
frighten a lady away and a protracted period of courtship
could mean that desire waned long before its object was
achieved. Wide experience of women had given him an intuition that rarely failed him and it was now encouraging
him to believe that Ediva, wife of the town reeve, did not
wish to waste too much time on the preliminaries. Her husband was away, she was alone, and Ralph was in the town
of Bedwyn for only one week in his entire life. This combination of factors dictated a certain speed. Ralph was delighted with this state of affairs.

"What kind of man is this moneyer?" he asked.

"Meet him and judge, my lord," she said.

"Your husband called him a curious fellow. In what way
does this curiosity show itself?"

Ediva smiled. "I would not spoil the surprise."

"This moneyer is a freak?" guessed Ralph. "He has two
heads, three arms, and four legs? What monster awaits us?"

"Eadmer is no monster," she promised. "Be patient."

They were walking past the church on their way to the
mint. She was wearing a russet gown and mantle in the style
of a Norman lady and the white wimple set off the sculp-
tured beauty of her features. When Ralph Delchard first arrived in England, he had little time for Saxon women and
Saxon ways, but twenty years had revised his opinion dramatically. His own wife had been from Coutances and was
without compare in his memory, but the finer points of an

English lady could now impress themselves very forcibly upon him. Ediva was more than lovely. She was stately and subdued, a woman of quality and intelligence who knew when to speak and exactly what to say. He felt drawn to her more strongly by the second.

Ediva was a married woman who needed to maintain her respectability. To accompany a stranger through the town would have been unthinkable, but the presence of a female companion gave it the necessary decorum. Two of Ralph's men marched in their wake to reinforce the sense of decency. Knowing their master of old, they realised what was actually afoot and their eyes glinted either side of their iron nasals. They were practised in their roles.

"This is the place," said Ediva at length.

"Thank you, lady. Will you enter with me?"

"I will wait for you here, my lord."

"But I would prefer your company within," said Ralph as he raised a roguish eyebrow. "This curious fellow may scare me, and your protection would be gratefully received."

She pondered. "Very well," she consented.

The woman moved to follow her, but Ediva stopped her with a gesture. The first part of Ralph's stratagem had worked. He had separated the two of them. The companion was now left alone with the two soldiers, and all three seemed happy with the potentialities of that situation. Even before he had reached the door and knocked, Ralph could hear the other woman laughing as his men began to joke with her.

A servant opened the door and conducted them within. They came to a smaller, stouter door that was studded with iron and clad with metal strips. Its lock would have done justice to a dungeon with a large key was needed to turn it from within when the servant pounded on the door. Ralph had sent word of his visit so that the moneyer would be there to receive him. The heavy door swung open on smooth hinges.

Ralph Delchard stared into an empty room.

"Where, in God's name, is the fellow?"

"He stands before you, my lord."

"Where?"

He looked down and stammered his apologies. Eadmer was curious indeed, a short, bent, wizened creature of fifty or more with a bearded face that sported a reddening nose and a pair of tiny, watchful eyes. A mere six inches in height saved Eadmer from being regarded as a dwarf. He was used to his deficiencies and made light of them. When introductions had been made, he brought the newcomers into his mint and slammed the door. As well as turning the key in the lock, he pushed home two solid bolts, then hooked a chain tightly across the door. A battering ram would have been needed to gain admission.

Ralph was impressed. "You keep the mint secure."

"I would lose my license else."

"And your money, good sir."

"Thieves lurk everywhere these days," said Eadmer. "A man may not be too careful with his property or his coin."

"I know it well."

Ralph placed himself where he could take inventory of the room and its other security arrangements. It was long but narrow and the ceiling was designed more for a person of Eadmer's stature than of his own. He had to bend his head beneath the low central beam as he looked around. All of the moneyer's equipment was there. His bench was pitted by long use and his dies stood ready in their tray. Hammers and other tools hung from racks on the wall. Two braziers were smouldering quietly in a corner. Moulds and tongs stood close by. Boxes and sacks which were obviously full did not disclose their contents. Two windows admitted light, but it was severely restricted by the thick iron bars that ran vertically down them. Ralph took a step closer to peer out and saw that the building hung over the river itself. Supported on wooden props, it stood fifteen feet above the waterline. Eadmer had his own moat.

"I congratulate you," said Ralph, then turned to the other

door on the far side of the room. It was even more barricaded than the first. "What lies behind there?"

Eadmer gave a hesitant grin. "Money!"

"You stand over the river like a mill," observed his guest. "While they grind out flour, you produce coin."

The moneyer let out an unexpected peal of laughter. It gave Ralph a moment to weigh their diminutive host. Gnarled and comical he might be, but Eadmer was a man of undoubted standing and wealth. Moneyers worked by royal license and played a fundamental part in the whole structure of royal finance. Their dies were issued centrally in London and they were entitled to keep six silver pennies from every pound that they struck in their respective mints. An industrious man could thus, literally, make a lot of money and further augment it by lending it out at interest. To this end, the more successful moneyers in the larger cities were already developing close and mutually beneficial relationships with goldsmiths. Eadmer was a nugget in himself.

"You work here alone?" said Ralph.

"With one assistant, my lord. The other stays at the mint in Marlborough."

"There are two so close together?"

"I am moneyer to them both," said Eadmer proudly. "In London, you will find a dozen or more mints, each with their moneyer's name on it. I rule this countryside and my name is legal tender on the face of every coin."

"Eadmer is greatly respected," said Ediva quietly. "My husband speaks highly of his integrity."

"He has good cause." The moneyer enjoyed flattery. "I work on here as I did under King Edward the Confessor, who knew the importance of a stable coinage. King William had made many changes to our country, but he was pleased to leave the mints alone. We know our trade better than the mints in Normandy, which are but two in number, Bayeux and Rouen. Our coins are never debased."

Ralph was happy to concede the point. The king had the sense to take over anything that operated efficiently so that he could use it for his own purpose, and the Anglo-Saxons had always understood the significance of an ordered coinage. Monetary reforms were constant and the system had been greatly improved by the time of Hastings. The face of King Harold stared up from coins of almost fifty mints at the time of his death. Conquest devalued him utterly.

"How may I help you?" said Eadmer.

"By looking at these," replied Ralph, taking out the two coins and holding them on his palm. "They are yours?"

Eadmer peered. "I believe they may well be."

"You are not sure?"

"I go by feel, not sight, my lord. May I?"

"Please." Ralph proferred the coins.

Eadmer selected one and took it to the window to stare at it more closely in the light. He then placed it in his own palm and judged its weight. A third test saw it slipped between his ancient teeth and bitten. He fingered the coin obsessively and clicked his tongue.

"Well?" said Ralph.

"Where did you find it?"

"That does not matter."

"It matters to me and to every honest man hereabouts. That coin looks like mine and would pass for mine to most of those who handled it. But I did not make it. It is too light and made of a compound unknown to me." Eadmer threw back his little shoulders and lifted an indignant chin. "This should be reported to the town reeve."

"My husband is away at present," said Ediva.

"Send him here as soon as he returns."

"I will do so. And promptly."

"May I keep this coin, my lord?"

"If you wish."

"It is essential," said Eadmer seriously. "I have to clear my own name here. Moneyers who turn forgers suffer mutilation or death." He looked at the coin again with faint disgust. "It is a fitting end for such an offence."

Ralph questioned him some more about his trade and the controls under which it operated in Bedwyn and Marlborough. After expressing their gratitude, he and Ediva took their leave and were shown to the front door by the servant. Once outside, they found themselves alone. Laughter from the rear of the mint showed that the soldiers were chatting with the woman beside the river. Ralph looked at her with masculine frankness for the first time and she shed a wife's enforced humility to stand before him in her own right.

"When may we meet again?" he whispered.

"As soon as may be, my lord."

"That lies in your choosing, lady."

"I'll send word of time and place."

"The evening finds me free."

"What of the night?"

She extended her hand for him to plant a chaste kiss upon it, then she leaned forward to touch his cheek with her lips. Her softness and her delicate fragrance enchanted him even more and he could not wait for the moment of consummation. He heard fresh laughter from his men and a giggle from the woman. Ralph Delchard and Ediva put on their masks again.

"Lady," he said respectfully, "allow us to conduct you home again. The evening has been a constant delight to me, but it has yielded all that it may."

Gervase Bret arrived at the abbey in the sober attire of his office. He had documents with him and he was admitted by the porter so that he could deliver them to Canon Hubert and Brother Simon. That, at least, was what he had told the monk in the gatehouse, knowing full well that the information would be swiftly relayed to Prior Baldwin. The documents could be handed over later. Other business had to be first discharged. Gervase had timed his appearance well. Vespers was held later in the summer and there was every hope that he might be able to locate Brother Luke before the bell tolled out its command.

The novice was in the garden, standing outside the empty workshop of Brother Peter. Red-rimmed eyes showed that he had wept copiously and his shoulders were bent in dejection.

"What ails you, Brother Luke?" said Gervase.

"I suffer another's pain."

"All Christians do that."

"Brother Peter has been beaten."

Gervase was taken aback. "The kind sacristan? For what offence could such a man be punished?"

"He has been lax in attendance once or twice."

"Is that a matter for harsh sentencing?" said Gervase. "Even the best horse stumbles. You do not thrash it with your whip for one or two mistakes."

"There was more beside, master, but I may not tell it. Brother Peter has sworn me to secrecy."

"Then I will pry no further." He glanced around. "Is there some place where we may walk in the garden and talk unobserved? I would value conversation."

"And so would I."

"Lead on."

Novices quickly learned the corners of the abbey where they could hide or seek respite. Brother Luke took him to the farthest edge of the garden where a cluster of crab-apple trees grew in the shade of the abbey wall. They would not easily be seen or interrupted there.

"Brother Peter is your closest friend, is he not?"

"My only friend within the enclave."

"No, Luke," said Gervase, slipping easily back into the reflex answers of his monastic days, "you have a friend above who looks down from heaven and pities you." He put an arm on the youth's shoulder. "Are you still troubled?"

"Mightily."

"What is Peter's counsel?"

"Watch and pray."

"But you still wish to leave?"

"Only to flee my persecutors."

"That would leave your dearest friend behind."

"I know," said the boy, sighing. "If I think of myself and

am released from my vows, I lose Peter. If I stay here, I will lose my freedom."

"To do what?"

Luke shrugged. "I do not know."

"Consider it well before you decide."

They heard voices and moved a few yards farther into their hiding place. The voices passed and they could resume.

"Why did you leave Eltham Abbey?"

Gervase looked into the open face of the novice and saw himself. His dilemma had been exactly that of Brother Luke except in one particular. To win the boy's confidence and to gain his help, Gervase knew that he would have to tell the truth. Even now, the confession could still touch off the pangs of guilt.

"I loved a woman."

"While you were still a novice?"

"She lived nearby the abbey. I saw her often."

"But we take vows of chastity here."

"I found that commitment too final a one to make."

Brother Luke looked uncomfortable, as if the same problem was vexing him but he was not able to share it. Instead, he asked for more detail, and Gervase supplied it with some misgivings. To talk of his precious Alys was always a source of immense pleasure, but it was soured a little by the present circumstance. He was not sure whether he was tempting Luke to flee from the order or convincing him that love of a woman was a sinful condition. What was certain was the rapt attention he was given. Luke was taking a first full and unequivocal look into a world to which he had been so far denied entry. Gervase was honest in the way that Brother Peter was honest. They answered his questions directly and did not obstruct or evade.

Gervase now sought his own supply of information.

"Brother Peter is surely not your only kind face in the abbey," he began. "What of the other novices?"

"They are too serious or too stupid for my liking."

"Abbot Serlo?"

"A blessed man, but he has no dealings with me."

"Prior Baldwin?"

"I fear him the most after Brother Thaddeus."

"Why?"

Luke talked freely about life within the confines of the abbey and described, without realising it, the whole political structure of the house. His comments on both prior and subprior had a youthful rawness to them, but their spirit accorded with Gervase's own observations. He eased the boy along until the latter was reminded of some happier incidents during his novitiate, talking himself into an appreciation of the values of the monastic life. Gervase heard him out until the bell for Vespers chimed. Brother Luke started. After the punishment meted out to Brother Peter, he did not want to be found wanting.

Gervase strolled back towards the church with him so that he could put a last few questions.

"Who is the oldest monk at the abbey?"

"The oldest?" Luke shrugged. "Brother John."

"Was he born in this area?"

"Not far from Burbage, I believe."

"What age would he be?"

"Oh, ancient," said the other. "I could not guess at his exact years, but he is weak and bedridden. The infirmarian sees Brother John the most. Seek of him."

"Have you met this reverend old gentleman yourself?"

"Yes, master. All the novices are presented to him when they join the house. Brother John tells us of the joys of the Benedictine rule and is living proof of its goodness. His body may be broken, but his mind is as clear as ever."

"Thank you, Brother Luke," said Gervase. "Go in to Vespers. Say a prayer for Brother Peter and meditate on your own confusion of heart."

The novice squeezed his arm in gratitude, then broke into a run as the last few monks converged on the church.

Gervase now had the information he needed.

* * *

Having escorted Ediva back to her home, Ralph Delchard and his two knights were still in the town when the commotion started. Men who had been given a name by Wulfgeat had now had a whole day to brood on it. Some had taken ale; some were intoxicated with revenge. All of them could wait no longer to bring the malefactor to justice. Arming themselves and gathering more people as they went along, they met in the market square at Bedwyn before riding off into the twilight.

"What's afoot?" Ralph asked of a passer-by.

"They know the killer of Alric Longdon," said the man.

"A wolf?"

"No, my lord. A dog that can savage like a wolf."

"Who owns it?"

"The Witch of Crofton."

"Who?"

"Emma is her name. She can weave spells."

"Can you be sure her dog was responsible?"

"No question of it, my lord."

"What proof do you have?"

"A stranger rode into the town this afternoon. He met Emma on the road and stopped to speak to her. He says the beast attacked him and would have torn his throat out if he had not run away." The man pointed after the horsemen. "They ride to Crofton to put an end to this terror we all feel."

Ralph had seen an enraged mob before and he knew how easily it could get out of hand. Though there was a number of respectable burgesses in the pack, it also contained more headstrong and violent characters. Whatever this Emma had done or not done, her chances of a fair hearing were non-existent. The best Ralph could do was to prevent bloodshed. He barked an order to his men and the three of them were soon leaping into their own saddles. It was not difficult to pick up the trail of the fury that thundered ahead of them.

Wulfgeat took no part in the communal vengeance and he was distressed to be its author. Emma's dog might well

100

have been the killer, but that did not necessarily mean that she had set it on to do the deed. It was often seen roaming on the edges of Savernake and was dispatched with a loud curse or a hurled stone. If the dog had strayed into the forest on the evening in question, its attack on the miller might have been a random act of madness or even provoked by his antagonism to the beast. A man who can beat a woman black-and-blue would not hold back his foot from kicking her dog.

There was another element in the situation which made Wulfgeat pause and showed him again how little he really knew and understood his only child. Leofgifu was alarmed when she heard how the other men had reacted that morning to the possibility—no more than that at this stage—that Emma of Crofton was implicated here, and she confessed for the first time that she had turned in extremity to the fearsome woman whom everyone called a witch. When her husband was slowly dying from a wasting disease, no doctor could find a medicine to soften his pain. It became so unbearable that he was ready to try anything, and Leofgifu sent to Crofton. Emma was quick to come and quicker still to prescribe a special potion for Leofgifu's husband. His condition did not improve, but the pain faded away completely.

"If that is witchcraft," Leofgifu had said, "then I welcome it, Father. My husband had suffered so much."

Those words were spoken at the start of the day. As it drew to its close, Wulfgeat and his daughter stood at the window and watched the horses ride past. The dog would be hacked down before its mistress was even allowed to defend it. Emma of Crofton was an eccentric and unappealing woman who eked out a life that disgusted God-fearing folk, but she did have someone to share her squalid and lonely life. That partner was about to be cruelly taken from her and she herself not spared.

"Stop them, Father," begged Leofgifu.

"It is too late, child."

"Go after them and turn them back."

"They would not listen to me."

"Emma of Crofton may not be guilty," she urged. "And even if she is, this is no civilised way to deal with her. Why does it take all those men to converse with an unarmed woman and her dog? That is bravery indeed!"

"They fear her witchcraft."

"My husband did not."

"Alric Longdon was killed," he reminded her.

"Yes," she retorted, cheeks aflame, "and there is not a man who gallops in that party who is not pleased with the death. They hated the miller and showed it in ways that beggar description. His widow has told me all."

"She also told you that Emma had put a curse on him."

"Would you not curse a man who beat you soundly?"

"A witch's spell can murder any man."

"Then why has she not murdered fifty or more who have reviled her these past years? Emma may be innocent."

"The widow does not think so."

"She speaks in sorrow and anger," said Leofgifu. "Hilda and the boy are in despair. Their man has been taken away. She named Emma, but she has no proof."

"Nor will they try to find it when they reach Crofton."

"Her appearance alone will condemn her."

Wulfgeat nodded and plucked nervously at his beard. He had been too swift to throw the name to the others. More evidence should first have been gathered against her and in a more discreet way. Wulfgeat was a hard man, but he prided himself on being a fair one. Setting a crazed mob on a lonely woman could not be construed as an act of fairness. He raised his shoulders in apology, but Leofgifu would not be appeased by that. If Emma and the dog were destroyed by the self-appointed posse, then she herself would be partly to blame for entrusting her father with what she had heard from the miller's widow. Another thought twisted a knife within her. Supposing that both woman and animal were subsequently cleared of blame when the real culprit was caught? Leofgifu and her father would be chained by guilt for the rest of their days.

"How can I make amends?" asked Wulfgeat.

"Speak to Hilda yourself."

"No," he refused. "That is asking too much. To give them shelter is one thing. But you promised me that I would never have to see either of them. Stand by your word."

"Things have changed," said Leofgifu. "See her, Father."

"What purpose is served?"

"A form of reconciliation. It is bad enough to lose a husband without being spurned by everyone who hated him. We are the only place who would take her in, save the abbey." She moved across to clutch his arm. "Listen to her for my sake. She rambles in her speech, but you will have a clearer understanding of it than I. It is not just his death that she talks about but the land that is now disputed before the commission."

"What land?" he said.

"Two hides alongside the river. Their mill stands on part of it. The abbey claims the holding."

"And so does Hugh de Brionne."

"There is a new voice raised," said Leofgifu. "She tried to tell me why but lost her way in tears. All I did gather was this. It was Alric who summoned the commissioners by letter. He started this debate."

Wulfgeat pondered. Fierce arguments over land were part of normal life in a town like Bedwyn. Boundary disputes had enlivened its temper for hundreds of years. Each time they were settled, they were redrawn; each time a new disposition was accepted, along would come Viking or Dane or rebel Saxon to redefine it again. Edward the Confessor's reign saw yet another shift in property, confirmed during the brief reign of Harold, but the whole process was started once again by the Normans. Ownership was at times a lottery. After the Conquest, when the invaders shared out the spoils of war, Wulfgeat had lost holdings of his own to the abbey and to Hugh de Brionne. It was a wound that had festered ever since. He had been dispossessed. If Hilda knew anything that might challenge the rights of a Norman abbot and a Norman lord, he was very anxious to hear it. There might be personal advantage for him as well as deep satisfaction. He assessed the implications of the new situation. Undying hatred of the miller fought with bald self-interest.

"I will see her," he decided.

They came out of the half-darkness at a mad gallop and descended the hill with reckless abandon. Emma heard them when they were half a mile away and she came out of her hovel to see what produced the frightening noise. Forty or more horsemen were swarming towards her and they had surrounded the whole property before she could even guess at their purpose. As they reined in their mounts, they formed a menacing circle that slowly began to close. The dog stood protectively in front of its mistress and growled its defiance. A spear sank into the ground only inches away from the animal and Emma recoiled in alarm.

"What do you want?" she cried.

"The killer," answered a spokesman.

"There is no killer here."

"That dog of yours was sent to murder Alric Longdon."

"He never leaves my side."

"You put a curse on the miller."

"He beat me till I bled," she retorted.

"And so will we," shouted another voice that was met with a rousing cheer. "Why do we stay our hands?"

It was a signal for the ring of hatred to tighten around them at a faster pace. A second spear all but hit the dog and a third grazed Emma's fat arm as it passed. The men began to chant, the dog began to bark, and the whole night seemed to fill with pandemonium. The Witch of Crofton and her miserable cur would be put down without mercy. A first sword was lifted to strike.

"Hold!"

Ralph Delchard's cry cut through the din as he came charging down the hill with his two men riding behind him. His appearance was so sudden and unexpected that some of the men thought that he and his knights were devils from hell who had been summoned to help the witch. Yells of fear went up. A few took flight at once. Others backed away out of caution. Horses bucked and neighed to add to the general chaos and the dog barked on with renewed frenzy.

Ralph's destrier cleared a path through the angry mob and came to a halt beside Emma. His men joined him and the three formed a triangle around her.

"Who speaks for you?" demanded Ralph sternly.

"I," said a voice in the gloom.

"Show your face if you have courage to do so."

"Keep out of this," ordered the man, remaining in the shadows. "You have no quarrel here."

"Forty men against a solitary woman is not a quarrel. It is a cowardly massacre and I will not allow it."

"Stand aside!" roared another voice.

"Yes!" supported a third, drawing strength from the over-whelming odds. "You will not save this witch. Stand aside or Norman blood will run."

This threat produced an ear-splitting shout of agreement. Ralph Delchard answered it immediately. His sword jumped into his hand, his horse reared up on its hind legs, and his challenge rang out across the field.

"If any man dare try me, here I am!"

Several riders inched their horses forward to take a closer look at him, then changed their minds at once. Here was no common townsman who wielded a sword or spear perhaps once in six months. Ralph was a seasoned warlord with twenty years of action behind him. He had killed his way into England with the rest of the Norman invaders and he thrived on battle. There were enough of them to overpower him, but he would reduce their numbers drastically in the process. His men were trained soldiers, too, and they kept their horses prancing on their hooves and ready for any en-counter.

Three men around a shivering woman and a barking dog. Who would strike the first blow or show the first sign of weakness? Both sides glared at each other for a long time.

"Give up this woman to us," called the spokesman.

"She has my arm to guard her."

"The woman is a witch."

"Even witches must stand trial in courts of law."

"*We* are a court of law!" he attested.

But the supportive yell was patchy and half-hearted. Ralph took his destrier in a circle so that he could taunt them and put them to shame.

"Go home to your wives," he advised. "Tell them what heroes you have been tonight. Boast about the woman you almost killed and the dog you all but slaughtered. Away with you all! Tell them how three Normans got the better of forty Saxons. Yes, you sturdy warriors, you have done noble work this day. Begone!"

There were token protests, but the heat and impetus had been taken out of the raid. Emma and the dog were an easy target on their own. Protected by Ralph and his men-at-arms, they were a different proposition, and however much the Saxons loathed the Norman usurpers, they had been taught to respect their military supremacy and the merciless swiftness of any reprisals. If a royal commissioner was cut down in cold blood with his men, a whole army would sally forth from Winchester to exact the most damning revenge. King William would not rest until every one of them had been hunted down and hanged.

"Well?" roared Ralph. "Will you fight or flee?"

There were some token jibes from the men, but they gradually drifted away and set off at a trot back towards Bedwyn. Ralph had savoured the excitement. Sheathing his sword, he jumped down from the saddle to introduce himself to Emma of Crofton. She was suffused with gratitude and the dog added a whining note of thanks.

Danger was over for a while. Ralph could take a closer look at this supposed witch. He grinned amiably, then saw the trickle of blood upon her arm. Gallantry and concern now prompted him.

"That wound needs dressing, lady. Let us go inside. . . ."

* * *

While a meeting was taking place between an outcast Saxon woman and a Norman lord, an even more unlikely encounter occurred at Wulfgeat's house. He consented to meet and talk to Hilda, widow of the deceased miller and thus his natural enemy. Her grief was quite disarming. As soon as he walked into the little room, he realised that she posed no threat and harboured no hostility. Hilda was curled up into a ball of misery in the corner, clutching her stepson for support and trying to make sense of what had happened to them both. She was so pathetically grateful to him for extending the hospitality of his home that he felt embarrassed he had not been courteous enough to welcome her before.

Leofgifu was with him and her gentle presence was a balm to the guests. Where her father might have disturbed Hilda with the urgency of his questions, Leofgifu was a model of patience and tact. She took time to get the woman talking before she let Wulfgeat join the conversation. When she had married the miller, Hilda had indeed been beautiful, but her charms had been buried along with her husband. Her face was now so white, pinched, and fraught that she looked fifteen years older. Wulfgeat's compassion rose, but he found it dry up when he turned to the boy, only nine but the image of his father. Cild was a hardy child whose young muscles were already used to work and strain. He not only had Alric's pallor and bovine ugliness, but there was the same sullen stare in the eyes. Cild could already nurse resentment with the slow intensity of an adult.

When Hilda was guided around to the subject of the abbey land, Wulfgeat took over the questioning.

"Your husband wrote to Winchester, you say?"

"That is what he told me, sir."

"He had a charter?"

"That is what he told me, sir."

"Where did he get this charter?"

"From my father, sir. In Queenhill."

"That lies in Worcestershire," explained Leofgifu.

"Yes, close to London," said Wulfgeat. "I knew that

Alric had to travel far to find himself a new wife." He was about to add that no woman in the locality would have cared to look upon the miller as a suitor, but he suppressed the comment out of consideration and turned back to the widow. "This charter of which you speak. Did you see it with your own eyes?" Hilda nodded. "What did it contain?"

The woman look bewildered and appealed to Leofgifu with a gesture. Wulfgeat needed no translation. Hilda had seen the document, but that was all. She could not read. He picked his way more carefully through her half-remembered story. Alric had gone to Queenhill, talked at length with her father, then wooed and won her. Money and charter had been exchanged between the men, but all detail was kept from her. It was plain that her heart would not have chosen Alric as a husband, but she was obedient to her father. A simple girl saw life in simple terms.

"I loved my father. I respected his choice."

Leofgifu shot Wulfgeat a rueful glance that made him sigh with regret. He concentrated on their visitor.

"Where is that charter now?"

"I do not know, sir."

"Is it at the mill?"

"I do not know, sir."

"Where did your husband keep his valuables?"

"We had none, sir."

"His money, his accounts. Where are they locked?"

"I do not know, sir."

Wulfgeat lowered his voice to a persuasive whisper.

"That document could help you," he explained. "It may not bring your husband back, but it may offer compensation of another kind. Commissioners are in the town. They need to see that charter. Help to find it and we may all benefit." He managed a smile. "Now, Hilda—where is it?"

"I do not know, sir."

"You must have some idea."

"I do not know, sir."

"She is telling the truth, Father," said Leofgifu. "She has

108

been kept in ignorance of the affairs of men. Duty to her husband was all she knew. Do not press her."

Wulfgeat nodded his disappointment. The significance of the charter was clear. Royal commissioners would not travel to Bedwyn unless they had good cause. Alric Longdon must somehow have convinced them that some gross abuse of rights had taken place, but only the charter could support him in his argument. It might still be at the mill, but Wulfgeat doubted it. Alric Longdon was known for being secretive. He would have hidden such an important article in a place where no one else could find it.

Leofgifu touched his shoulder to indicate that they should withdraw. Hilda was plainly tired and needed all the recuperation that sleep could bring. Wulfgeat made to leave. He thanked the woman for her help, then flicked a glance at the boy. Cild was watching him intently. It was eerie. Wulfgeat found himself looking straight into the eyes of Alric Longdon once again. There was bitterness and envy and hatred in the boy's gaze, but there was something else as well. It was a sense of quiet triumph. His father's death had snatched everything away from him except one last precious possession. It gave him a power that he never looked to have and it might be used to hurt.

Cild knew where the charter was.

Chapter Seven

NIGHT ENTICED NEW SOUNDS FROM SAVERNAKE FOREST. Owls hooted from their perches, badgers snuffled in their dingles, and strutting wildcats screeched their furious messages at the moon. Deep in thick woodland, a rutting stag mounted its doe with noisy love-play. Other creatures came out to hear and swell the nocturnal discord. The whole forest was an echo chamber. Two pairs of heavy feet added to the mild uproar of the night as they scrunched over grass and twig and bracken. The verderers were returning to Bedwyn from their patrol on the northern margin. Poachers had been their quarry, but they had also searched yet again for the mystery wolf. Daylight and long staves made them brave enough to take on any beast that walked, but darkness ambushed their courage and left them fearful. When an anonymous yowl rose high above the cacophony, they lengthened their stride and quickened their pace. Savernake was no place in which to be caught at night. Other beings ruled its rough domain.

They came over a hill and saw light in the distant town to revive their spirit. If they skirted the wood and cut down towards the river, they would be home and safe in less than half an hour. It made them jocular and they discovered tongues that had been lost in the heart of the forest. Oak and elm rose up on their right with a reassuring solidity to provide a defensive wall against any dangers that might lurk in the undergrowth. Good ale and good wives awaited them in Bedwyn. A long day's work would end in restful ease.

"Stay!"

"Why?"

"Listen!"

It was the bigger of the two men who heard it first and who made his companion halt. The latter grew impatient.

"I hear nothing."

"Listen!"

"Let us get on."

The bigger man hissed him into silence and pulled him close. They peered into the darkness of the trees, then ventured in a few yards. Both had their ears pricked and their staves at the ready, but they detected nothing untoward until they were about to move on once more. Then the voices of the night fell silent for a moment and a different sound came through, a long, loud, slow dragging noise, accompanied by a grunt of pain. Was it a wild boar dragging its prey? A wounded fox pulling itself along? Some larger beast lumbering blindly across the ground?

Stifling the urge to run, they communicated with a glance and knew their duty. With a concerted yell, they used their staves to thresh the undergrowth as they stumbled towards the sound. The grunt became a strange, high-pitched cry and the bushes ahead of them shook violently. All they could see in the moonlight was a sight so weird and unexpected that they refused to believe it.

"A sheep?" said one.

"It cannot be."

"A goat?"

"Not here in the forest."

"Was it, then, a pig?"

"A pig does not have fleece."

"What did we see?"

"Who knows?" said the other. "The wolf of Savernake?"

Whatever the creature had been, it had been frightened away, and that gave them some comfort. The bigger man used his stave to prod his way forward, then almost tripped over a large object on the ground. He regained his balance, then looked down. It was a rock, a big, smooth piece of sandstone which had been towed across the floor of the forest with such effort that it had left a channel gouged in the earth behind it. No wolf could pull a boulder such as that. Only a bear would cope. Wooden staves would not hold off such an animal. If it attacked, their chances would be slim.

A loud and unexplained roar came from the distance.

They took to their heels and ran all the way home.

Gervase Bret and Ralph Delchard had much to discuss that night as they compared their findings and speculated afresh. Both were pleased with their researches. Gervase felt quite at home within the confines of the abbey walls and Ralph had found his natural milieu of strife and action at Crofton. The one could look forward to a talk with an ancient monk, while the other could dream of more intimate conference with the wife of the town reeve. Before they retired for the night, Ralph first yawned, then rehearsed their findings.

"This miller was a hoarder of forged coins," he said reflectively. "He hid them in a chest within that yew tree. When he took a fresh haul to put it with the rest, he was attacked by wolf or dog or some such sharp-toothed cur. His treasure was removed. When and by whom?"

"Know that and we know where to find the charter."

"Find the charter and we set the abbey in a turmoil."

"No," said Gervase, "it already has turmoil enough beneath that placid surface. Monks are men and all men have their failings."

"Start again with the miller," suggested Ralph. "His widow may know of the coins as well as of the charter."

"I think not. A man as close as Alric Longdon would not take a woman into his confidence. He married her for other reasons and they have been man and wife too short a time to grow together. Queenhill is a lengthy ride to find himself a bride. He needed a charter to make him go so far afield. The silver may have helped to buy the girl." Gervase shook his head. "No, his widow will know little. We must not expect too much from her. The miller worked alone."

"I disagree, Gervase." Another yawn surfaced. "My bed

112

calls me, so I will not delay. I say but this. The dead man was no forger. Those brutish hands could shift great sacks of flour but not take on the subtle task of minting silver coins. That needs Eadmer's skill. You see my mind?"

"He has an accomplice. Who stole the hoard himself."

"We shall see, we shall see." He winked a farewell and rolled towards the staircase. "In the morning."

"Will the widow be called before us?"

Ralph turned. "One of us will speak privily with her."

"You?"

"A quieter voice will get more from her. Good night."

"God bless!"

While Ralph hauled himself upstairs, Gervase went back to the satchel of documents on the table and took them out. He studied one by the light of the candle and ran his finger along the neat calligraphy. Ralph Delchard had a practised eye that could weigh up a man at a glance, but Gervase worked by other means. He could read between the lines of a charter and extract its hidden secrets. The parchment before him was the one from the abbey, which claimed rights to the disputed holding of two hides. Couched in legal terms, it was so clear and persuasive that his predecessors waved it through as a binding document, but he had serious doubts. As soon as he had handled it, he felt a vague unease that was well founded. When Gervase stamped the charter a forgery, Prior Baldwin and Subprior Matthew protested so long and so vigorously that he knew his instinct was right, but that instinct now had to be buttressed with proof so that deception could be both rectified and punished.

He took two other charters from the satchel and laid them beside the first. All were from Bedwyn, all were dated the same, and all were allegedly the work of the same scribe. Gervase went through each one with painstaking care to catch the trick of the man's quill and the hint of his character. It was a steady hand that flowed fast and smooth without losing definition, but there were quirks to be discerned. His head went from one to the other as he compared each detail of the scribe's handiwork. Something was wrong with the abbey charter, but he could not yet tell what it was. He scrutinised the parchments for almost two hours before he got his proof. It was worth a chuckle of triumph. Prior Baldwin and Subprior Matthew would rant and rave once more, but he now had the full measure of them. One tiny squiggle of ink had left the pair of them impaled upon the point of a quill.

Gervase was still smiling as he fell asleep in bed.

Word of the latest sighting in the forest had permeated the whole town by early morning. Verderers were men who knew the native denizens by sight, sound, and smell, but they could not place the creature they had glimpsed in the dark. Their report sent new tremors through the community and produced a fresh crop of breathless invention. Most people inclined to the idea of a bear that had escaped captivity and returned to the wild, but they could not account for the absence of any spoor. When the verderers and others went back at first light to the scene of their unnerving encounter, the stone had gone completely and left no further indentations in the ground. A scattering of red flakes suggested that the creature had smashed it into smaller and more manageable lumps before carrying them off. Hounds picked up a scent, but it died when they reached a stream.

The latest discovery did not exonerate Emma and her dog. Some still believed she had caused the miller's death and a few were even heard to argue that the witch had transformed her familiar into a bear so that it could forage in the woodland. Why the bear should be shifting a boulder of sandstone in the darkness was not explained and the more just townsfolk came round to the view that Emma might not, after all, be culpable. They still argued that the dog should be caught and destroyed on the grounds that it was a danger to others, and the evidence of the traveller who had accosted Emma was repeated time and again. His version of events had been carefully shaped to present himself as an innocent victim rather than as a red-blooded man who was driven by an impulse of abstract lust.

114

The link between catastrophe and the commissioners was further strengthened. Since the visitors arrived, Bedwyn had been plagued with tragedy and mishap, and Ralph Delchard's heroics in Crofton on the previous night had exacerbated the general animosity. If they could rid themselves of the Norman interlopers, it was thought, they would regain the safety of their streets and the contented rhythm of their lives. Ralph Delchard symbolised the horrors of the Conquest. It was his name that was spat with contempt in the marketplace.

Ralph was blithely unaware of his growing notoriety.

"Row me downstream," he said.

"But we could ride there much faster, my lord."

"I wish to take to the water."

"I am no boatman," admitted the man. "Your legs would take you quicker than my arms."

"There is no hurry. Row on."

The river was no distance from the hunting lodge and they could see the boat that was moored to a post. Ralph commandeered it and ordered one of his knights to strike off downstream towards the mill of Alric Longdon and beyond. He sat in the stern and trailed a lazy hand in the water while the other man struggled to come to terms with oars. There was more splashing than forward movement, but at least they moved in the right direction. When they reached the middle of the river, the current helped to speed them up.

Ralph studied the sluice-gate that lay ahead and saw its function at once. The miller was clever and far-sighted, though he had probably met the expense of construction from a hoard of forged money. Unwitting carpenters who had sunk the mighty timbers in the water to take the weight of the gate itself would have spent their silver long ago and put the counterfeit coins into circulation. The fact that they had not yet been detected was proof of their quality. Eadmer provided the currency for Bedwyn. His mint was controlled by the warden of the exchange, who sold him his bullion, then received back the newly struck coins to check

115

them with meticulous care. Only if they were up to standard would they be released for public use. Nothing which left Eadmer's expert hands was ever rejected.

"Slow down," ordered Ralph.

"We are being swept along, my lord."

"Dip your oars and hold them still."

"Yes, my lord."

He experimented a few times and finally got a small measure of success. The boat slowed a little and allowed Ralph to take a more leisurely view of the mill that they were about to pass. It was a suitable habitat for Alric Longdon. The ugly shape of the building, the neglect of its exterior, the relentless power of its now-silent wheel, and its isolated position on the river all defined the character and person of the man. He lived on the very fringe of Bedwyn, like a scavenger who skulks in his lair until a prey approaches. As they floated past its massive bulk, Ralph looked up and felt a shiver of distaste. This was no fit home for a family. It was a place of work that had been battered by half a century of constant usage, a cold prison which forced hard labour upon its inmates for the whole of their lives. Happiness had never penetrated its stout walls. It was a monument to the miller's meanness of spirit. Ralph was glad to drift on by.

"How much farther, my lord?" asked the oarsman.

"Row me back to Winchester."

"My arms are aching already."

"When they fall off, I will take my turn."

"It is no joke, my lord."

"No," agreed Ralph, then burst into laughter. "Pull on your oars again. Take me towards the church."

The man made the fatal mistake of looking over his shoulder, and the small craft went out of control and all but turned in a circle. It took minutes to right it again and to row it along a straighter course. Ralph Delchard sat back and surveyed the scene with growing admiration. Bedwyn had a pastoral setting of undeniable loveliness and it was hard to believe that the air of serenity it now exuded was hiding a cauldron of rage and dissension. When the church finally climbed into view, he told his man to ship the oars and let the boat drift into the bank. They had come to the end of their voyage.

"Where are we?" asked the man, now panting freely.

"About to lay a siege."

"A siege, my lord?"

"Of that."

The boat thudded into the bank and the man grabbed at an overhanging branch to steady it. He was then able to look across the river to the object of Ralph's curiosity.

"You saw the mint but yesterday," he complained.

"Only from the inside."

"My lord?"

"There is a castle. How do we take it?"

The soldier recovered his humour. Fighting was his trade. He was on firm ground now and entered willingly into the game with his master.

"Storm it from the front."

"It is too well fortified."

"Approach from the sides."

"Both have solid walls with tiny windows," said Ralph. "You would be picked off with arrows by an enemy that you never even saw."

"Then take it from the river," rejoined the man. "Scale the walls and enter by force."

Ralph clicked his tongue. "Ladders could not be used from boats. They need firm foundation. Ropes could not be thrown to the roof. There is no place to get a purchase." He pointed at the windows. "How would you get past those iron bars if you ever managed to reach them? No, my friend. Stones and boiling oil could be poured onto your boats and a man foolish enough to scale that wall would be exposed to attack from every window. You are no siege-master."

"I would starve them out."

"There is an easier way if you but look."

The soldier studied the building with more attention to

the detail of its construction. It was half-timbered but used solid brick where others settled for wattle and daub. Around each window was a protective square of sharp iron spikes. Its roof was thatched and might succumb to fire, but he sensed that Ralph had found an easier mode of entry. He turned back to his lord and shrugged his failure.

"Think of a *real* castle," advised Ralph.

"This is but a well-defended mint."

"Place a motte and bailey on the same spot. Raise your walls and reinforce them at their weakest points. Build your keep so that it uses the river as its moat, just like the mint. Now," said Ralph with a knowing smirk, "what would you set over the river itself? What use would you make of this convenient water?"

The man realised and laughed coarsely. A garderobe or two would be built at the rear of the keep. The castle inhabitants would relieve themselves into the water below. If a concerted attack could not be made, one stealthy man might gain entrance through a garderobe under cover of darkness and find a means to open the main gate. The soldier grinned his admiration, but he had only learned how to take a mythical castle on that same spot. Ralph Delchard had discovered how to gain access to a royal mint.

"Take me across there now," he said, "and go in under the building that I may gaze up at Eadmer's recreation. Silver bullion may go into the place, but I warrant that a baser metal drops out."

Their raucous laughter skimmed across the water.

"You have a visitor, Brother John. Will you receive him?"

"Gladly. Who is he that calls so early?"

"A young man from the king's household."

Slight alarm showed. "I am summoned by his majesty?"

"No, brother. Your visitor only pays you his respects."

"What is his name?"

"Gervase Bret."

"Norman or Breton?"

"I vouch the fellow has more Saxon in him."

"Show him to me."

"Wait there, Brother John."

A croak of a laugh. "God leaves with me no choice."

Gervase Bret reached the abbey before Prime and gained entry through the gatehouse. Monastic architecture obeyed a set pattern, so he needed no direction to the infirmary range. It consisted of a hall, chapel, and kitchen and stood east of the cloister, so it was well away from the noise of the outer court to the west. Sick or ancient monks who could no longer meet the demands of claustral life were cared for here by the infirmarian and his assistant. Gervase had been a regular caller at the infirmary in Eltham Abbey and he knew that even monks of advancing years retained a vestigial discipline whenever possible. Confined to bed, they could still wake when the bell rang for Matins and join in each service of the day with gladsome hearts.

Brother John was such a faithful servant of the order. Approaching seventy and racked with disease, his old bones still rustled at the fixed hours of the day. He lay propped up on his bed, with a rough blanket over his meagre body. His face was gaunt and shrunken, but there was still a glimmer of light in his watery eyes. When he was shown into the hall by the padding infirmarian, Gervase Bret walked past the other patients and gave them each a respectful nod. He was then introduced to Brother John and offered a low stool. The infirmarian warned him that his visit must be short, so that the oldest occupant of the abbey was not tired by the effort of speech and concentration. Gervase was left alone with the remarkable Brother John, looking at the blue-veined skull, which still displayed a silver tonsure, and wondering how such a narrow head could hold in so many long years of prayer and meditation.

"Why did you come?" asked a reedy voice.

"Brother Luke talked of you," said Gervase.

"Do I know Brother Luke?"

"He is one of the novices."

"There was a Brother Luke here when I first joined the

119

order," recalled the old man. "The precentor, no less. He died the year that poor King Harold died."

"After the Battle of Hastings?"

"Oh, no, young sir," said John with a throaty chuckle. "I talk of King Harold who followed King Cnut and was himself then succeeded by King Harthacnut."

"How long have you been a brother here?"

"Through six reigns. King William is my last."

"Luke tells me that you hail from Burbage."

"Brother Luke the Precentor?"

"The novice."

"Burbage was my home until I found God."

"You have seen many changes during all those reigns," noted Gervase. "Has it vexed your soul?"

"Profoundly at times, but I have prayed for help." The old man wheezed and brought a trembling hand up to his mouth as he coughed. "Who are you, young man? I see by your manner that you are no stranger to these walls."

"I was a novice myself at Eltham Abbey."

"Eltham!" Brother John pursed his lips in a weak smile. "I went to Eltham once with gifts from this abbey when it was first raised. The abbot received me himself. What was his name now . . . Abbot Waleran?"

"Abbot Maurilius," corrected Gervase, knowing that his word was being tested. "He was still Father Abbot when I wore the cowl. You will also remember Prior Richard?"

"Indeed I do. He showed me much kindness." He nodded his approval of his visitor's credentials. "You come from Eltham, a place of blessed memory. How may I help you, my son? My strength is waning and you must ask before I doze off once again."

"Brother Luke told me . . ."

"The precentor?"

"The novice."

"Oh, yes. Of course. The novice."

"He says you know this stretch of country well. If I wish to hear the history of this part of the shire, you are the person who can best advise me."

"Use me in any way you may."

"You must be well acquainted with abbey lands."

"Bless my soul!" said Brother John, and he went off into such a paroxysm of coughing that Gervase had to pass him a cup of water and hold him up so that he could drink it. The fit finally subsided. "I am sorry, but you made me laugh."

"If that was laughter, I will not provoke it again," said Gervase with sympathy. "Wherein lies the humour?"

"Ask Brother Luke."

"The novice?"

"The precentor. He would have told you."

"But he has been dead these forty years or more."

"He saw my mettle and urged my appointment." The old man crooked a finger to beckon him closer. "I was born near Burbage and given the name of Brungar. That is no fit title for a Benedictine monk. Brother Brungar murders the mouth, so I took the name of John." He smiled wistfully at the memory. "My father was a sokeman with many rights. I was brought up on the land. I am withered now, but I was a lusty fellow then and chosen by the precentor because of that."

"Chosen, Brother John?"

"You talked of abbey lands."

"You worked a plough upon them?"

"No, young sir," replied the other. "I am no Brother Thaddeus who beats the oxen to drive them forward. My furrows went through the purses of our tenants. I was the rent-collector for this abbey."

Gervase seized on this stroke of luck and plied him with many questions. The rent-collector for the abbey visited every patch of land that housed a subtenant. He knew the size of every holding and could put an accurate figure on its value. Boundaries had changed repeatedly, but Brother John had taken it all in his stride. Six reigns accustom a man to violent alteration. He was philosophical in his reminiscences.

"Who paid the rent for those two hides?" said Gervase.

"It was not owned by the abbey."

"Can you be certain, Brother John?"

"As certain as I am about anything," returned the other with mild offence. "I collected rents for almost forty years on abbey lands. Those two hides were held directly from the king by Heregod."

"Heregod?"

"The father of Alric the Miller."

"Directly from the king?"

"For services rendered." The monk shook his head. "I know not what they were, but King Edward showed his gratitude and Heregod held that land. He used it to grow his own corn for the mill. And I will tell you something else." Gervase was again motioned closer. "It was not two hides but four. King Edward was a man of generous temper."

"How did they abbey secure the holdings?"

Brother John paused. Happy to wander through his past with his rent-collector's bag slung round his shoulder, he was now more cautious. The abbey had been his life and he did not wish to show disloyalty. The blue-veined skull was wrinkled with doubt and hesitation. He had said enough. Gervase tried to prompt him over the last important details.

"I will not ask you more," he said, "but let me put a case to you. That land was held by Alric's father thirty years ago. The abbey now takes rent from it and disputes that income with Hugh de Brionne. How did this come about? I hazard a guess. Say nothing, Brother John, for I would not put you in that position. Simply hear me out. . . ."

Gervase spoke quietly and concisely, piecing together all the evidence he had so far gathered, then adding what his keen intelligence told him. The old monk did not need to say a word. His rheumy eyes began to run so freely that his visitor was given all the confirmation he needed. He thanked Brother John for his help and stood up to take his leave.

"You should have stayed in Eltham Abbey," said John. "The order always has need of a sharp brain."

"I was called elsewhere."

"That was Eltham's loss."

"Good-bye, Brother John. . . ."

"Give my regards to Brother Luke."

"The novice?"

"The precentor. . . ."

Wulfgeat reasoned long and hard with Hilda, but he could not get her to understand the importance of it all. She was still too dazed by the heady passage of events. A week ago, she had been the dutiful wife of a miller and had hopes of bearing his child before another summer came around. Now she was bereft of everything and saddled with a stepson for whom she had learned to care but whom she could never truly love. When Hilda was still reeling from the shock of her husband's death, Prior Baldwin had come to offer her solace and walked away with the key to the mill. Now Wulfgeat was asking her to prise the whereabouts of the charter from her stepson, but she refused to believe that the boy knew anything, and he himself denied it flatly. Failing with this first, rushed approach, Wulfgeat was now soliciting permission to visit her home to look around for himself. Hilda was frightened and bemused.

"What must I do, Leofgifu?" she asked.

"Nothing you do not wish."

"Your father presses me too hard."

"I will speak to him to let you both alone."

"Yet this is his house," said Hilda. "He has rights."

"I brought you here and I will tend your needs. Tell me what they are and I will guard you against all anxiety."

"You have been very kind."

"I know what it is to lose a husband."

"And to marry one who has not touched your heart?"

Leofgifu bit her lip. "That, too, Hilda. . . ."

"Could I hear the story?" Her friend looked around guiltily. "Cild is not here. I let him out to walk. He is a fretful boy penned up in one room. He will come to no harm."

"You trust him, then?"

"I have to trust Cild. He is all I have." She took Leofgifu by both hands and held them tightly. "Tell me about your husband. Show me that I am not the only one. . . ."

When persuasion failed, it was time to resort to more desperate action. Wulfgeat was an honourable man with a law-abiding attitude, but the pressure of circumstance can turn a saint to sin and misdemeanour. Since he could get no key to the mill, he resolved to enter it by other means and took a trusted servant with him along the river. They were grateful that the mill stood in such a secluded spot. Nobody could see them about their stealthy work.

"Shall I break down the door?" asked the servant.

"Find some other way if you can."

"This lock will be hard to force."

"Try a window or the roof."

"Leave it to me, sir."

The servant was young and nimble. He went quickly round mill and house to look for modes of entry. The one he chose was at the very top of the building, a small window that was slightly ajar but too far from the ground to invite the interest of a passing thief.

"How will you reach it?" asked Wulfgeat.

"I think I have a way."

"You'll sprout a pair of wings?"

"I'll use the miller's wheel."

It was a tricky ascent. The huge slats of the wheel were soft with age and slippery with years of accumulated slime, but the servant got a firm grip and pulled himself slowly up towards his target. It took him several minutes before he balanced on top of the wheel and reached for the sill of the window. Hauling himself up, he nudged the window fully open, then slithered straight inside. Wulfgeat rushed to the back door to be let in as it was unbolted.

They were thorough. Wulfgeat did not expect to find the

124

charter, but he hoped the mill might have some clues as to its whereabouts. The place was cramped and airless and he was retching as soon as he went through the door. The musty atmosphere in which the miller lived attacked their lungs and they held hands to their mouths until they had got used to it. Room by little room, they searched diligently for any letters or maps or written evidence. None could be found and it drove them on to a more frantic search, but it was still to no avail. An hour later, they gave up.

Wulfgeat left the mill and waited while the servant locked the door from within and then climbed upstairs to the window to leave by the same route as he had entered. There was no charter inside the mill and not even the slightest hint that such document existed. Wulfgeat was beginning to feel ashamed. They had rifled a dead man's house. He could justify his behaviour to himself only by remembering the great significance of the charter. It would cause enormous upset to the abbey and to a Norman lord, and it would bring untold benefit to the distressed widow. On behalf of all Saxons who had been dispossessed of land, himself among them, Wulfgeat had to track it down.

"Let us go," he decided.

"Shall I search around the vicinity?"

"There is no point. Alric was too wily. His hiding place might be a mile or more away." He looked up. "Did you leave the window as we found it?"

"Yes. And each room in the house."

"Hilda will never guess that we have been here."

Wulfgeat led the way back along the path. They had gone fifty yards before there was a splashing noise in the river and a figure came to the surface beside the mill-wheel. He had been there throughout their visit and watched them every time he came up for air. Looking sadly up at the home they had violated, he made a grisly promise to himself and to his father, then he turned to push himself off from the wheel. He swam powerfully across the river and climbed out on the opposite bank, trotting naked along it until he found the brake where he had left his clothes.

Cild was glad that he had followed Wulfgeat all the way from the house. He now loathed him more than ever. Help from such a man was no help at all. Wulfgeat had taken them into his home but not to offer consolation. He plainly resented them and he had driven the boy's stepmother to tears by the force of his questioning. Being under the roof of such a man was an insult to his dead father. Cild knew his duty. He had to avenge that stinging insult and repay the other countless acts of malice which Wulfgeat had committed against his father. He had much to brood upon as he headed back towards the town.

The abbey delegation had been called to the shire hall that morning at ten o'clock, but it was Hugh de Brionne, lord of the manor of Chisbury, who first came striding through the door. He brought no escort of knights this time, but his entry still caused a mild sensation. Marching up to the table where the four commissioners sat, he snarled a greeting and flung down a parcel of documents in front of them with such contemptuous force that he sent a dozen other charters flapping in the air like startled doves. Brother Simon tried to pluck them to his breast in midflight, while Canon Hubert issued an astringent rebuke. Gervase Bret immediately undid the ribbon which held the new submission together and unrolled its yellowing contents. Ralph Delchard remained calmly authoritative.

"Respect is due to royal officers," he warned. "The writ of King William runs here in Bedwyn. He has a low opinion of lords who seek to flout him."

"Read my charters," insisted Hugh. "Discharge me from this enquiry and let me go about my business."

"What is the hurry?" said Ralph.

"Matters of greater weight require my presence."

"Nothing can outweigh the substance of our findings here. You are a soldier and understand a soldier's needs. William has to muster an army to repel a promised invasion from the Danes. He needs a precise inventory of the holdings of his feudal lords, including your good self. When he

126

can see exactly what lands his vassals have, he can raise his revenue accordingly."

Hugh stamped a foot. "Give me no lectures on war. I know how armies march. The king is entitled to his levy, but it must be fairly taken and not forced unequally upon us. But this enquiry—this Domesday Book of yours—has a second and a larger purpose."

"Who gives the lectures now?" mocked Ralph.

"It legalises all the changes that took place when Norman feet trampled first on English soil." He pointed to his documents. "See what your predecessors saw. Behave as they did. Ratify my claims. And trespass no more upon my indulgence."

"Yes, my lord," said Gervase. He rolled up the documents and tied them once more with a ribbon. "They appear to be in order but refer to holdings that are outside the scope of this examination. Our interest is in two particular hides."

"Stolen from me by the abbey!"

"No, my lord," replied Gervase. "Taken into your demesne from one Heregod of Longdon. Four hides in all are thrown in question here, either side of the boundary between the abbey lands and the manor of Chisbury. I see a charter in your parcel to challenge the abbey land but none to enforce the two hides of your own."

"They are mine by royal grant."

"Show us the proof and you may go."

"The document is mislaid."

"Then maybe the land was mislaid, too."

"Do you accuse Hugh de Brionne of dishonesty!" howled the other. "Take care of your manners, young sir, or I will have to teach you some."

Ralph smiled. "Forgive my colleague's rudeness. It is but the folly of youth and will improve with time. Let him have his answer and our dealings with you will conclude."

"That land has always been part of my demesne."

"But by what right, my lord?" said Gervase.

"Royal grant!"

"We find no record of it back in Winchester."

"Word of mouth will uphold me," argued Hugh, trying to hurry the business through. "Call my subtenants from those same hides and let them speak under oath. I'll wager my ten best horses that each man swears for me."

"We may all rely on that," said Ralph, knowing that any subtenant of Hugh de Brionne would be terrified into saying precisely what he wanted him to say. "Filling this hall with the oaths of wretched Saxons will not content us. We need firmer proof."

"In writing," said Gervase.

"Find this charter you mislaid," suggested Canon Hubert with irony. "Its disappearance has been too convenient."

Hugh de Brionne seethed with rage and stamped his foot again, but they were unmoved by his show of temper. Flicking his mantle over his shoulder to display the black wolf on his tunic, he emitted a low animal growl.

"I will be back!"

Then he snatched up his documents and stalked out.

Living alone for so long had given Emma of Crofton a fierce independence. Rejected by all and feared by most, she had learned to cope with the sneers and the taunts that came her way each day, and she had also taught herself how to dodge a stone or take an occasional blow. A bloodthirsty mob, however, was a different matter, especially when it descended on her so violently out of the gloom. Ralph Delchard's intercession had saved her life. There was no doubt that she and the dog would have been torn apart and she was equally certain that nobody would have grieved for either of them. No sheriff would be summoned to investigate her murder, no action taken against the killers. A witch and her familiar had been destroyed. Their remains might not have been found for weeks. The kindest thing that would have happened was for someone to dig a hole and kick them into it. She and her dog would have shared the same unmarked grave, two dead animals found lying on the ground and tossed with cold indifference into oblivion.

A Norman lord had come to her rescue and bound up her wounded arm, but he could not stand sentry all night. When he left, others might sneak back to finish the execution that he had interrupted. That fear took her out of the house and up into the wood nearby. She and the dog dug themselves a pit in the soft earth and curled up together in the safety of nature. Exhaustion made her sleep well into the morning.

The journey back to her hovel was made with furtive steps. Enemies might lurk to ambush her again. She sent her dog on ahead and watched from behind a thick hedge as it sniffed its way around their home. Its wagging tail was a signal that bore relief. Emma dared to venture out of cover.

"Wait there, wait there!"

She tensed with apprehension, but it was no threat to her life that came scurrying towards her. It was the same peasant woman to whom she had given the potion for the family's stomach pains. The ragged newcomer was moving with such freedom that her indisposition was clearly gone. The woman had been waiting for Emma to return.

"I heard about those men," she sympathised.

"They have gone now."

"But they may come back one day."

"I have lived with that fear a long time now."

"Come to me."

"What?"

"If you are in danger," said the woman, "come to me. Our house is small, but you are welcome to hide there with your dog. Do not sleep in the wood again. Come to me."

Emma was touched. Everyone else rejected her. Even the patients whose health she had restored stayed out of her way thereafter. Yet she was now being offered a refuge. A woman who had almost nothing of her own was willing to share the last thing she had—a mean dwelling which would be taken from her if her husband was found guilty—with an outcast. She was willing to risk the danger of having a reviled witch under her roof when armed men were out hunting her. Emma came close to real tears and she looked into the willing face of her new friend.

"Why do you help me in this way?" she wondered.

"You cured our pain; you gave us bread."

"Bread?"

"Your prayer was answered, Emma. We thank you."

The woman leaned forward to kiss her on the cheek, then she turned on her heel and hurried back in the direction of her home. Emma could not comprehend such kindness. As she walked on down to her own house, she tried to puzzle it out. Yesterday, she had faced death in the night; today, she was being shown the face of true friendship. It was baffling.

Her dog came bounding up to her and nuzzled her fat thigh as she trundled on, then he ran back to the front door of the house and crouched excitedly over something. Emma at first thought that he had caught a bird or mouse, but she soon saw otherwise. As she reached the door and moved the animal back with her foot, she saw something scattered across her doorstep. They were silver coins.

Chapter Eight

BROTHER PETER BORE HIS TRIBULATIONS WITH NOBLE equanimity. The punishment he suffered would have disabled most of the monks for days and introduced at least a hint of bitterness into their relationship with Brother Thaddeus. Peter rose above the common experience and astonished the whole house by appearing at Matins next morning to take his appointed place. He was evidently in considerable pain and moved with some difficulty, but the face that was bowed humbly before God contained neither reproach nor suffering but shone with its usual blithe religiosity. When the sacristan picked his way gingerly across the cloister garth after Prime, he was even able to acknowledge the cheerful greeting of Brother Thaddeus. Not a breath of personal animosity stirred. The happy ploughman was but an instrument of harsh discipline and therefore not to blame. Peter even found a moment to ask kindly after the oxen in the field. Like him, they had felt the wounding power of Brother Thaddeus's strong arm.

It was after Terce when Brother Luke at last found him.

"How are you, Brother Peter?"

"I survive."

"Reports had you half-dead."

"Brother Thaddeus would have cut me in two if Abbot Serlo had not curtailed my beating." He gave a weary smile. "It is all over now. I will not dwell on it."

Luke studied him with almost-ghoulish fascination. They were in Peter's workshop and the brazier was still glowing quietly in the corner. The novice could not understand how his friend could so soon and so readily return to his holy labours after such a terrible ordeal. Peter's stoic attitude was quite inspiring.

"Does it not hurt?" murmured Luke.

"Like the Devil!"

"Then should you not rest?"

"I have done so already."

"Wounds need time to heal."

"They may heal just as well if I stand on my feet," said Peter bravely. "Brother Infirmarian has been extremely kind to me. He has washed my body clean and applied ointments as a salve. His tender ministrations have softened the pain, if they have not relieved the stiffness."

Luke was aghast. "Are you not *angry*?"

"With whom?"

"With anyone or anything that can do this to you. With Abbot Serlo or with Brother Thaddeus. With the strictures of the Benedictine rule. With the brother who informed on you in the first place." Luke bristled. "I would be enraged."

"My only anger is reserved for myself."

"Yourself?"

"I transgressed, Luke. I paid the penalty."

"You are truly sainted."

"We all have our cross to bear," said Peter as he took the silver cross from its drawer and held it up. "This is mine and I was crucified for spending too much time on it."

"The abbey does not deserve such a wondrous gift."

"It does, Luke. Do not be blinded by friendship to me from seeing duty to the order. I am but one obedientiary who went astray and have been whipped back into line. I accept that without complaint. Do you likewise."

Brother Luke made the effort to do so, but it was way beyond his competence. His eye kept roving over Peter's cowl and he eventually asked the question which had brought him there.

"May I see?"

"No."

"The others say that Brother Thaddeus is vicious."

"I have not seen his work and nor will you."

"But you bear it upon your back."

"Out of sight to both of us."

"Can I not wash it for you? Apply more ointment?"

"I am too afraid for you, Luke."

"Afraid? Of what?"

"If I lift my cowl to any other brother, he will see no more than the retribution of Father Abbot." He put concerned hands on the young shoulders and looked the novice full in the face. "If I show you my wounds, you will see the exit from the order. And I would keep you here."

"To suffer the same treatment myself?"

"To avoid it by due observance of the rule."

Peter clapped his hands to change the subject and put the crucifix away once more. His manner was almost spry, though there was still an aching slowness in his motions.

"What have you been doing with yourself?" he said.

"Praying for you."

"Your prayers were answered. Here I am again."

"Praise the Lord!" Luke remembered something else. "The young commissioner came to call upon me."

"Gervase Bret?"

"We talked in the garden."

"Upon what subject?"

"His reason for leaving Eltham Abbey."

Peter frowned. "He tried to tempt you away?"

"No, he was careful not to influence my decision in any way. But he was honest about his own travails and that made an impression on me. He spoke in the roundest terms and did not shirk my questions."

"What else did he say?"

"He was intrigued by the abbey itself," explained Luke, "and asked me about its working. That was the curious thing. When I met him, I was disposed to be released from my vows and leave the order, yet when I spoke with him about our life together here, I did so with such zeal that I came to see how much I had grown into it."

"We are a family and you an honoured son."

"The master of the novices does not honour me."

"He will in time, Luke. If you stay." Peter's frown deepened. "What did you tell Gervase Bret?"

"All that he asked."

"Did he mention Prior Baldwin?"

"Many times. He has seen through that sacred tyrant."

"And Subprior Matthew?"

"He questioned me about the subprior's work."

"Beware, Luke!"

"Why?"

"He is trying to entrap you."

"But he came here as a friend."

"A friend to you, perhaps, but not to Bedwyn Abbey. He is a royal official, sent here on a mission. Our prior and subprior represent the abbey. You weaken their position if you divulge any information about our community." Brother Peter fixed an admonitory gaze on him. "I warned you before. This man was here to use your inexperience against you. The abbey has to fight the commissioners. You give them ammunition to use against your brothers."

"I did not think him so sly."

"He has his warrant, Luke."

"Then all he told me was false?"

"I think it was."

"No, no, it cannot be," exclaimed the youth with spirit. "He spoke so openly about his own novitiate and suffered once more the pains of separation from the order as he talked. It was a dreadful choice he had to make and doubts will pursue him all his life." Luke gritted his teeth and thought it over. "Gervase Bret is a straightforward man. He did not lie to me about Eltham Abbey."

"Why did he leave it?"

"He yielded to temptation."

"Ambition?"

"A woman."

Peter sighed. "Each man has his own peculiar weakness. My own lies wrapped in cloth inside that drawer. For Gervase Bret, it was the wonder of a woman." He sighed again and put an arm around his friend. "We all have fatal flaws, Luke."

"What is mine?"

The message arrived before noon and it threw Hilda into a panic. Leofgifu read it out to her and saw the rising terror in her eyes. A frightened creature at the best of times, she was particularly vulnerable at the moment, and Leofgifu had to spend a long time calming her down before they could even begin to address the problem. Authority unnerved the widow.

"They have sent for me!" she whimpered.

"But they have not," said her friend. "This is not an official summons. One of the commissioners simply wishes to speak with you about your husband."

"I know nothing, Leofgifu."

"Then you will have nothing to tell them."

"They will be angry with me."

"I think not," said Leofgifu, glancing at the missive once more. "The man who sent this letter shows you much consideration. He apologises for intruding on your grief. He knows your situation. But your husband brought them all to Bedwyn, so they must talk with you."

"I will not see them."

"They have the power to enforce it," warned the other.

"Tell them I am too ill."

"It will not deflect them from their purpose."

Hilda looked anxiously and helplessly around like a small animal caught in a trap. Alric's death was shock enough to bear without having Prior Baldwin and Wulfgeat bearing down upon her. Now another man was trying to get something from her which she did not possess.

"See him," advised Leofgifu.

"Will you be with me?" pleaded Hilda.

"Every second."

"May we receive him here?"

"I am sure my father will consent."

"What is this commissioner's name?"

135

"Master Gervase Bret."

"And you say he will not scold me?"

Leofgifu gave her pledge. "Not while I am here."

A change of tactics allowed Prior Baldwin and Subprior Matthew to exhibit a more compliant attitude to the quartet who sat behind the long table in the shire hall. Baldwin sounded a conciliatory note at the start and Matthew was there to throw in a funereal smile of agreement whenever he deemed it necessary. Having antagonised the commissioners during earlier exchanges, the two men now seemed keen to mollify and compromise. Brother Simon was taken in by the apparent change of heart, but Canon Hubert treated it with an unconcealed scepticism and snorted in disbelief more than once. Ralph Delchard was diverted by the manoeuvres, but he left it to Gervase Bret to lock horns with the prelates.

"I have spoken with Abbot Serlo today," said Baldwin, "and he agrees that a misunderstanding has arisen. The two hides which arouse this unfortunate controversy were willed to us when he and I first came to Bedwyn. You have the charter which sets the truth before you."

"But it is a forgery," affirmed Gervase.

Baldwin smiled sweetly. "No, sir, you *allege* that it is a forgery, and that is a different matter. That document has been signed, sealed, and proved. Your predecessors found no fault in it. Why must you?"

"Because we have a counter-claim."

"Could that not be a forgery?"

"Indeed it could," said Ralph heavily. "The more I see of Bedwyn and its ways, I begin to wonder if anything here is what it seems. We have had so many lies and prevarications that I am coming to think the town itself does not exist! It is a forgery practised on the eye."

"Leave off these jests," said Canon Hubert. "They do not advance the case. What we talk of here is the burden of proof."

"Thank you," said Baldwin pleasantly. "You are right as

136

usual, Canon Hubert, but the burden of proof lies with you."

Gervase Bret lifted up the abbey charter to peruse it.

"It is false," he said quietly.

"How do you know?" challenged Baldwin.

"Intuition."

"Really!" said Matthew, stirred from his mourning. "Are we to decide the fate of two hundred acres or more by the intuition of a callow youth?"

"I may be callow, Brother Matthew, but I am not blind."

"Substantiate your allegation," said Baldwin. "If the document has been falsely drawn up—prove it."

"Prove it," echoed Matthew somnolently.

Their confidence had clearly been revived by their long discussions back at the abbey and they had returned with more composure. If they could discredit the word of Gervase Bret, they had won the day for the abbey. Baldwin had already manipulated the Bishop of Durham and his co-commissioners to good effect. He now carried the fight to a mere clerk of Chancery with every hope of success. Instead of his earlier red-faced bluster, he used a patronising gaze that could quell most opposition by its concentrated power.

All eyes were on Gervase Bret as he fingered the charter before him. He seemed uncertain. Ralph looked worried, Canon Hubert shifted in his chair, and Brother Simon developed a nervous sniff. The abbey delegation grew more complacent.

"We are waiting, Master Bret," said Baldwin.

"Waiting in vain, it seems," added Matthew.

"Will you speak or may we have leave to go?"

"Prove it!" hissed Canon Hubert.

There was an even longer and more stressful pause. It was finally broken by Ralph Delchard, who pounded the table.

"God's tits!" he yelled. "Prove it, Gervase."

"Very well," said the other calmly.

He set the charter before him and put two others beside

137

it. Chairs grated as everyone pulled in closer to view the evidence. The visitors were still supremely assured. Prior Baldwin's smile now had a touch of studious arrogance.

"Before you are three charters," said Gervase evenly. "All are reputedly the work of the same scribe, one Drogo of Wilton, much employed by Osmund, Bishop of Salisbury. You will recognise his hand. It is most distinctive."

"We know it well," said Baldwin. "Drogo was a friend to our abbey. His handiwork adorns many of our charters. He was only a scribe, but we appreciate quality in any man. If he were here, he would own that he had written all three charters." More arrogance came into the smile. "But he is not here, Master Bret. The poor man is buried in the parish churchyard in Wilton."

"You seem to have a problem with your witnesses," said Matthew with a rare flash of humour. "When you wish to call them to your aid, you find that God has issued his summons before you. That is Drogo's work in all three cases."

"How can you be so certain?" asked Gervase.

"Because we *know*," said Matthew.

A wry eyebrow was raised. "Intuition?"

"We still require your proof," muttered Canon Hubert.

"Ralph has loaned it to me."

Gervase slipped a hand into the purse at his belt and took out three silver coins. He put one on each document, then invited the others to examine them as closely as they wished. The prelates were irritated by what they saw as a pointless game, but they consented. Canon Hubert and Brother Simon took longer to inspect the coins, while Ralph Delchard sat back and pretended he had no idea what was going on.

"Well?" said Gervase at length.

"They are the same," said Baldwin. "Minted here in Bedwyn by Eadmer. They bear his name and mark."

"I agree," said Matthew.

"And so do we," added Hubert, speaking for Brother Simon without even consulting him. "Three identical coins. What is the point of this demonstration?"

"To show how easily we can be deceived," said Gervase. "The two coins on the outside are genuine, but the one in the middle—on the abbey charter—is counterfeit."

"How do you know?" said Baldwin.

"Eadmer confirmed it," explained Ralph, relishing the chance to join in. "He knows his coinage as well as a mother knows her own children, and our moneyer rejected the one in the middle at once. It is a clever forgery."

"Like the charter," continued Gervase, moving the coins aside. "See here, if you will. Two documents bear the work of Drogo so manifestly that it cannot be denied. Watch how he loops this letter and turns that and note that flourish on his capitals. Now compare them with your abbey charter. It is so close to Drogo that it could be him and yet, I fear, it is not." He beckoned them forward. "You see this tiny upward stroke of the quill at each sentence's end? It is so small a defect in the hand of Drogo that it is hardly worth notice except that it does not occur in the abbey charter. Nor do his ligatures—look here, and here and here. And one thing more, this Drogo was a scribe and not a scholar. His Latin falters briefly in both the genuine documents and he makes neat alteration." He sat back in his chair. "I spend my whole life sifting through such charters and scribes are all my friends. Drogo's work has only trifling blemishes, but they single him out. The abbey document is too perfect to be his."

There was stunned silence as the two prelates stared first at the abbey charter, then at the others, then at each other, then back at Gervase. He couched his accusation in the softest terms.

"A scribe is a scribe," he said gently, "who writes but as directed. We must not expect more of him. But the hand which framed this abbey charter has a keener edge and a higher intelligence. It cannot bear to make even the most paltry mistakes. My guess would be that this is no scribe at all but a master of the illuminated manuscript." He smiled benignly at Matthew. "The subprior will know that errors may not be tolerated in a scriptorium. Drogo would not have gained acceptance there."

Baldwin and Matthew had been struck dumb yet again. They dared not look at each other and neither lowered his eyes to the abbey charter. It had been torn to shreds. Gervase addressed himself to Prior Baldwin.

"How many other of your charters are the work of Drogo?" he enquired. "We shall need to see them all to pick out any more that are as false as this. Drogo may be dead, but he can speak to us from beyond the grave."

Ralph Delchard was determined to have the last word. Scooping up the coins, he shook them in his hands, then opened his palm, pointing to each in turn.

"True—false—true." An expansive grin. "But do not take my word for it. Eadmer the Moneyer may be brought here at your request. He is one witness who has not yet vanished below ground." A ripe chuckle followed. "Though he seems to be on his way in that direction."

Wulfgeat's quieter persuasion finally achieved its aim. He talked with Cild for almost two hours before the success. Reason made no headway. The boy was too stubborn to listen and too young to understand the meaning of the lost charter. It was pointless telling him how much he and his stepmother would gain from it all. Why should he trust the word of his father's enemy? Alric would never have done so and Cild was like him in every way. It was this fact which eventually told. Wulfgeat appealed directly to the boy's self-interest.

"I will give you money, Cild."

A defiant shake of the head.

"You may have it now, if you wish."

"No!"

"We all need money. Your father taught you that."

"No!"

"You are a clever boy to hold out for it. I admire that. Put a price on all things, Cild. As your father did." He regarded the boy with interest. "What would you like to buy?

140

What do you need? Have you ever had money of your own to spend before?"

Cild had not and the flame of curiosity was ignited. Wulfgeat did not rush. He fanned it gently until it leapt and danced. His method of approach had been completely wrong until now. Logic had failed and bullying had produced only a deeper resistance and resentment. An offer of money put an end to the long negotiation at last.

"Show me where the charter is," said Wulfgeat, "and I will give you more money than you have ever seen before."

Cild glared at him stonily for a couple of minutes.

"How much?" he grunted.

The afternoon released them from their deliberations. Lesser witnesses were due to give statements, and Canon Hubert was more than capable of collecting the evidence alone and ordering anything of value to be recorded by Brother Simon. It had been a productive day so far. Hugh de Brionne had been effectively quashed and the abbey representatives had been more or less demolished. Four hides in the Bedwyn returns were spreading utter chaos.

Ralph Delchard and Gervase Bret mounted their horses. It was a dull afternoon, with dark clouds trying to shoulder the town into submission. Ralph looked up.

"This is a day to stay within-doors," he said. "Where do you go now, Gervase?"

"To visit the widow."

"I visit a wife."

"Ralph!"

"She sent me word. I cannot disappoint her."

"Think of her husband."

"He is my chiefest reason for going. That self-serving reeve deserves to be cuckolded. It is my bounden duty."

"Consider the lady."

"I have considered nothing else since we met."

"Pull back before it is too late."

"Did I obstruct you when you courted Alys?"

"Well, no, but that is different. We are betrothed."

"So are Ediva and I." He beamed. "For today."

He rode away before Gervase could offer more protest. Two of his men followed, but the others remained in the shire hall to act as ushers and guards. Ralph and his escort kept up a steady canter until they reached the hunting lodge. He went inside to wash and to change his attire, glad to shake off the day's business in favour of pleasure. Ediva was awaiting him. All else paled beside that promise.

One of his men knocked on the door of his chamber.

"She is here, my lord."

"Here!" The tryst had been arranged elsewhere.

"She waits in the stable."

"Stable!" He would not roll in the hay with a woman of her quality. "What does she say?"

"Only that we must fetch you instantly."

"No more?"

"She became unruly."

Ralph liked nothing that he had heard and he hurried downstairs with some apprehension. The soldier was at his heels. They came into the stable-yard and looked around. Ralph could see nothing but a huge pile of rags in one corner. Only when it moved did he realise that he was looking at Emma of Crofton. It was her message that had been relayed and which had brought him down so speedily. He grimaced at the thought of a rendezvous with her. The hirsute face emerged from the bundle and she dragged herself up. Something lay on the ground like a nest of eggs on which a hen has been sitting. Emma reached down to pick it up and offer it to him. It was a basket of wild fruit.

"For me?" said Ralph, pleased.

"I picked them."

"Thank you, Emma."

"No, my lord"—she gave him the basket—"thank *you*."

"Where did you pick all this?"

But she was already gone. A bark showed that her dog was waiting for her in the trees. Ralph was both moved and delighted. Emma had walked all the way from Crofton to deliver her gift and taken severe risks to get to him. This was a rare act of gratitude for the help he had given.

He looked down at the fruit and selected a red berry.

"No, my lord!" exclaimed the soldier. "The woman is a witch. That may be poisoned."

"I rescued her," said Ralph, popping the berry into his mouth without hesitation. "Even witches do not poison their saviours." He offered the basket. "Try one. . . ."

Hilda's anxieties were soon put to rest by Gervase Bret. He was young and personable and spoke in her own language. He was not there to accuse or interrogate; indeed, he told her much more than he asked and his questions were merely gentle enquiries. Sensitive to her distressed condition, he was tender and unhurried. Hilda was so used to hearing bad opinions of her husband that it was refreshing to be with a man who accorded him the respect due to all the dead. She let him win her over and slowly dropped her guard.

If Hilda was reassured by their visitor, Leofgifu was greatly impressed. Her father had spoken slightingly of the commissioners and she had a Saxon's wariness of any Norman, but Gervase did not conform at all to her idea of a member of the king's household. He was altogether too honest and considerate and unjudging. The mixed parentage so obvious in his appearance gave him an insight into the heart and temperament of the Saxons. Though he was there on a serious errand, she found herself hoping that she could detain him later with an offer of refreshment.

Absorbed with Hilda and her predicament, Gervase was not unaware of his attraction to the daughter of the house. It was mutual. He could see her quality at a glance and sensed the total dependence of the other woman on her. Leofgifu was an act of compassion in herself and truly personified her name of "love-giver." They provided a stark contrast. Both were beautiful women who had suffered a bereavement. Sadness rested upon them with almost tangible force, but the resemblance ended there. Hilda's looks had been extinguished by her ordeal and only the remnants of her handsomeness remained. Leofgifu was different. The pain of loss had somehow enhanced her charms and given her whole face a wistful glow that was quite enchanting. Gervase was reminded of his first meeting with Alys.

The information he had to impart was private, but Hilda insisted that her friend remain to hear it. Leofgifu could be trusted. Neither she nor Gervase even questioned the widow's wishes. All three stayed sitting where they were.

"We need that charter," Gervase said with soft emphasis. "It tells the truth about the contested land and puts your future in a kinder light."

"My future?" Hilda was lost.

"The document names you."

Alarm flickered. "Me?"

"Your father or his heir, to be precise," he resumed. "And since your father is now deceased, the holding passes to the next in line. Women may inherit just as men."

"But not as often," said Leofgifu with asperity.

"Thus it is," he said, taking it stage by stage so that she would not be too confused. "Heregod of Longdon was given that land by royal grant. King Edward the Confessor gave him four hides adjoining Savernake Forest."

"Why there and not in Worcestershire?" asked Leofgifu.

"We do not know for certain, but the king was fond of hunting. Even piety likes to chase a deer through a wood." The remark left Hilda baffled, but Leofgifu smiled. "King Edward knew and liked this shire. He came to Bedwyn with his retinue and stayed at the hunting lodge where we now rest our heads. His gift was land that stands nearby. Heregod of Longdon brought his family to a new home in Bedwyn." He gave a sigh. "It was not a happy move. . . ."

Hilda was entranced. Facts which had been kept from her by her father now tumbled out in profusion. Impressions she had gathered as a child and as a wife now took on substance. The detail confused her and the interplay between events and the passage of time left her further bewildered, but a vague sense came through to her of what she stood to gain. Another thing became clear. Gervase Bret was on her side. This only served to increase Leofgifu's admiration. A blunter recital of the facts could cause Hilda great pain. Gervase chose his words with utmost care, gliding over the courtship that had taken place in Queenhill in such a way as to conceal its essence. Alric Longdon had not married her out of love and his clumsy wooing had been crude pretence. He bought his wife from a dying man so that he could regain the holdings that his father had lost. Hilda was no more than an agreeable factor in a financial transaction.

"And that is why we need the charter," he concluded.

"I do not know where it is."

"Give him the key to the mill," urged Leofgifu.

"The charter is not there."

"I know," said Gervase, recalling the futile search made by Prior Baldwin, "but it is a starting place. It will tell me something of the character of your husband—and of his father, Heregod. All that may be relevant. I would like to see inside the mill."

"I will go with you," volunteered Leofgifu before she could stop herself. "I can show you to the place."

"Thank you. I would value your help."

"You will have the key," said Hilda.

While she crossed to the table to get it, the others let their eyes connect for a moment. Frank admiration flowed freely between them, but it was soon stemmed. Hilda could not find the key to the mill and was deeply disturbed.

"Who has taken it?" she said.

Light rain was falling as Cild ran along the river-bank. He reached the mill and used the key to let himself in, going straight into the storeroom at the back and choosing one of the empty flour sacks. He banged it against a wall and sent up a cloud of white particles, inhaling the familiar smell with a distant pleasure. Then he went out into the rain once more, locked the door, and vanished into the copse at the rear of the property. He threaded his way between the trees until he came to a willow. Beneath its swaying branches was a box. Like his father, he had his own hiding place in woodland, but Cild's treasure was of a different order.

The box was no more than rough timber nailed hastily together, but it served its grim purpose. Reaching behind it, he pulled out a stick with a forked end. Cild was cautious but unafraid. He lay the sack on the ground and peeled back its top in readiness, then he used the stick to lift the latch on the makeshift door. The moment the latch moved, he jumped behind the box and waited. Nothing happened for minutes, then the snake came out in a determined slither. Two feet of squirming life had been set free, its fangs bared and its tongue darting in and out with random malice.

Cild moved fast. The stick fell, the forked end trapping the snake's head from behind. The boy's other hand inched the sack nearer. As the creature writhed and spat, he put a foot under its body and flicked it into the open mouth of the sack, closing the neck tightly and using a piece of twine to secure it. The operation was over. He was now holding a venomous cargo that threshed wildly around in the sack. A treasured pet had been transformed into a deadly weapon against an enemy.

The forest was patrolled in all weathers, so he used cover wherever he could. Eventually, he came to the stream and followed it up the hill. When Cild finally got to the yew tree, he did not linger. It was the place where his father had been killed and he shuddered at the memory, but one death could be answered by another. The forked stick was used to explore the hollow cavity and he felt the solid object at its base, still wrapped in its sacking. With the snake now flinging itself around inside its prison, he lowered the sack down into the tree, making sure that its neck was uppermost. It was too far down inside the hollow to be seen and a hand would need to grope down to make contact. The trap had been set. Cild shivered with cold joy.

He was suddenly afraid. The enormity of what he was doing seemed to hit him like a huge fist and the hideous significance of the scene pressed down upon him. His father had been savaged on this very spot, his throat torn out by ruthless teeth, his body knocked into the stream to lie there undiscovered for half a day. Cild could almost hear the menacing growl of a wolf. He took to his heels and raced down the hill as fast as he could. His fears had not been imaginary. Two dark and malevolent eyes watched him from the undergrowth.

Heavy rain now hurled itself at the windows and ran in careless rivulets down the panes. As afternoon merged into evening, the force of the storm increased. Ralph Delchard and Ediva did not even hear it. They were still entwined on the bed in languid happiness, their hands now absently caressing where they had grasped and squeezed only minutes before. Ediva was a willing lover and threw off inhibition. A virile Norman lord was fitter company for her appetite than a fussy, preoccupied, half-hearted man whose work preceded all else. Ralph was strong and urgent. He had brought out her full, rich sensuality and satisfied her with an intensity that she had never known in her marriage. She nestled into him and purred softly. He had reminded her that she was a woman.

"Are you content?" he whispered.

She murmured with pleasure.

"This place is safe?"

"Yes, my lord."

"I would not put a lady in danger."

"You would and did." She gave him a teasing kiss. "That is why we are here."

They were in a small cottage in a wood to the north of the town. It was barely furnished, but the bed was large and soft enough and the place offered all the privacy that they needed. Two of his men were in the trees outside to ward off interruption. It was an ideal choice for a tryst.

"I must ride this way again," he said.

"My lord will always be welcome."

"Does your husband often travel from home?"

"Too often," she said with a slight edge, "and when he is there, I do not get my due of attention."

"His folly is my gain."

He kissed her forehead and ran a hand through the long, loose hair whose scent was so enchanting. It was minutes before he picked up the conversation once more.

"Does the reeve own this cottage?"

"No, my lord," she said, "but we have the use of it."

"On whose land are we, then?"

She hesitated. "A friend of my husband."

"A good friend if he lends him such a place to rest." He touched her cheek with the back of his hand. "Who is this man?" He sensed her reluctance and stroked it gently away before pulling her face to his and giving her a long, slow kiss that sucked out all resistance. "Tell me now, Ediva," he said. "Who is he?"

"Hugh de Brionne."

Gervase Bret had stayed much longer at the house than he had intended, but he felt no regret. He was sheltering from the rain and quite content to stay there until the key to the mill was found. If Cild had taken it, as now seemed likely, he would return in time. Gervase was happy to loiter in such pleasant company. Leofgifu had brought him back downstairs to leave Hilda alone in her room to rest. As they sat opposite each other at the table, they drank cups of wine and permitted a subtle change to come over their relationship. He was touched by her forlorn beauty, while she was drawn by his easy benevolence. He had learned of her own grief, while she had sensed brutal losses on his side. Both felt the pull of a closer friendship which they knew was beyond their grasp and so they settled for an affectionate togetherness that left them free to explore each other's minds. He asked about her family and she talked as openly as if she had known him all her life.

"My father hates the Normans," she said.

"It is to be expected."

"Do you hate them, Gervase?"

"Sometimes."

"Yet you are one of them."

"I am and I am not," he confessed. "Ralph teases me about it all the time. He calls me an English mongrel and says that I have learned to bark like a Norman but will never have his true breeding."

"Does that offend you?"

"No, Leofgifu. It comforts me."

"What of your father?"

"A Breton, and long since dead."

"He would be proud to see his son rise so high."

"Not as a clerk of Chancery," said Gervase. "My father was a soldier and would have wanted a son to fight. Ralph Delchard is the same. Fighting is in his blood. He mocks me for my love of a peaceful life. Had he been my father, he often says, he would have strangled me at birth to escape the humiliation of raising such a son."

"A man of peace is worth a hundred soldiers."

"If he can manage to stay alive."

He studied her face and her quiet dignity once more and saw the marks of Wulfgeat clearly imprinted. She had his self-possession and his fearless eye. She had the strength of character he had seen on display in the shire hall.

"We met your father with the other burgesses."

"He told me of the encounter."

"I would like to meet him again."

"His manner would not flatter you."

"I would not seek for praise. Where is he now?"

"He had business in the town but would not tell me what." Her lips tightened. "My father thinks that women may not understand. We are here only to adorn the life of a man and not to share it with him."

"Did your husband take that view as well?"

"He worshipped me."

"But did he treat you as an equal?"

"No."

"Did you choose him for yourself?"

"No."

149

"Why, then, did you marry?"

"My father has a strong will. I was forced to obey."

"Did you not resist?"

"For several weeks, but I was overwhelmed. It was my duty to follow his wishes." She glanced upwards. "You know how Hilda was given in marriage to the miller. It was not exactly so with me, for my husband was kind and loving, but there was the same contract. The marriage was made between two men and not between two lovers."

"Did you resent your husband?"

"I came to respect him."

"You mourn and miss him now?"

"Greatly."

Gervase could see that she wanted him to ask the next question. "Did you love him?" he said.

"I cherished his goodness."

"That is not what I mean, Leofgifu."

"I honoured and obeyed him as I vowed."

"No more than that?"

"It was all that I could offer him."

"Why?"

"I loved another."

"Did your father know this?"

Her face puckered. "He despised the man."

Gervase took her hand to offer consolation. Wulfgeat had been cruel to name her Leofgifu. This beautiful Love-Giver had so much love to give, but it was callously stifled. Thrust into a marriage she did not want, she was grieving for a husband she could never admit into her heart. What made her plight even more pitiable was that she had been forced to live once again with the very man who ground the hope and passion out of her between the mill-wheels of his ambition.

"Are you happy with your father?"

"No," she confessed. "Life here is an oppression."

Wulfgeat trudged along with a cloak over his head and shoulders. The rain had eased to a drizzle now, but the great black sky was a blanket that pressed down on Savernake to smother it to death. Birds and animals were muffled. Insects were suffocated into silence. Even the trees were hushed. The only sound that came from the forest was the swift rushing of its intersecting network of streams as they raced with swollen rage to join the river below and speed its wild current.

Cild met him at the mill and led the way. The gloom served them well, but the boy still moved with caution. He was fearful of being seen with Wulfgeat in case a witness guessed at the dark nature of his purpose. It hung so heavily around his neck that he dared not even look up at his companion. Guilt was tempered with remorse. As soon as he thought of his father and the hatred daily heaped upon the miller, his intent was reaffirmed. Wulfgeat was not just one of the most powerful enemies whose spite had to be endured; he epitomised the attitude of the whole town. In Wulfgeat's unrelenting acrimony, the boy saw the vindictive face of Bedwyn itself.

"How much farther?" said Wulfgeat.

"Not far."

"Are you certain you know the way?"

"Yes."

"And the charter is there?"

"Yes."

"Safe from this weather?"

"The chest is wrapped and hidden."

"Did you tell your mother?"

"My mother is dead."

"Hilda takes her place now," he said brusquely. "Look to her for comfort. Does she know of this?"

"No."

"Good."

"You told nobody else?"

The boy shook his head.

"Good."

They pressed on side by side. Wulfgeat was conscious of the irony of the situation. Nothing in creation would have made him stroll companionably with Alric of Longdon, yet he was now accompanying the boy eagerly along the river-bank. He had no pity or liking for the child. Cild was simply a means to an end and Wulfgeat had bought his cooperation. He did not regret that. The charter would repay him generously.

"Why have you stopped?" he complained.

"I may go no farther."

"You must take me there."

"No."

"I paid you, boy."

"No."

"Lead on!"

Wulfgeat grabbed him roughly to shake him into obedience, but the boy's tears made him stay his hand. Cild was terrified to go farther. He sobbed his excuses until Wulfgeat came to see his refusal in a more sympathetic way. They had reached the junction of river and stream. Light woodland covered the hill before them. They were patently close to the hiding place itself, but the boy could not bring himself to approach closer. His father had been killed and the spot harboured memories too awful for Cild to confront. Nothing would make him venture one step farther and Wulfgeat had been unwise to resort to force. The boy had his father's mulish stubbornness. Threaten him again and he might renege on the bargain that had been struck.

"Teach me the way," said Wulfgeat.

"Follow the line of this stream."

"How far?"

"Till it goes from sight. Higher up."

"What do I look for?"

"A yew tree."

"I see a dozen already from where I stand. How will I know I have the right one?"

"It is by the stream where the water comes out from under the ground. It is split in two."

"By lightning?"

"Yes."

152

"And then?"

"Reach deep into the hollow."

"That is the hiding place?"

"Your hand will touch a sack." Cild's heart was pumping as he rehearsed the execution, but his voice did not betray him. "Untie the cord and thrust your hand right in."

"The box is there?"

"Box and charter. My father showed me."

"You have earned your money, Cild."

"I know."

"But if you have lied to me . . ." warned Wulfgeat.

"No, no, I swear it! The sack is in that tree!"

The man could see the boy was speaking the truth. He adjusted his cloak on his shoulders, then followed the trail as he had been directed. Cild was still shivering with fear when Wulfgeat left him, but it was soon replaced by an evil smirk of anticipation. He had planned it all with care. Only he and his father would ever know what had happened.

Wulfgeat climbed on with awkward steps, cursing the slippery incline and grabbing at roots and branches to steady his ascent. The stream soon vanished, but he could see no yew tree. Had the boy deceived him, after all? But farther up the hill, the water broke through the chalk once more and he was reassured. He grunted on upwards through the dark.

He was out of breath when he reached the yew tree and he rested hard against it for support. Alric Longdon had died here at this hiding-place, but the memory only served to curl his lip. The boy was rightly afraid, but Wulfgeat felt no fear. Where the loathsome miller fell was consecrated ground to him. Wulfgeat peered into the hollow of the tree, then put an inquisitive hand inside. He felt the sack and smiled. All was as the boy had explained.

He flung off his cloak so that he could untie the sack unencumbered, but his hands never even reached the twine. As he stretched upwards to fling back the garment, a creature of fur and teeth and claws came leaping from the bushes to bowl him over and snap at his unguarded throat.

Wulfgeat was strong, but the force of the attack overpowered him within seconds. His neck and face were eaten voraciously away and his twitching carcass soon lay still in a pool of gouting blood.

When Cild crept up on him twenty minutes later, he did not even recognise the man. Nose and eyes had both gone and the head was almost severed from the body. Wulfgeat's clothing had been ripped apart by claws and one of his hands had been bitten half-away. The boy screamed out in horror.

The wolf of Savernake had another victim.

Chapter Nine

GERVASE BRET WAS NEEDED ELSEWHERE, BUT HE WAS quite unable to leave. Conversation with Leofgifu was so interesting and so pleasurable that an hour slipped past with the speed of a minute. She was indeed an unusual young woman with qualities that reminded him of his dear Alys back in Winchester—thus causing him a twinge of guilt—but these were offset by characteristics that were entirely her own. What astounded him was her complete lack of bitterness. Most daughters who had been through her ordeal would have been alienated from their fathers, consumed by self-pity and animated by deep resentment at the severity of their fate. Leofgifu, by contrast, was an image of acceptance. She was honest about her unhappiness, but she did not thrust it upon all around her. She had learned how to suffer in silence and to find relief in helping others whose predicament was worse than her own. Gervase was entranced. He felt that he was watching true heroism on display and it moved him.

By the same token, Leofgifu was increasingly attracted to him. His youthful candour was underpinned by a restraint and discretion that were uncommon in someone of his age. Because Gervase was so unthreatening, she was able to relax with him and to talk openly in a way that she had not done for years. Leofgifu had never been short of male attention. As soon as she was widowed, she sensed lecherous eyes falling upon her once more and it was not long before lonely and desperate men were whispering in corners with her father about the possibility of a second marriage. The very notion of tying herself to another man appalled her and she treated all approaches with an icy contempt that her father's entreaties had been unable to melt. Leofgifu had earned and now cherished her independence. Yet all those emotions which had once made her want to yield totally and uncritically to a man came flooding back as she talked with Gervase. He was not for her, but she could share briefly in the joy of his life.

"Are you betrothed?" she asked softly.

"Yes."

"What is her name?"

"Alys."

"She is most fortunate."

He smiled. "Alys does not always think so."

"When will you marry?"

"When we may find the time." He hid his frustration in a sigh. "My work must come first and it keeps me away from Winchester too often and too long. Ralph tells me that a man can understand real love only when he is separated from his beloved, but it makes for much suffering as well."

"I know." Wistfulness descended. She studied him for a moment before speaking. "You said earlier that you entered the abbey at Eltham. Why did you leave?"

"Alys."

"Was she the sole reason?"

"No."

"What else drove you out?"

"I was too weak to withstand the monastic discipline."

"Too weak or too worldly?"

"Both," he said. "I failed the test. Self-denial was too high a price for me to pay."

"How do you look at monastic life now?"

"With admiration."

"And with regrets?"

"No, Leofgifu. With fear. I am in two minds about this assignment of ours in Bedwyn. Part of me is still drawn to the beautiful simplicity of life within the cloister, but another part of me shudders whenever I see the abbey. It is too demanding, too searching, too overwhelming. I could never envisage taking the cowl again."

"Supposing that you had never met Alys."

"I would still have escaped the order."

"How?"

"By meeting you."

It was such an innocent and natural expression of affection that she was lit by a glow of uncomplicated delight. Years suddenly fell away as she recaptured, for an instant, another time with another man when this same feeling had infused her. Leofgifu and Gervase stared at each other for a long while before they realised that they were still holding hands. Self-consciousness made them loosen their grasp and sit apart. It was only then they became aware that they were no longer alone.

Standing in the open doorway was a sorry figure with the rain beating at his back. Cild was drenched. He was panting with his exertions and bent double by his woes. But it was his face that caused real alarm. It had turned to such a ghastly whiteness that he looked positively ill and his mouth was agape with frozen terror. Gervase and Leofgifu rose at once and moved across to him with concern.

The boy collapsed in a heap before them.

Bedwyn was drowned in a sea of hysteria. The first wave had come with the death of Alric Longdon, but this, it now appeared, had merely lapped at the communal fears of the town. When the news of Wulfgeat's grisly end spread, it was a tidal surge that swept all before it. Every man, woman, and child gibbered helplessly as gushing water claimed them. Bedwyn was doomed. The whole community was at the mercy of some supernatural creature which could take its prey at will and with complete impunity. There was nowhere to hide. The wolf of Savernake would eat its way through the entire town.

A forester had heard the scream from half a mile away and ran to the spot where the faceless Wulfgeat was splattered upon the ground. Nobody else was in sight, but the shadow of the animal still seemed to lie across its victim. The forester raced madly to the town to summon help and he set off the typhoon which now engulfed them. Only the monks from the abbey had courage enough to venture into the danger area to rescue the fallen man. The brutalised remains of Wulfgeat were borne back to the mortuary chapel with all due haste. Those who were charged to clean the body had never been given a more repellent task. As they tentatively bathed the mutilated torso, they were convinced that they were dealing with the work of the Devil.

The Witch of Crofton came quickly back into fashion as the most likely suspect. It was Wulfgeat who had first pointed to her as the author of the first outrage. This was plainly Emma's revenge. She had killed Alric because he had beaten her and she had murdered Wulfgeat because he had instigated the raid upon her. Nothing could be clearer. Her dog was the agent of her heinous crimes. Transformed by a spell into a giant wolf, it patrolled the forest and lured its victims to an isolated spot so that it could savage them to death. It then resumed its form as the black dog which kept the witch company as her familiar. Hatred of Emma reached new heights, but it was moderated by naked fear of repercussions. Those who wished to ride off again to slay her and her hound now thought about possible consequences. Alric and Wulfgeat had both offended her and both had died as a result. Even from beyond the grave, her potent charms could mean damnation. Her destruction had to be plotted with great care.

Ralph Delchard did not even consider the name of Emma. Witchcraft did not intrude upon his common sense and he was still grateful for the basket of wild fruit which Emma had picked for him. Such a gesture could not have come from the cold-blooded monster created by common report. When the news of Wulfgeat's death was brought to him at the hunting lodge, he called for his horse to be saddled and galloped to the abbey, arriving in time to see the body while it was being washed and to scrutinise its wounds without revulsion. He then spoke with the forester who had discovered the corpse. The man had just given a full account to Abbot Serlo of what he had seen and hazy impressions had already hardened into solid fact. A sturdy fellow of middle years, he trembled as he went through the details again.

"Wulfgeat was mauled by a huge wolf," he said.

Ralph was unpersuaded. "Did you see the animal?"

"No, my lord, but I heard it."

"That distinctive howl?"

"It was more like a scream of triumph."

"Wolves do not scream."

"This one did, my lord."

"Then it was no wolf. A fox might make such a noise. Or at least, a vixen might during mating. But foxes would never attack a man in that way. Was that the sound you thought you heard? A high-pitched cry?"

"I did hear it, my lord. Clear as a bell."

"Shriek or howl?"

"A scream."

"Animal or human?"

"I took it to be animal."

"You are a forester, man. You should *know*."

"It frighted me out of my wits," said the forester as he rubbed his rough beard. "I thought it was the beast, but it might have been Wulfgeat himself, calling out for help."

"How would he do that with his throat bitten away?" said Ralph irritably. "If Wulfgeat had time enough to yell out, then he had time to draw his weapon; yet his sword was still in its scabbard when you found him."

"That is so, my lord."

"You saw nobody else?"

"Nobody."

"And no sign of a sudden departure?"

"Some fur caught on the brambles, that is all."

"How was he lying?"

"Upon the bare earth."

"But at what angle? Facing what direction? How close to those brambles? How near to that yew tree?" Ralph put a

159

hand on his shoulder. "Steady your nerves and tell me the truth. Much may depend on it. Give me no more talk of huge wolves and wicked witches. Speak only of what you *saw*. Now, you came rushing upon him by that stream. Describe how he lay."

Ralph Delchard slowly dragged the details out of him and gained an approximate knowledge of what had taken place. The man was still far too scared to give an objective report, but he no longer slid into assumptions about a phantom wolf which had been conjured up by the black arts of the Witch of Crofton. Something had killed Wulfgeat and the forester was the first on the scene. His garbled account yielded a number of valuable facts.

Their discussion took place near the abbey gatehouse and so they were on hand to hear the mild commotion that ensued as eager visitors arrived. A distraught Leofgifu was demanding to be admitted to the mortuary chapel to view the body of her father and to confirm the terrible news which had just reached her. Hilda was trying to hold her friend back and Gervase Bret was doing all he could to persuade the stricken daughter against such a course of action. The porter attempted to calm them down, but Leofgifu insisted on her rights as next of kin. Ralph Delchard stepped in to introduce himself and to add his voice to that of the others.

"Lady, you have my deepest sympathy," he said quietly.

"Where is my father?"

"Beyond recall. Let him rest in peace."

"I must see him."

"It is not a sight fit for your young eyes."

"I am his only child."

"Then remember him for his goodness and do not vex his poor body now. There is nothing you may do to bring him back and the manner of his death will haunt you forever if you persist in looking upon him once more. Spare yourself that agony."

"Come away, Leofgifu," said Gervase gently. "This is no place for you."

She was adamant. "I wish to see my father."

"Let Gervase take you home," advised Ralph. "You will live to thank me for this wise counsel. I have seen the body and it is no longer that of the man you once knew. Your father's soul is in heaven. Pray for him."

But even the concerted efforts of four people could not dissuade her from her intent. Fired by a duty that grew out of a sense of guilt, Leofgifu stood her ground. They had no power to prevent her from seeing the body. Her voice became shrill as she reaffirmed her demands.

Monastic authority interceded in the dispute.

"What means this unseemly noise?" asked Prior Baldwin as he swooped down on them. "Peace, peace, good lady!"

Leofgifu was finally subdued. The sight of the prior and the sacristan had a calming effect on her and their words added further balm. Ralph had no respect for monks, but he had to admire the practised way in which both Baldwin and Peter offered their condolences to the bereaved daughter. They were professionals in the service of death. They knew exactly what to say and exactly how to say it. All of Leofgifu's truculence disappeared and they talked her out of her purpose before she even had chance to state what it was.

Prior Baldwin's tone had a distant condescension in it, but Brother Peter's voice was soft and sincere. When he looked at Leofgifu, there was a world of sadness in his expression. He spoke as a monk, but she heard him as a friend. She could only respect Baldwin. It was Peter who inspired trust and who offered her real support. He told her that she was to call on him at any time if she needed spiritual sustenance or practical help of any kind, and she knew that it was no idle invitation. During her brief stay at the abbey, Hilda had been greatly buoyed up by the gentle assistance of the sacristan. Now it was Leofgifu who felt his natural generosity reaching out to her. Something in his manner both rallied her and confused her, lifting her up from total despair and yet adding a new bewilderment to her situation. Leofgifu wanted his help but was somehow

161

unable to grasp at it. Prior Baldwin tried to ease her on her way, but Peter detained her with further promises and advice. It was to the latter that she addressed her final question.

"Was he killed by a wolf?"

"We believe so."

"May I see him?"

A kind pause. "We think not, Leofgifu."

There was a sharp intake of breath, as if she was in great pain for a second, then she nodded her agreement. Prior Baldwin offered her accommodation at the abbey, but Leofgifu had no reason to be there any longer. Her mind had been slightly eased. Her father was forever beyond her now. Supported by Hilda, she turned towards the gate and went through it. Ralph Delchard collected his horse, then followed with Gervase Bret in order to lend assistance if needed, but Hilda was in control now. Having been helped through her own ordeal by Leofgifu, she could now return that loving kindness.

The men dropped back a little so that they could converse without being overheard by the two women ahead of them.

"What did you learn?" asked Gervase.

"He was killed on the same spot as Alric."

"By a wolf?"

"By an animal of some kind."

"What was Wulfgeat *doing* in such a place?"

"There is only one explanation," decided Ralph. "He knew about the hiding place in the yew tree. Wulfgeat was Alric's accomplice."

"But they hated each other."

"A mask to their true relationship."

"No, Ralph," said the other. "I talked with the miller's widow and I could see that the hatred was genuine on both sides. Those men would not have worked together no matter what rewards were offered. Look for some other reason that puts them both in the same part of Savernake when they died."

162

"There *is* no other reason."

"There must be."

They walked in silence for a while and saw Hilda's arm tighten around Leofgifu's shoulders as the first tears of remorse began to flow. Ralph still felt that there was some collusion between miller and burgess, but Gervase pursued a different line of thought.

"Why did Wulfgeat visit that spot?" he resumed.

"To search for the chest."

"If he had been Alric's accomplice, he would have known that the chest was not there. All that the yew tree holds is a block of wood in a sack. Why go after that?"

"Why indeed?" conceded Ralph.

"Someone took him there."

"Wulfgeat?"

"Someone showed him the way and led him to his death. He would not have gone to such a place unless he had expected to find something to his advantage—the money or the charter. That was the lure to get him there."

"But who set it, Gervase?"

"I do not know as yet. Let us remember the moneyer."

"Eadmer, the dwarf?"

"You thought you had spied a way into his mint."

"Yes," said Ralph sadly. "Until we rowed beneath his building and looked up into the throne where Eadmer sits. I guessed at a weak link in the chain of his defences, but I was wrong. The moneyer has too small a bottom for my device. No man would ever be able to crawl through that hole and up into the mint. His shoulders would be too wide."

"No man, you say?"

"It is quite impossible."

Gervase turned to face him with a quizzical smile.

"What about a boy?"

Cild lay curled up on the mattress in the tiny room he shared with his mother. He was still in a state of shock and his young mind was trying to make sense of what he had seen and what it all meant. His had been a harsh life so far and it had lacked all the pleasures of childhood, but there had been compensatory joys. In spite of a strict and punitive upbringing, he had loved his father deeply and relished those moments when he was taken into the latter's confidence so that he could help to outwit rivals and enemies. Alric sowed corruption in his son at an early age to ensure that he had an ally in the ceaseless battle against an uncaring world. Women never understood the nature of such conflicts. Cild's mother and his stepmother had, therefore, been kept ignorant of what their menfolk did outside the mill. It had bonded father and son together and it was that bond which now came to the boy's aid. He reconstructed the progress of events once more in his fevered brain.

Wulfgeat had not been killed. When Cild looked down upon the prostrate body, he had seen his own father. It was Alric who was the victim of the wolf and his cruel and unnecessary death had ruined the futures of his son and of his second wife, putting an unbridgeable gap between them. Anger displaced fear as he reflected on the situation. Shock gave way to cold rancour. Wulfgeat had loathed his father and gloried in his downfall. He and his servant had broken into the mill to search it without permission. His only interest in Alric Longdon lay in finding the miller's chest so that he could use the charter it contained for his own personal gain. Wulfgeat was no caring friend who took pity on the widow and her stepson. He was a greedy and selfish man who tried to exploit the death of his arch-enemy. Sympathy was wasted on such a person. He deserved to perish in the most violent way. One death answered another.

Cild had set his trap, but the burgess had met a deadlier foe than the snake in the flour sack. The boy should be grateful. He himself had survived and was free from all suspicion. The murder he had plotted did not, in fact, take place. Fate had contrived better than he himself. His father had indeed been avenged and Cild was now lying in the house of the man who had tormented him. That only served to complete the sense of triumph. Instead of being huddled into a frightened ball, he should be full of exultation. Cild had conquered Wulfgeat and taken possession of his home. The son of a mere miller had outfoxed one of the leading burgesses in the town of Bedwyn. It was a signal victory.

The boy slowly uncurled and let his arms and legs stretch right out with growing freedom. Then he began to laugh. It was not the normal happy chuckle of a boy of nine but the weird, uncanny, unsettling, high-pitched cackle of some demented creature of the forest. He was possessed. Caught up in the wildness of his cachinnation, Cild began to twitch and writhe about on the mattress like a poisonous snake that has just been liberated from its irksome prison inside a sack.

Hugh de Brionne chose his moment well, riding into Bedwyn at the break of day on his destrier, with his huntsmen in support, bringing a pack of baying hounds to wake anyone still abed and to announce his bold purpose. Where the Warden of Savernake's men had failed, Hugh de Brionne would succeed. He would sift through the forest until the wolf was tracked down and caught. Bedwyn might still be immobilised by terror, but a Norman lord was determined to take action. He was also grateful of anything which diverted attention away from the land dispute in which he had become embroiled. Success in Savernake would make him a hero in the locality. A man who was usually despised for his arrogance would now be praised for his bravery and there would be none of the usual complaints about the damage done to farming land over which he and his huntsmen had to ride to reach the forest. If he could kill the wolf, he could rid the town of a menace that banished all sleep and he would also impress the leader of the commissioners who sat in judgement upon him. A keen huntsman himself, Ralph Delchard would be the first to commend a successful sortie in the forest. Hugh de Brionne had everything to gain.

His horse pranced in a circle around the marketplace

while its master waved his stump of an arm to keen onlookers and collected their good wishes.

"Fortune attend you, my lord!"

"Kill the wolf!"

"Run it to ground!"

"Show it no mercy!"

"Unleash your hounds!"

"Bring it back dead!"

"Destroy it!"

The shouts brought more and more heads out of windows and the whole town was soon urging Hugh de
Brionne to remove the bane of their existence. He was an
unpopular man who could yet turn out to be their saviour,
and even the most loyal Saxon was ready to applaud a Norman if he could catch the wolf of Savernake. The name of
Emma was hurled into the air, but Hugh de Brionne did not
deign to hear it. Witchcraft did not murder Wulfgeat. Only
feeble minds could believe such nonsense. In the opinion of
Hugh de Brionne, the burgess was brought down by the angry fangs of a lone wolf. His job was to find it before it
could strike again.

"Sound the horn!" he ordered.

The blast reverberated around the town and set off a
frenzy among the hounds. With Hugh in the lead, they scurried off eagerly in the direction of the forest, borne along
by the cheers of the people and by an overweening confidence. Men with weapons and trained dogs might prove to
be their salvation. Bedwyn was certainly able to face the
new day with more fortitude than had hitherto been the
case.

It soon evaporated. An hour passed and the sounds of
the hunt could no longer be heard. The wolf had evidently
outrun its pursuers. A second hour rolled by and the Witch
of Crofton was resurrected once more as the culprit. Hugh
de Brionne was searching in the wrong direction. There
was no wolf in the forest, because it was now a black dog
that guarded its mistress. Reality succumbed to superstition
as the anxieties of the long night took hold on minds once

more. Nobody could hunt down a wolf that existed only when it was called into being by black magic. Hugh de Brionne and his men were chasing shadows in the forest.

The passage of a third hour reinforced the feeling that the whole venture was a waste of time. Those who had trusted in a Norman lord now reviled him for his false promises and they also noted the recurring link between invasion and affliction. When the commissioners came, Alric Longdon died; while they stayed, the town was being rent apart by boundary disputes and their evil influence had culminated in a second gruesome death. The Normans were not simply there to enforce the king's business. They were a curse on the community. This thought made people recall the Saxon spirit which had inflamed Wulfgeat throughout his life.

"Down with the Normans!" someone dared to shout.

"Wulfgeat was right! Never surrender!"

"Drive them out!"

"Grind them under the heel!"

"Save a Saxon town for true Saxons!"

"Normans are a plague upon us!"

"Remember Wulfgeat! Resist them!"

"Be true to his memory!"

"Who will stand against them?"

A great cheer went up, but it was marketplace valour. They knew in their hearts that they did not have the skill or the numbers to defeat their Norman overlords and their morning rebellion was, in any case, misjudged. One blast on a hunting horn dispelled it completely.

"They're coming back!"

"I see Hugh de Brionne."

"The riders are all scattered."

"But they are bringing something."

"They have a kill."

Speculation grew to bursting point as they watched the huntsmen canter down the hill and into the town. Hugh de Brionne was at the head of his entourage, a smile of satisfaction on his scarred face. His armour glinted in the sunshine and his mantle streamed behind him in the breeze. As he opened up an avenue in the busy marketplace, two of his men came forward. Each held the end of a long branch of wood from which a dead carcass dangled. The animal was hacked into shreds and dripping with blood, its great mouth open to reveal its murderous teeth, its tongue drooping uselessly. On their master's command, they let their quarry drop to the floor and it spewed out even more blood in front of the awe-struck townsfolk.

Hugh de Brionne pointed with his stump of an arm.

"Behold the wolf of Savernake!"

Abbot Serlo was omniscient. Although there were things that he chose not to know because they interfered with the higher matters to which his life was dedicated, he nevertheless had an instinctive grasp on them. When Prior Baldwin called on him that morning after Prime, the abbot did not need to ask about the latest development in the battle of wits with the commissioners. He sensed at once that there had been setback and threat and relegated the matter to the end of their discussion. Of much more immediate concern to him was the grotesque corpse which lay on a bier in the mortuary chapel. His eyes protruded beyond their customary danger point.

"Should we not send for the sheriff, Prior Baldwin?"

"No, Father Abbot."

"This is a second tragedy within days."

"But not brought about by human agency," said the prior. "A wolf struck down both men. We cannot call on the sheriff to do our hunting for us, especially when there is no work left for him to do."

Serlo was pleased. "The animal has been caught?"

"Caught and killed, Father Abbot."

"By whom?"

"Hugh de Brionne and his men."

The eyes wobbled upwards as the portly abbot mixed gratitude with regret, offering up a prayer of thanks for the removal of the troublesome beast while wishing that someone else could claim the credit for its death. Hugh de Brionne was a thorn in the side of the abbey at the best of times. With something of this order to boast about, he would become even more insufferable.

Prior Baldwin took a more expedient view of it all.

"Set a wolf to catch a wolf," he said.

"One danger at least is past."

"Hugh de Brionne will be famous for a week."

"And notorious for the rest of his days."

"Let us forget the noble lord," said Baldwin, anxious to move away from the subject of a man who was still implicated in the boundary dispute with the abbey. "Our thoughts must be with Wulfgeat."

"Prayers have been said for him at every service." Abbot Serlo turned his bulging eyes once more upon his guest. "No man deserves to die in such a hideous way, but one is bound to look for purpose in the nature of his demise. Christ went into the wilderness for forty days and forty nights and emerged untouched by the snarling denizens of that place. Goodness is its own protection. Brothers from this house go into the forest every day and come to no harm. Yet Alric and Wulfgeat met with evil among the trees." He spread his palms questionably. "*Why*, Prior Baldwin? What marked these men out for such horror? How did they incur God's displeasure? Wherein lies their sin? These were no random killings by a crazed animal. They were a judgment from heaven upon two men who transgressed. In what way?"

"I do not know, Father Abbot."

"Is there any link between them?"

"None save the heat of their enmity."

"They were yoked together in wickedness."

"I fail to see how."

"Think hard, Prior Baldwin."

"I am exerting my brain to its utmost limit."

"The answer stands all around you."

"Does it, Father Abbot?"

"That is my conjecture."

His eyelids closed to narrow his gaze to the merest dot, but there was no loss of power. Indeed, Baldwin began to feel distinctly uncomfortable beneath the force of the scrutiny and it helped to concentrate his mind.

"All around me?" he said.

"Even so."

"You speak of the abbey?"

"Of what else?"

"How are the two men implicated?" wondered Baldwin. "Both were brought here, it is true, and both have lain in our mortuary chapel to await a Christian burial. But neither has been a friend to us. Indeed, it was Alric who brought these inquisitive commissioners down upon us once more."

Serlo nodded imperceptibly. "That is my point."

Baldwin finally understood. Alric had challenged the abbey and he had died. Wulfgeat was no benefactor of the order and there had been a series of acrimonious disputes with him over the years. Both men would have been in a position to embarrass the abbey further in front of the new commissioners, yet both had been eliminated from the enquiry in the most dramatic way. Baldwin smiled inwardly. God did indeed work in mysterious ways. Weak minds fell back on superstition in times of stress, but strong hearts held true to their Maker. The wolf of Savernake was no agent of the Devil trying to avenge personal slights on behalf of a miserable outcast woman from Crofton. It was a hound of heaven sent down expressly to lend aid to Bedwyn Abbey in a time of trial. In accusing the monks, Alric and Wulfgeat had overstepped the bounds of decency and they had to be chastised firmly for their audacity. The wolf was a sign from above. Notwithstanding its precarious position, the abbey would still secure a victory in its fight against other claimants. God was self-evidently on their side and a thousand commissioners could not prevail against His might.

Abbot Serlo watched a sense of profound relief seep its way through his prior. No more required to be said on the issue. He could now leave it once more in Baldwin's hands.

The abbot indicated the little altar which stood in the corner of the room and they knelt beside each other in prayer. Serlo went into his normal ritual, chanting quietly to himself in Latin, exuding purity of heart, rehearsing for sainthood, eyes hooded but mind wide open to view the full wonder of God. Here was prayer as true supplication.

Baldwin likewise went through a set order of worship, but he soon diverged from it. While his abbot was on high beside him, the prior had more earthly concerns. He was not yet ready to advance his claims to canonisation. What he was praying for was another murderous attack from another wolf in Savernake Forest and he nominated the victims.

Ralph Delchard and Gervase Bret.

The two friends spent a dull morning in the shire hall with their colleagues, taking statements about the disputed land from a variety of witnesses and building up a more complete picture of the situation. It was uninspiring work and Ralph Delchard seized the first opportunity to unload it on Canon Hubert and Brother Simon. As soon as he heard the uproar in the marketplace that was occasioned by the return of the hunting party, Ralph was on his feet and shuffling his papers. Gervase Bret, too, wanted to be nearer the centre of the action. They excused themselves politely and aroused no protest by their withdrawal. Hubert was delighted to resume control of affairs once more and Simon felt that his own status was also now elevated. The questioning continued.

Ralph and Gervase reached the marketplace as the crowd was clustering around the dead wolf. Hugh de Brionne was savouring his moment of celebration and he gave them a mock bow when he saw them. Ralph was anxious to examine the wolf itself and forced his way through the press, but Gervase was more squeamish and lurked on the fringes. There was no pleasure for him in the sight of a mangled animal and he could not understand the blood-lust which seemed to excite everyone else who was present. Ralph spoke with the lord of the manor of Chisbury, then left him to enjoy his sudden prestige and made his way back to Gervase. He took his friend aside so that they could speak in private.

"Let us go," he suggested. "I am out of place here."

"Why, Ralph?"

"Because I am a heretic among believers."

Gervase grinned. "That is nothing new."

"Those who wanted a wolf have now found one."

"The animal has terrorised the whole town."

"No, Gervase. What they have been frightened of is the *idea* of a wolf. Hugh de Brionne has simply put flesh and blood on that idea by dumping a carcass in the market-place." He glanced over his shoulder at the happy throng. "I would not trust that arrant knave for a second. How Alric and Wulfgeat were killed, I do not know, but of one thing I am quite certain. That bleeding mess on the cobbles did not attack either man."

"How can you be so sure?"

"Look at his huntsmen and his hounds," said Ralph. "They would be heard from miles away and smelled long before they got close enough to corner the beast. Hugh admitted to me that the wolf was lame. My guess is that that is why it was driven out of its pack and forced to hunt alone. And that is why the hounds were able to track it down and overhaul it. A wolf with a damaged front paw did not make those marks on the chest of the dead men." A rousing cheer went up as Hugh de Brionne rode off with his retinue. "Let him have his hour, Gervase. He has caught *a* wolf in Savernake but not *the* wolf—if, indeed, such a creature exists."

"*Something* must have been up in those trees, Ralph."

"I believe it is still there. Let us search for it."

"Now?"

"Would you rather sit in commission with Hubert?"

Gervase chuckled. "Lead on. . . ."

They found their horses and set off, leaving the four men-at-arms in the shire hall to bolster Canon Hubert's authority and to enforce his wishes. Ralph and Gervase rode along the river at a rising trot. The heavy rain of the previous day had left the leaves damp and the ground sodden, but sunshine was slowly drying everything out. Birdsong seemed much louder and more melodious. They went past Alric's mill without comment and rode on until they reached the point where the stream fed into the river. Dismounting from their horses, they tethered the animals and continued on foot. Though the woodland was suffused with light and vibrating with the happy buzz of insects, Ralph nevertheless drew his sword as they began the ascent. Alric and Wulfgeat had made this same journey without due care for their safety. Whatever else happened, Ralph would not be taken unawares.

He led the way uphill, picking a route through the undergrowth and using his sword to lever himself along. They eventually reached the blasted yew tree beside which two men had already met their deaths. There were clear signs of a struggle. Wulfgeat had put up more resistance than Alric and the earth was churned up into mud where the burgess had apparently wrestled with his attacker. Wisps of fresh fur were caught up in the brambles to suggest that the bush had once again been the place from which the ambush had been launched. Ralph applied his imagination to the facts he had gleaned from the forester and he walked through a version of the fateful encounter, pretending to be man and wolf by turns and experimenting with possible positions. Gervase watched with interest and admiration. A death-grapple belonged firmly in his friend's province. His own territory lay in the thickets of the law where the wolves walked on two legs and savaged their prey with charters.

Ralph Delchard was eventually satisfied with his improvisation. It had proved conclusively to him that the wolf captured by Hugh de Brionne had not been the killer. He now turned his attention to the yew tree which had brought both men to that spot in the first place. Alric had come to deposit silver coin, but Wulfgeat was there in search of something to take away. Ralph was about to thrust a hand into the dark hollow when a sixth sense warned him. He used his sword to probe around and the steel saved him from a very painful end. The sack into which it cut suddenly burst into life and threshed around inside the trunk. Pushing Gervase back out of the way, Ralph jabbed his sword point into the sack, then lifted it right up and tossed it onto the open ground. Its angry inhabitant became even more agitated and the sack twitched violently.

Ralph's curiosity made him reach forward to tug at the twine around the neck. He stepped back instantly, but there was no response at first. It seemed as if the creature inside the sack was either dead or spurning the opportunity to escape. Gervase moved in for a closer look, but Ralph's blade stopped him in the nick of time. Out through the folds of the sack came the head of the snake, its eyes alert and its tongue darting. Its slither was slow and measured until it saw them, then it quickened its pace considerably, making a determined wriggle towards Ralph's ankles. Its fangs were bared to inflict a venomous bite, but it never got close enough to him. His sword point came down with stunning accuracy and pierced through the back of its neck, sinking deep into the ground and leaving it impaled lifelessly.

"That creature was waiting for Wulfgeat," said Gervase.

"How do you know?"

"Look at the sack."

"Another from the mill."

"It was put there to welcome Wulfgeat's hand."

"Who would want to set such a trap?"

"Alric's accomplice."

"And who is that, Gervase?"

"The same person who gained entry into Eadmer's mint."

"You told me that it might be a boy."

"It was. Cild, son of Alric. This is also his work."

They handled the sack to make sure that it had come from the same mill and noted Alric's mark upon it. Ralph now retrieved his sword to make further careful investigation of the yew tree, but there were no more poisonous snakes guarding the absent treasure. All that remained was the block of wood and purse that he himself had put back inside the original sack. Wood and sacks were replaced inside the tree as the two friends considered their next move.

"We must question this boy closely," said Ralph.

"Not yet," argued Gervase. "Cild needs time to recover from the shock. He conducted Wulfgeat to this part of the forest, then waited while he came in search of the chest. The boy expected to find him dying from a snakebite and instead stumbles on his half-eaten remains. No wonder he was still reeling with horror when he returned to the house."

"Speak to him when you judge it to be fit. You have access to the place. A softer tongue than mine is needed in a house of mourning."

"I will wait and watch. Cild is still a boy, but he has the cunning of a grown man. He will not confess easily. It will have to be wormed painstakingly out of him."

Ralph nodded, then turned back to the tree, staring down at the thick tendrils which encircled it with such proprietary zeal. Gervase gave a wry smile.

"This town was well christened," he said.

"Bedwyn?"

"Its name derives from the Latin for bindweed. Look at this yew tree and you have a symbol of our stay here. All is intertwined confusion." He gazed back in the direction of the town itself. "A simple assignment brought us here. There was an irregularity in the abbey returns. That is all we knew. Yet from that one tiny seed of doubt has grown this endless convolvulus that twists and turns its way through the whole community. We have met death and decay, fraud and forgery. And much more may await us before we are done."

"You are too philosophical," said Ralph bluntly. "I am no gardener, but I know the way to deal with bindweed." His sword flashed and the yew tree was freed from its coils. "Cut it away without mercy."

Gervase was ready to head back to the town, but Ralph

175

was in an exploratory mood. He wanted to see more of Savernake. If the dead wolf had not been responsible for the two deaths, then something else had, and the only place they would find it would be in the forest. With his sword still at the ready, he climbed farther up the hill until he reached the top. He and Gervase could now survey a wooded slope that swept down into a valley that was more densely timbered. His inquisitiveness was inflamed even more.

"Let us go down there," he volunteered.

"It will take too long, Ralph."

"Are you frightened?"

"Of course not."

"Do you wish to borrow my weapon?"

"I have a dagger in my belt."

"You are afraid of the exercise, then?"

"That is not so, Ralph."

"So why do you drag your feet? Am I to tell Alys that you were either too weak or too worried to take a walk among the trees?" He gave a coarse laugh. "If *she* were with you at this moment, you would stroll through the forest all day."

"The hunt has already been through here this morning," said Gervase reasonably. "What can we possibly find that thirty men and a pack of hounds contrived to miss?"

"A great deal," promised Ralph. "Follow."

The gradient was steeper on the other side of the hill and they had to grasp at the trunks of saplings to steady themselves. When they reached the valley floor, they heard a stream bubbling nearby and they traced the sound until they found the water. It was a much deeper and wider stream than the one which they had just left and it provided them with a meandering path through this thicker part of the forest. Trees rose up all around them and the overhanging branches sometimes excluded all light, giving a sense of privacy in the half-dark. Birds and insects abounded and smaller animals would occasionally dart from cover for a second before vanishing just as swiftly. Ralph felt a vague sense of menace that kept his sword up, but Gervase began to warm to this new habitat and to be glad that his friend had made him come on the visit. This section of Savernake was enclosed and well protected. It held no threat for him.

While Ralph Delchard shouldered his way unceremoniously through the undergrowth, therefore, Gervase Bret took the time to look and listen. He played with leaves, he fingered bark, and he picked the wild fruit. He liked the brush of grass against his shins and the swish of bushes against his arms. There was so much to see and enjoy that he wanted to slow down to absorb it all properly, but Ralph was restless. When they stepped into a small clearing, the older man gave it no more than a glance before crossing towards a clump of birches.

"Wait!" said Gervase.

"Why?"

"Hold there!"

"For what reason?"

"Can you not see?"

"No. Let us move on."

Gervase grabbed him. "Look around you, Ralph!"

He did as requested but still saw nothing that should detain him. The clearing was oval in shape and no more than thirty yards in diameter. Around its perimeter was a number of mounds of earth that had grassed over. Ralph Delchard had dismissed them with a glance, but Gervase Bret was intrigued. Running to the first misshapen lump, he bent down to examine it, then pulled away the turf which had been used to cover it. What had looked like a natural mound was, in fact, a piece of red sandstone set carefully in the earth. The stone was no more than eighteen inches high, but it had been crudely dressed to shape. Gervase was thrilled with his discovery. He scampered around the clearing and snatched the turf away from each of the mounds until all were uncovered, then he moved to the centre of the clearing with Ralph. The grassy lumps on the ground were now revealed as a circle of stones set at regular intervals. Gervase was fascinated.

"It is like Stonehenge!" he said.

"Yes," agreed Ralph with a grin. "This must be Eadmer's home. It is a Stonehenge for dwarves."

"See there!" said Gervase, pointing. "That stone has not yet been dressed. It has only just been put into position. What we saw on Salisbury Plain was a dead place, but this is alive. Can you not feel the presence of worship?"

"No, Gervase."

"I sense it very strongly."

"All I see is a random collection of stones."

"Look for the pattern. Follow the scheme." Gervase moved to the largest stone and bent to try its weight. "I cannot even budge it. What strength must have been needed to bring it to its resting place?"

Ralph Delchard could not resist a physical challenge.

"Leave it to me," he said, sheathing his sword.

He crouched down to get a firm hold on the sandstone before jiggling it to and fro to loosen it from the earth. Then he gathered all his energy and put it into one mighty heave that saw him lift the object right up from the ground. It was an appreciable feat of strength, but Gervase was not allowed to admire it for long. No sooner did Ralph strain to stand upright than there was a roar of protest from the undergrowth and a startling figure came bursting out to confront them. It was short, stocky, and quivering with rage. There was so much hair and so much fur, both heavily clotted with filth, that it was impossible to tell whether the creature was human, animal, or some outlandish compound of the two.

It roared with anger again and bared pointed black teeth at the intruders. Ralph Delchard dropped the sandstone at once and grabbed his sword. Gervase reached for his dagger. Before either of them could strike, however, the newcomer let out a dark babble of noise, then vanished into the trees. They went after it, but they had no chance of catching it in such a warren of trees. Both were breathless when they abandoned the chase and leaned against an outcrop of chalk for support.

"I was right," said Ralph proudly. "That lame animal was no more than sport for Hugh de Brionne and his men. The real killer lives here in this place. We have just been face-to-face with the wolf of Savernake."

Ralph Delchard spoke as a soldier who had just been roused to combat. When an enemy appeared, his only thought had been to reach for his weapon and attack. Gervase Bret had listened as well as seen. The creature's loud gabble had just been a howl of anger to his friend, but he had caught something of its meaning.

"That was no wolf, Ralph," he said confidently.

"You saw the creature stand right in front of me. Wolf or bear or whatever it was—*that* was the killer we seek."

"I think not."

"We had to fight the monster off!"

Gervase shook his head. "It was a man."

"You heard its roar; you marked those teeth. I'll wager a month's pay that that was no human being. It was some freak of nature who haunts the forest like a foul ghost."

"No animal would build a circle of stones."

"He howled with fury when we invaded his lair."

"He was only defending his temple," explained Gervase. "And he did not attack us. He merely sought to frighten us away with that noise. It may have sounded like the cry of an animal to you, but I could pick out words from it. He is a man, Ralph, of that there is no question. He spoke in Welsh."

Chapter Ten

BROTHER LUKE'S TRIBULATIONS DID NOT BECOME ANY easier to bear with the passage of time. Indeed, the closer he came to the end of his novitiate, the worse was his anguish of body and soul. It made him careless and unreliable in his devotions, so the wrath of the master of the novices was visited upon him with greater severity. Luke smarted with indignation and took the earliest opportunity to seek out his one haven of rest in the abbey. Brother Peter, as ever, was bent over the table in his workshop as he put the final touches to his silver crucifix. He gave his own young friend a cordial welcome, waved him to a stool, then sat opposite him. Though Luke was caught up in his agonising, he did notice that the sacristan was still moving stiffly and with barely concealed pain.

"How are your wounds?" he asked solicitously.

"I see them as marks of favour, Luke."

"Do they not *hurt*?"

"Only to remind me of their presence."

"Brother Thaddeus might have crippled you."

"The abbot knew when to stay his strong arm," said Peter easily. "But enough of my condition. That is old news. Tell me about Brother Luke and how he fares."

"Very ill."

"How do you sleep?"

"Fitfully."

"How do you study?"

"Unevenly."

"How do you pray?" The youth bit his lip and Peter leaned in to repeat the question. "How do you pray?"

"Without conviction."

"These are indeed sad tidings. Tell me all."

Luke poured out his troubles yet again and spoke of fresh anxieties that had attached themselves to his ever-growing burden of doubt. He talked freely and without shame to Brother Peter. Nothing could shock his friend. Thoughts which had no place inside a man's head at any time—let alone when he was living an exemplary life within the enclave—were now put into words. He bared his soul, then tried to lessen the impact of his drift away from the demands of the order by quoting from St. Augustine.

" *'Da mihi castitatem et continentiam, sed noli modo.'* "

Peter smiled as he translated. " 'Give me chastity and continency, but not yet!' Yes, my friend, St. Augustine had to wrestle mightily with the sins of the flesh. But he chose the true course in the end. Lay another of his edicts to your heart: *'Salus extra ecclesiam non est.'* There is no salvation outside the Church.' "

"Salvation may wait. I seek experience of life."

"Even if it corrupts you entirely?"

"That is my dilemma."

"I was led astray and found my redemption within these four walls. You may not be so fortunate, Luke. Leave now and you may never be readmitted. Stay with us and you need fear none of the evils of the outside world."

The novice rubbed sweaty palms together and looked up.

"Can love be called an evil, Brother Peter?"

"In itself, no," said the other, "but it may lead on to evil-doing. Love diseases the heart and unbalances the mind. It makes people do terrible things in its name."

"But I wish to *know* love," insisted the youth.

"Then find it within the order. Love of God transcends all other earthly passions and brings rewards that are truly everlasting. Look inwards, Luke. Seek for love there."

"I have done so, Peter, but my thoughts still wander."

"School yourself more strictly."

"I may not. He is inside my head all the while."

"He?" echoed the sacristan. "Do you mean God?"

"No. Gervase Bret."

Sudden anger surfaced. "You should never have listened to him!"

"I was only listening to myself," owned Luke. "What I have imagined, he has had the courage to reach out and take. Gervase Bret is betrothed to a lady called—"

"We have heard enough of this young man," said Peter sharply. "I am trying to fit your mind to life inside the abbey and he is trying to tempt you away. Remember the Garden of Eden, my dear friend. You are sitting in it right at this moment. Listen to that serpent—take the apple from his Tree of Knowledge—and you will be cast out."

"Gervase is no serpent," protested Luke.

"Choose wisely and choose well!"

Peter's unaccustomed asperity jolted the novice. The sacristan was normally the soul of affability and he was possessed of almost unlimited forbearance. Yet the young commissioner had somehow caught him on the raw and brought out a more waspish side to him. Peter saw his friend's obvious dismay and patted his leg reassuringly.

"You are wrong," he said in a gentler tone. "I do not dislike this Gervase Bret. I found him a charming young man with an intelligence far greater than that of his blunt companion. But he represents a temptation. Look at the world through his eyes and you will drift towards damnation. View it through mine and you will serve God gladly for the rest of your days."

"I am still sorely vexed."

"Ponder anew."

"I do nothing else."

"Remember St. Augustine's trials."

"Chastity and continency, but not yet!"

"Subdue all fleshly inclination."

"How, Peter?" wailed the other. *"How?"*

"Brother Thaddeus will teach you the way."

A visible shudder ran through Luke as he saw the

182

brawny ploughman at work with his birch twigs. Thaddeus could beat the desire out of anyone, but it was a martyrdom that had no appeal for the novice. There had to be another way to come to terms with the promptings which were turning his nights into long and uneasy assaults upon his virtue. Peter had given him food for thought which he could digest when he was next alone. Time was running out and he would soon have to return to his studies. Another subject now called for discussion and it brought a fresh burst of remorse from the novice.

"I am deeply troubled by death," he announced.

"So are we all, so are we all."

"I speak of Wulfgeat," explained the other. "We are forbidden to visit the mortuary chapel, but I could not keep myself away and I saw what the wolf had done to his poor body. How can any man deserve *that*, Peter? What happened to Alric Longdon was harrowing enough, but this sight turned my stomach. Wulfgeat was eaten alive. Why? Why?"

"Stay calm and I will instruct you."

"Abbot Serlo speaks about justifying the ways of God to men. Is it possible to justify such butchery?"

"I believe it is."

"Wulfgeat was a good man by all account."

"Even good men have a streak of badness in them at times," said Peter evenly. "Whenever you meet with horror or disaster, look for a sign. It is always there if you know where to find it. God is the fount of all joy, but he is also the engine of retribution."

"Alric and Wulfgeat were killed by a stray animal."

"Who put that animal in Savernake?"

"It fled from its pack."

"Who drove it out?"

"The other wolves."

"At whose behest?" When he saw Brother Luke hesitate, he supplied his own answer. "God arranges all things. Alric and Wulfgeat died violent deaths that others might be warned."

183

"But what did they do, Peter?"

"They threatened the existence of this abbey."

"Could a simple miller do that?"

"Alric was by no means simple," corrected Peter. "He had low cunning and enough education to be able to read and write. It was he who summoned these commissioners here and brought this Gervase Bret to cloud your thoughts. I do not know the full details, but Prior Baldwin has told me that Alric posed a serious threat to this foundation. How and in what precise manner, I may only guess, but I accept the prior's word without question."

"What of Wulfgeat?"

"Likewise. He, too, sought to challenge Bedwyn Abbey through the agency of these commissioners. Can you not discern a connection here, Luke? Two men set themselves up against a house of God and they are struck down by Him."

"Is that the sign of which you made mention?"

"It is. Could it be any clearer?"

"So Alric and Wulfgeat were victims of the Almighty?"

"He fights at our side," reinforced Peter. "Stay with us and He will always guard you. Leave the abbey and you will lose His protection."

"But what of the commissioners?"

"The commissioners?"

"They are here to confront the abbey." Brother Luke swallowed hard. "Will they be slaughtered, as well?"

Peter smiled. "No, my friend. It is not needful. They are birds of passage who will soon be gone from this place. Gervase Bret and his colleagues are no longer a source of jeopardy for this house. Prior Baldwin has seen to that. He assures me that God has guided him in his disputations. He vows to send the commissioners on their way at once."

The afternoon session at the shire hall was the most lively and contentious so far. Ralph Delchard and Gervase Bret had barely resumed their seats alongside their colleagues when the abbey delegation sailed in with a new buoyancy.

Prior Baldwin had the unassailable self-assurance of the truly blessed and the doleful Brother Matthew, weighed down though he was with a large satchel of documents, had found a sombre smile to wear upon his face. Beaten men when they last left the hall, they were returning as smug conquerors. Without being invited, Baldwin lowered himself into his chair; without being asked, Matthew flung the satchel down upon the table as if delivering the Ten Commandments to a wayward people. He, too, sat back with unruffled calm. For a few minutes, the commissioners were quite dumbfounded.

Ralph Delchard was the first to locate his voice.

"What is the meaning of this?" he demanded.

"You have our documents," said Baldwin, flicking an eye at the satchel. "Show us yours."

Matthew continued. "Every charter before you is legal and binding. It will stand the closest scrutiny. We must now examine your evidence of a counter-claim. Let us see it."

"Let us see it," asserted the prior, "or let us go. We have played your little games far too long as it is."

"They are not games," rumbled Canon Hubert. "The abbey is under suspicion because of an irregularity. The charter relating to a specific piece of land is a forgery."

Baldwin preened himself. "We are *told* that it is a forgery by our young friend here, but the only person who could weigh the document fairly in the balance is the scribe who wrote it out, and Drogo, alas, is no longer among us. We rest our case on custom and usage. The terms of this charter reflect what has happened to those two hides over the last twenty years. Those terms will stand in any court of law unless you can produce a counter-claim which negates them."

"We have such a counter-claim," said Ralph.

"It predates yours and is genuine," added Hubert.

"Then where is it?" said Matthew tonelessly.

"We have a right to see it," said Baldwin. "If our abbey is accused, we wish to see the face of the accuser. Give us this charter so that we may peruse it with care and answer its monstrous impudence. Our integrity has been put in question and we demand the opportunity to vindicate ourselves." His eyes blazed. "Where is your charter?"

Ralph's temper flared. "It is we who are empowered to call for evidence and not you, Prior Baldwin. The abbey is on trial because it has overreached itself out of sheer greed. We have taken statements from many witnesses and all attest that the abbey seized that land shortly after Abbot Serlo was brought here from Caen."

"You dare to impugn the name of Abbot Serlo!" exclaimed the prior. "He is a saint."

"Then others have done his dirty work for him."

"God will punish you for such blasphemy!"

"He has already done so," moaned Ralph, "by making me sit on this commission and listen to such holy nonsense as you keep thrusting upon me."

Canon Hubert intervened. "Abbot Serlo is above reproach," he said. "Nobody can meet such a man without being aware that they are in the presence of someone who has been touched by the hand of God. But that does not exonerate his abbey. All that we have learned from witnesses supports the claim that brought us to Bedwyn in the first place."

"What witnesses?" hissed Baldwin.

"Subtenants on the land in question."

"Ignorant men with a grudge against the abbey."

"They have long memories."

"Long and unforgiving, Canon Hubert. This is not just a battle between abbey and town. It is a feud between Norman and Saxon. Subtenants have no rights of ownership. They merely till the land and pay rent for that privilege. If they can find a way to flail at their landlords, then they will take it out of Saxon malice. Times are hard and that spreads even more bitterness. The abbey has become its natural target."

He turned to his subprior for endorsement and Matthew cleared his throat to make way for a sepulchral comment.

"The subtenants bite the hand that feeds them. Their

word has no merit in a dispute of this kind. We hold that land from the king. No worthy voice contests that."

"Yes, it does," said Gervase.

"To whom does it belong?" asked Matthew.

"Brother John."

There was mild consternation in the two chairs opposite him, but prior and subprior recovered with impressive speed. Baldwin sighed and gave an indulgent smile.

"Brother John is very old."

"It is the reason I spoke at length to him."

"His memory is no longer sound."

"I found it as sharp as a razor," said Gervase.

"Brother John is close to death."

"That is why he values truth so highly."

"You misled him, I think."

"I merely asked him about his days as the abbey rent-collector. Before you and Abbot Serlo arrived. Ten minutes with Brother John were most revealing. His account was full of detail to support the counter-claim."

"Canon Hubert," said the prior, turning rudely away from Gervase. "You will best understand our position here. An ancient monk is being asked to betray the house which has nurtured him. Brother John is a dying man who wastes away on his bed at the infirmary. His mind wanders and he does not always know what he says. Explain to your colleague here, if you will, that an obedientiary is not able to bear witness against his abbey. He would never be permitted to come into such a place as this to make a sworn statement." He threw a disdainful glance at Gervase before he continued. "I appeal to you as a man of God. Insist on just practices here. We must set an example to the laity. Judge us if you must, but do so by fair means."

Canon Hubert ran a tongue over dry lips as he heard the plea. Much as he disliked the prior, he had to concede that there was some truth in what had been said, and he had his own reservations about Gervase's methods of gathering evidence. Baldwin was encouraged. His plan to create a rift between the lay and clerical members of the commission was working. He tried to open that rift still further.

"You have tested us in this hall, Canon Hubert, but you have done so with scrupulous fairness. We have no criticism to make of your conduct." His eye moved to Gervase Bret and then on to Ralph Delchard. "But we have been treated with less respect by others. How has your young colleague sought to overthrow us? By means that are honest, open, and legal? No, Canon Hubert. He has gone behind our backs to speak with the youngest and the oldest members of our house. He has listened to the gossip of a novice and to the ramblings of a venerable monk. Traduce us, if you must. Bring down the full majesty of the law upon us, if you so desire. But do not insult us and the whole Benedictine order by calling the fledgling Brother Luke and the failing Brother John as your witnesses. They fit into no definition of justice." He rose imperiously to his feet and addressed his final taunt to Gervase. "Where is your charter?"

"We do not have it here," admitted the other.

"Call us back when you do," said Baldwin with a polite sneer, gathering up the satchel of documents and handing it to Subprior Matthew. "We will then return with *our* written evidence. Your accusations are wild and hurtful, but they carry no substance. Without a charter, you have no case."

He nudged Matthew to his feet and they made to leave.

Ralph bridled. "Who gave you permission to withdraw?"

"God," said Baldwin.

He swept out with his subprior and left the commission in turmoil. Canon Hubert blamed Gervase and tried to lecture him on legal procedure. Ralph defended his friend and cursed all clergy. Even the laconic Brother Simon was drawn into the vicious argument, and it raged for a long time. Gervase eventually brought it to a halt by standing up and waving them into silence.

"Our case is unanswerable," he said quietly, "but it lacks one vital element. We need Alric's charter. When that is in our hands, we may confound Prior Baldwin and his windy rhetoric. The charter is the key to it all."

"Yes," agreed Ralph, "and it will not only light a fire under the abbey. Hugh de Brionne's fat arse will burn, as well. He gained his two hides of that land unlawfully with the help of that insidious reeve, Saewold. I had testimony from the most impeccable source."

"I tremble to think how you obtained it," said Hubert.

"The charter will corroborate all that I learned during my researches." Ralph pushed his chair back from the table. "We must suspend our deliberations until we have found it."

"If it exists," wondered Brother Simon meekly.

"It exists right enough," said Gervase confidently. "And I will not return to this hall until I have tracked it down and verified its contents. Be of good cheer. That charter is out there waiting for us. Somewhere . . ."

Living alone in such an isolated place, Emma was free from the tensions and upheavals that characterised life in the towns and villages all around her. She set her own pace and fulfilled her needs in ways of her own choosing. Whenever she was given an insight into the communal experience, she quickly withdrew in disgust to the sanctuary of her mean hovel. Emma could preserve a tattered self-respect there. Events in Bedwyn had spilled over into her private world, putting her in mortal danger, and only the courage of a Norman lord had saved her and her dog. It made her even more wary of straying too close to her fellow human beings. A woman who aroused great caution in others had now developed more elaborate safeguards herself.

When she was summoned to the cottage, therefore, she approached it with the utmost care, sending her dog on ahead to scout for possible dangers. Because the dwelling was only half a mile from Bedwyn, she kept glancing nervously at the town itself, as if fearing a second attack. But none came and her dog scented no peril. Emma walked slowly towards the cottage, her senses still alert. An ugly, thickset man in his thirties opened the door to give her a gruff welcome. He was a villein on the estate, a peasant who gave service to his lord in return for the humble abode and the patch of cultivable land on which he and his family subsisted. His words drew her into the cottage, but his eyes were full of dread. It had clearly not been his idea to summon the Witch of Crofton and he suffered her presence reluctantly.

Emma saw the sick child at once, lying on a crude mattress in considerable discomfort. The anxious mother sat beside her and bathed her daughter's fevered brow with brackish water from a wooden pail. Like her husband, she was fearful of their visitor, but she had called her as a last resort. Nobody else could revive the poor child whose fever had worsened day by day. Too weak to cry out, the little girl yet registered great alarm when she saw the strange figure moving towards her and she clutched at her mother with pathetic urgency. Both parents tried to soothe the child before handing her over to the ministrations of Emma.

The visitor made her diagnosis within seconds. The patient had a high fever and her face was covered in red blotches. A dry throat was producing a hoarse cough and her condition showed that she had been unable to keep food down for some days. The girl was slowly fading away. When the parents had subdued their daughter, Emma moved swiftly to confirm what her eyes had already told her. Big, coarse hands were surprisingly tender as they felt brow and throat and arms. Dirty fingers were delicate as they parted the child's lips so that Emma could peer into the mouth.

"You called me just in time," she concluded.

"Did we?" said the mother.

"She will live."

"Thank God!"

Emma rummaged in her bag to bring out a handful of tiny stone bottles. She selected two and put the others away. She held up the smaller of the vessels.

190

"Give her two drops of this in a cup of water every four hours. Sit with her and bathe her as you have been doing. The fever should break by morning." She displayed the other bottle. "This contains an ointment for her face. Apply it gently every six hours. It will take the sting from those red blotches and they will vanish within a few days."

She held out the bottles, but husband and wife hesitated as if suspecting witchcraft. How could they trust Emma? The potions might indeed help to cure their ailing daughter, but they might equally turn her into a black cat or set her hair alight or kill her on the spot. Emma of Crofton saw their dismay and moved to counter it.

"Give her the medicine," she said, "or she will die."

The mother made the decision and nodded vigorously. Her husband agreed and crossed to an earthenware pot, into which he thrust a hand. When Emma was given two silver coins, she gazed down in amazement at their sparkling newness. She had seen money like this before.

"It is ours to spend," said the man defensively. "And there is no better way to use it than to save our child. It was a gift from heaven. Someone left it outside our door."

Gervase Bret was stung repeatedly by angry questions that buzzed around his brain like wasps whose nest has been disturbed. What creature had killed Alric Longdon? Where was the miller's hoard? Who had been his accomplice in producing counterfeit coinage? Why had Wulfgeat been attacked, as well? What hope had drawn him to the blasted yew and how had he persuaded a surly boy to take him there? Where was the charter which would link and explain all these strange happenings? In what way did Bedwyn Abbey fit into the scheme of things? Who stood most to gain from the turn of events?

Where was the real wolf of Savernake?

As he rode alone through the streets of Bedwyn, he shook his head to escape the assault, but the questions buzzed on in his mind. Relief would come only when he found the answers, and they lay at his destination.

191

Wulfgeat's house held all the secrets. The widow of the miller and the daughter of the burgess had been plunged into misery and could not even begin to see beyond it at this stage. But they had also inherited a dark truth about their respective menfolk and Gervase had somehow to identify the corruption that had bonded the two victims together. Cild was also living at the house with guilt too heavy for any boy to contain forever. Two grieving women and a boy of nine would be unwilling partners in his investigation. Gervase would have to tread stealthily.

He reached the house, dismounted, and knocked on the door. A servant admitted him, then took charge of his horse. Gervase was left alone in the room where he and Leofgifu had had such a long and soulful conversation. It seemed bleak and empty now. Wulfgeat had a personality that spread right through his home, but it had suddenly vanished. The house itself was in mourning for its master.

The door opened and Hilda took a step into the room.

"Leofgifu thanks you for your concern," she said.

"I did not wish to disturb her," apologised Gervase. "I simply came to see if there was anything at all that I could do to ease her suffering at this time."

"I will tell her that."

"She may contact me at the hunting lodge."

"I will tell her that as well."

"Thank you, Hilda." He looked upwards. "How is she now?"

"Deeply upset."

"They were cruel tidings."

"You were with Leofgifu when she heard," said the other. "She was grateful. You helped her."

"I did what I could in her hour of need."

"It mattered."

Hilda was now hovering uncertainly and wanting him to leave. It was too much to expect that Leofgifu might receive him and confide in him about her father, but he had hoped for something positive from the visit. He tried a new gambit.

"Has Cild recovered yet?" he asked.

"Cild?"

"From his illness."

"He is well enough," she muttered.

"But he collapsed on the floor yesterday."

"He had been out in foul weather."

"A hardy young boy like Cild would not be troubled by wind or rain. That lad could walk through a blizzard without fear. Yet he fainted before us. He went down on this floor as if he had been struck." He moved closer to her. "Are you sure that your son has not been sick, Hilda?"

She was noncommittal. "He is well enough now."

"Did he say where he had been?"

"To the mill."

"Is that why he took the key?"

"Yes."

"Without asking your permission?"

"Yes."

"Did that make you angry?"

She took time to think it over. "Yes, it did."

"Will you punish him?"

"I do not know."

"What would your husband have done?"

Hilda winced. "He would have beaten Cild."

"Why did the boy go to the mill?"

"He would not say."

"Did you ask him?"

"He would not say," she repeated helplessly.

Hilda was still trying to cope with her own distress and yet she was sharing the sorrow of another woman as well. The effort had drained her to the limit. It would be callous to press her any further and Gervase pulled back. She and Leofgifu were in no fit state to face his enquiries. He could best show his consideration by leaving them alone at this trying time. Mumbling a farewell, he moved to the door.

"Wait," she said. "I have something for you."

"For me?"

She crossed to place a strip of iron in his hand. Gervase

looked down and his spirits revived at once. Hilda could not tell him anything, but her gesture was eloquent. He was now holding the key to Alric Longdon's mill.

Gervase Bret went off like a hound that has finally picked up the trail. Reclaiming his horse at once, he mounted swiftly and cantered off to the hunting lodge to collect Ralph Delchard. They were soon riding side by side in the direction of the river. The mill looked grimmer and more derelict than ever now, its silent wheel still buffeted by water but no longer able to grind out its rough music. The two friends tethered their horses and used the key to let themselves into the premises. Both coughed as they entered the musty atmosphere and they recoiled from the cheerless interior of the miller's home. They split up to begin their search and went through every part of the building, but they found no more than Prior Baldwin or Wulfgeat had done. Alric had writing materials with his account books, but there was no royal charter. Nor were there any further caches of silver coins. The miller kept his valuables in Savernake Forest.

"Let us look outside," said Gervase at length.

"For what?"

"Fresh air at least."

Ralph coughed aloud. "I need that most of all." He led the way to the door. "Just look at this pigsty, Gervase. Why ever did a respectable woman like Hilda share it with him?"

"She had no choice in the matter."

They came out of the mill and inhaled lungfuls of air before locking the door behind them. Then they began to walk around the immediate vicinity. Gervase soon found exactly what he had expected. He smacked the wooden box with the flat of his hand.

"Here is it, Ralph. The adder's home."

"God in heaven!" exclaimed the other. "What sort of boy would keep a poisonous snake for a pet?"

"The son of a man like Alric Longdon."

"I had a mouse at his age."

"You had something more important than that."

"Did I?"

"A proper childhood."

They resumed their search, and it was Ralph's turn to make a discovery. He pointed excitedly up into a tree.

"Do you see it, Gervase?"

"It is only a rope."

"But it has a hook at the top."

"Only to make it easier to secure it to the bough."

"This is where he practised," said Ralph. "I know it!"

"Did you never swing on a rope as a boy?"

"Not in this way."

"What is so unusual about it?"

"This, Gervase."

Ralph took the rope and looped it up before snapping it quickly in his hand. He stepped back as the hook dislodged itself from the bough and fell to the ground. Ralph grabbed it once more and moved to another tree. Aiming at a branch that stood out almost horizontally, he chuckled with glee as the hook settled firmly into place. He tested the rope then held it tight, inching his way upward with his hands as his feet made slow progress up the trunk itself. Ralph was soon ten feet from the ground and laughing his approval. Gervase now understood the purpose of the demonstration.

"The latrine at the mint!"

"Eadmer's seat of meditation."

"That is how the boy was taught to climb up it."

"I must visit the little moneyer again," said Ralph before dropping heavily to the ground. "He assures me that nothing was stolen from his mint, but Cild did not go up that foul channel simply to view the dwarf's workplace. He was sent for a purpose." He punched his friend's chest. "Come with me, Gervase. Your brain is more acute than mine and you will enjoy meeting Eadmer."

"I have business elsewhere, Ralph."

"With whom?"

"A friend."

He took hold of the rope and jerked it hard so that the

hook was lifted off its branch and sent hurtling to the ground. Gathering it up, he coiled the rope carefully, then brandished it in front of him.

"I may need this," he said.

Piety is its own best advertisement, and Abbot Serlo merely had to appear in the abbey church for his godliness to inspire all around him. He inhabited a higher world but was never patronizing to those of lower station; he was devout but never sanctimonious. The obedientiaries were adoring sons of their Father Abbot. Prior Baldwin could exert a powerful influence, as well. When he appeared at Vespers, he was in a mood of blithe religiosity and the monks read its meaning and rejoiced. The battle had evidently been won. On their behalf, the prior had defended the abbey against the depredations of the commissioners and the day had been his. It put a heartiness into the choral work and mellifluous sound filled the nave before soaring straight up to heaven. Bedwyn Abbey was indeed blessed. Abbot and prior were striking individuals with complementary virtues that served the house superbly well. The combination of holiness from the one and hard bargaining from the other made them invincible.

Serlo was still singing his thanks to the Lord as he returned to his lodgings after Vespers. One of his monks followed him at a discreet distance.

"Excuse me, Father Abbot," he said deferentially.

"Brother Peter!"

"I crave a brief moment with you."

"But you will miss your supper," noted Serlo with paternal interest. "Bread, fruit, and ale are being served in the refectory. Take your place there and eat."

"My request has precedence, Father Abbot."

Serlo invited the sacristan into his lodging and moved across to lower his bulk into the high-backed oak chair. Peter waited until the abbot was properly settled, then he knelt before him and offered up his gift. It was a solid object that was wrapped in cloth and tied with a ribbon.

"What is this, Brother Peter?"

"Proof of my dedication."

"But we see that every day."

"I fell from grace and I was justly disciplined," said Peter, "but I never strayed from the path of righteousness. When my duties were neglected, this is what absorbed my time and my talents. Open it, Father Abbot."

Serlo obeyed and his eyes strained at their moorings for an instant before running with tears. He was so moved by the beauty of the silver crucifix and by the implications of its existence that he was overcome. It was to produce such a work of art that a master-craftsman had laboured so unremittingly, stealing time wherever he could, even when he knew it might lead to stern reprimand. The crucifix was the latest and finest example of Brother Peter's skills and it would be given pride of place on the altar. Abbot Serlo rolled his moist eyes over it and stroked the silver with reverential fingers. Like everything else in his life, it was truly a gift from God.

He put a hand on the head of the kneeling sacristan.

"Bless you, my son."

"I put my poor abilities at the disposal of the Lord."

"You have made me ashamed."

"Why, Father Abbot?"

"No man should be punished for *this*."

"It made me wayward in my other duties."

"You should have spoken up and explained, Peter."

"That would have ruined the surprise."

"It would have saved you a beating."

"Pain brings me nearer to Christ," said the other. "The hand of Brother Thaddeus nailed me up on the cross. Do not weep for me, Father Abbot. I was content."

"Can you forgive me, Brother Peter?"

"There is nothing to forgive."

"Can you still love and respect me?"

"More than ever."

Abbot Serlo set the crucifix on the little table beside him

and examined it afresh. Its proportions were perfect, its sheen mesmeric, its enamel figure of Jesus almost lifelike.

"It is a miracle," he pronounced. "For so much beauty to come out of so much pain. For so much faith to triumph over so much oppression. This crucifix is a miracle in silver. It tells the whole story of Christianity at a glance."

Brother Peter wept tears of joy and prostrated himself in front of his abbot. He was in a state of exultation.

Gervase Bret had to ride for a couple of miles before he found what he needed. Leaping from the saddle, he checked the stone for size and shape, then reached for the rope. After tying up his cargo, he clipped the hook around the pommel of his saddle and put a foot in the stirrup once more. His horse made light of the added burden, dragging it along over grass and through bracken as if it were no more than a trailing rein. The sandstone bit and bounced its way along until they reached the wooded slope. Gervase now took over the task of heaving the object on his own, guiding it between the bushes and around the exposed roots of trees and over the recurring undulations of the terrain. His horse cropped grass beside the stream below while its master sweated and pulled.

Gervase reached the summit and paused to catch his breath. Descent was altogether swifter. Once the sandstone was in motion again, it gathered impetus and chased him down the incline, hacking a shallow trench through the undergrowth and sending birds and animals into dramatic retreat. A stout elm finally halted its passage, but the stone was undamaged. Winding the rope around his shoulders once more, Gervase towed on. The rock seemed heavier than ever now, but he struggled bruisingly on through the denser woodland like a sinner performing an especially onerous penance. Twigs lacerated his face, bushes threshed at his shoulders, and the rope started to eat its way through his skin, yet he did not dare to stop. Only when he finally hauled the sandstone into the clearing did he take note of his aching limbs and his pounding head. Breathing stertorously, he dropped to one knee and let go of the rope. They were still there. The other pieces of sandstone were all hidden beneath their grassy disguise, but they were still in position.

He waited until a semblance of a voice returned. When he was able to call out, he did so in faltering Welsh.

"Are you there!" There was no answer. "I come as a friend!" Still there was no response. "I bring a gift for you!" he cried. "Come and see what it is."

His voice rang down the valley, but it seemed to reach no human ears. Gervase paused to rest further. He studied the circle of stones again and tried to fathom their meaning. Stonehenge had been vastly larger in scale and set on an open plain. Was that to make its statement loud and clear? Or was it to catch the sun and to use the movements of the heavens? This circle was small and private and hidden away at the heart of a timbered valley. Why had such a secluded spot been chosen? If it was a temple, what was the object of worship? When he had walked among the sarsens on Salisbury Plain, he had felt the throb of a primitive power that stretched back endlessly in time. The clearing had resonance more than power, the hum of recent activity, the distant echo of a religious service that had been performed there. And yet it was not a religion that Gervase knew or understood. Stonehenge was a place of light and affirmation. This was a darker manifestation of the human soul. He felt like an intruder from another world.

The sky was filming over now and shadows lay across the ground like felled trees. He became aware of the potential danger. Gervase was relying on his own instinct and ignoring that of his friend. Ralph Delchard had sensed hostility in the clearing and struck at a wild animal. The figure they had seen was certainly big enough and strong enough to overpower men like Alric and Wulfgeat, especially when it had the advantage of surprise. Even a battle-hardened veteran like Ralph had been shocked by its unexpected arrival out of the undergrowth. Two armed men might put the creature to flight, but one tired Chancery clerk might be deemed more easy prey. Gervase looked up at the fading light and the chill hand of fear touched him. It was time to flee.

"Who are you!"

The voice boomed out in Welsh and seemed to come from behind every tree. Gervase was being watched. He stood in the middle of the clearing and rotated slowly as he tried to work out where the man was standing. It was a deep, rough, and uncultured voice, but it belonged to a human being.

"Who are you!"

The question battered at his ears and he gave answer.

"A friend."

"What is your name?"

"Gervase."

"Why are you here?"

"To bring this stone for you."

"Keep away!"

"It is my gift to you."

"This place is sacred."

"Put my stone in your circle."

There was a long pause, followed by a rustling among the leaves. Gervase had the impression that the man was circling him to make sure that he was quite alone and did not have any confederates hiding in the undergrowth. Earlier, two armed men had treated him as an enemy. One of them was now claiming to be his friend. He was right to be sceptical.

"I need your help," Gervase shouted.

"Leave me alone."

"You dwell in the forest. You know its ways."

"Go now while you still can."

"This is your home. Teach me to understand it."

"My world is not yours."

"Answer my questions and you will be left in peace."

"You will come back with others."

"No!" promised Gervase. "I give you my word. Nobody will hear of this; nobody will search for you and drive you out. You will tell from my voice that I am not Welsh, but neither am I from this place. I will soon leave Bedwyn. You will never see me again."

There was another long pause and the bushes were parted. Gervase felt the intense scrutiny and tried to meet it with an affable smile. The voice was still cynical.

"Why should I trust you?"

"Because I brought that stone all the way here."

"Who knows you have come?"

"Nobody."

"Why do you wear a dagger?"

Gervase took it out of its sheath and threw it a few yards away. He was now quite defenceless. Against a man as powerful as the one he had glimpsed at their previous encounter, he would have little chance. Common sense told him to brace himself against attack, but he knew it was important to show no fear. The stone he had lugged there was not simply a present to the man but an act of apology. He waited patiently until the voice boomed forth again.

"What do you want?"

"Guidance. Two men have been killed in Savernake."

"I know."

"Was it your doing?"

A roar of protest came from the bushes and they shook violently. Gervase tried to retract his question, but his uncertain grasp on the language let him down and he had to resort to placatory gestures. There was wounded pride in the undergrowth, but it was eventually soothed.

"You are a hermit," said Gervase. "I respect that."

"Then go your way."

"You love peace, but it has been disturbed by this strife in the forest. I can take that strife away." He took a step in the direction of the bushes. "A wolf was caught here yesterday. Did the animal savage those two men?"

"No."

"Can you say who did?"

"No."

"Do you *know* who did?"

201

Such a long pause ensued that Gervase began to wonder whether the man had quietly withdrawn and left him alone. He took another step in the direction from which the voice had come.

"Stay where you are!" came the warning.

"Why are you afraid of me?"

"I live alone."

There was a rugged dignity in the way he said this that was an explanation in itself. The hermit had created his own private world in the forest and he survived there with the guile of an animal. No other human being could enter or share his leafy domain. Darkness was now threatening and Gervase did not wish to be lost in Savernake. He made one last attempt to get through to the invisible listener.

"Help me, my friend. I must find out how these two men died. Something was stolen from the place where they fell. That, too, must be found." A third step took him closer to the bushes. "Please help me. I am staying at the hunting lodge near Bedwyn. Help me in my work and we will move on. You will be free to roam the forest as before."

Gervase strained his eyes to peer through the foliage, but it was too thick to admit his gaze. As he leaned forward to take a closer look, he heard a rustling noise behind him and turned. Strong muscles were pulling on the rope so that the rock was being dragged into the safety of the trees on the other side of the clearing. Gervase was content. His strange interview was over, but it had ended with a small measure of success.

His gift had been accepted.

Eadmer the Moneyer was in a testy mood when Ralph Delchard called on him without warning. He admitted the unwelcome visitor to his inner sanctum and shut its fortified door with a thud to show his displeasure. His day's work was now over and he was ready to douse the candles that flickered in their holders, then leave. Ralph was keeping him there against his will. The slight figure grew combative.

"Have you reported to the town reeve?" he asked.

"Not yet."

"But you were here with the man's wife."

"That was a separate transaction," said Ralph with a nostalgic smile. "Saewold is due home tomorrow and he will be told of the forgery in due course."

"There is no time to waste, my lord!" insisted Eadmer.

"I delay out of policy."

"Policy?"

"Yes, my friend. These counterfeit coins are no stray accidents. They have been steadily minted over a period of time. I believe that the forger is still busy at his nefarious trade. If I raise the alarm through Saewold, then the criminal will be frightened away and may escape our net completely."

"You know, then, who the villain is?"

"We soon shall," said Ralph confidently, "and we will catch him in the act. But that requires patience. He must be stalked before he can be taken."

"I will cut off his hands!"

"The law will do more than that for him, Eadmer."

"Forgery is worse than murder."

"You will be able to tell that to the wretch one day."

"Bring him before me!"

Eadmer grabbed a hammer and brought it down onto a metal tray with such force that the clang made Ralph's ears sing. The moneyer was small but vengeful. His trade lent itself to fraud and corruption of all kinds and strict procedures were in force to ensure that high standards of professional integrity were maintained at all times. One dishonest moneyer could give the rest a bad name. Debased coins could drive out good ones. Eadmer wanted action.

"Get out there and find the rogue!" he urged.

"I must speak with you first."

"You have questioned me already."

"Confirmation is needed." Ralph looked around the room. "Are you quite sure that nothing is missing from the mint?"

203

"Certain."

"What about your strong room?"

"Everything is accounted for."

"No possibility of error?"

Eader was emphatic. "None!"

"What would a forger need to produce coins?"

"A black heart and a pact with the Devil!"

Ralph grinned. "But what materials must he have?"

"Silver bullion with means of heating and handling it. Then there are these," he said, indicating the tray of dies. "They are issued in London under special licence. The die is the essence of the whole process."

"Yet none of yours have been stolen?"

"No, my lord."

"What of your mint in Marlborough?"

"It is even more of a fortress than this one."

Ralph nodded and sauntered around the room until he came to the rough curtain across an opening in the wall.

"What is in here?"

"That need not concern you."

"May I look?"

"Hold your nose if you do."

Ralph twitched the curtain and peeped into the tiny chamber. It contained four bare walls and a raised block of stone. Aromatic memories of Eadmer's use of the chamber rose up to offend his sensibilities, but Ralph forced himself to lean over and gaze down through the hole that was cut in the stone. Seen from below in a boat, it had looked smooth and regular. Viewed from above, it was almost conical in shape and tapered upwards. The stone was rough-hewn and pitted with droppings. One more feature now declared itself. Two feet down the aperture was a thin iron bar that bisected the narrow space. Only a man as stunted as Eadmer could squeeze through such a gap. The bar was an effective precaution, but it could also become a useful accessory. A rope with a hook on the end could be thrown up to gain a purchase on it.

Ralph stepped back into the room and dared to breathe

204

again. If the boy had climbed up that way and entered the mint, what had he stolen? Everything remained unharmed and in its place. Perhaps he did not need to take anything from the premises. Cild might have gained entry in order to unlock the door and admit the forger.

"Would you know if someone had used your materials?"

"Of course," snapped Eadmer.

"How?"

"The brazier would still be hot. Smell would linger."

"That I can vouch for!" said Ralph ruefully.

"My tools would be moved. Each has an exact place and I could tell if one was an inch from where it should be."

"Nothing taken, nothing moved."

"Only genuine coins leave this mint."

"Then how did they do it!"

Ralph stamped a foot in exasperation, then moved to the window. Evening was drawing in and the river was dappled with pools of darkness. A lone heron was skimming the water aimlessly. On the opposite bank, the little Saxon church had become a murky blur. Somewhere in its graveyard, the body of Alric lay buried. Nobody would visit such an eerie spot at night and a boat which came downriver at that time would be in no danger of being seen. A boy who swam beneath the house with a rope around his shoulders would risk even less chance of detection. But what was the point of getting Cild inside the mint if nothing was to be taken from it? Ralph scratched his head in bafflement.

An acrid stink made him turn round again.

"You must go," said Eadmer, licking a finger and thumb so that he could snuff out the tallow candles. "I am wanted elsewhere and you may not stay here alone."

He extinguished another flame and the wick smoked on pungently. Ralph Delchard watched him with growing curiosity, then a smile spread slowly across his face until he was beaming. Without knowing it, the moneyer had just provided the vital clue which his visitor was seeking. A daily chore had unlocked a nocturnal mystery. Surging gratitude made Ralph burst into wild laughter. His companion shrunk back in alarm.

"What is the matter, my lord?" he asked.

"Eadmer," said Ralph, arms out wide, "I love you."

Chapter Eleven

IT WAS NIGHTFALL BY THE TIME GERVASE BRET FINALLY picked his way back to the hunting lodge, and the servant who greeted him was carrying a blazing torch. While the man took the horse off to be stabled, the weary Gervase went into the building, to find his companion seated alone at the long table. Ralph Delchard was in a jovial mood. The remains of a roasted chicken lay on a pewter dish before him and he was washing it down with a cup of wine. He waved his friend across and Gervase sank gratefully down on the bench opposite him. Ralph reached for the jug to pour out a second cup of wine, then pushed it across the table.

"Drink deep and think of Normandy."

"It is French wine?"

"No," said Ralph, "it comes from the vineyard at Bradford-on-Avon, but its grapes were grown by a Norman hand and it will quench your thirst well enough." He emptied his own cup, then refilled it. "It was the one great mistake that the Conqueror made," he observed sagely. "A Norman army marches on its supply of wine. When we set sail for England twenty years ago, no proper thought was given to the matter. We landed at Pevensey and made our position secure before we headed across country towards Hastings. The army was hungry, so we killed and ate whatever lay in our way. We were also thirsty, but what little wine we had brought soon ran out and we had to drink their foul English water." He grimaced at the bitter memory. "It did almost as much damage to our host as King

Harold and his housecarls. That water poisoned our bellies and opened our bowels with a vengeance. If William had only carried enough wine in his invasion fleet, we would have been in a fit state to win the battle of Hastings in half the time."

Gervase smiled obligingly. He had heard the story before, but he did not mind the repetition. Ralph's high spirits showed that his visit to the mint had been profitable. He was still glowing with pleasure, but he wanted to hear from his friend before he divulged his own news.

"Where have you been, Gervase?"

"To the forest."

"Alone?"

"No, I had a piece of red sandstone with me."

"Can you be serious?" said Ralph, sitting up. "When you took that rope and told me you were off to see a friend, I thought you had arranged a tryst with one of these lovely Saxon women. I hoped you were going to tie her down and have your way with her like any red-blooded Norman."

"Do not make a jest of it, Ralph," reproved Gervase. "You know my lineage and you know my fidelity. Alys waits for me in Winchester and no woman could take me from her."

"Not even Leofgifu?"

It was a question that halted him and he took some time to compose his answer. There was more than a tinge of regret in his voice when he eventually spoke.

"No," he said. "Not even Leofgifu."

"So what did you do with this rock and this rope?"

Gervase gave a terse description of events and saw his friend's amazement turn into apprehension. Ralph could not believe that he had been so careless of his safety.

"Two men have already been killed in Savernake."

"Not by his hand."

"How do you know that?"

"He is a gentle creature at heart."

"Gentle!" exclaimed Ralph. "Can you call that thing of hair and fur which jumped out at us in any way gentle? I took it for a wolf, but you say it is a man. I hold to my conclusion, Gervase. The Welsh are untamed. They are far more animal than human. I have fought against them on the border and I know them to be savage barbarians with not an ounce of gentleness between them." He shook his head in disgust. "And you faced such an ogre on your own in Savernake!"

"He did not harm me," said Gervase simply.

Ralph snorted. "I'll take my men out at first light tomorrow and hunt this wild beast down."

"No! I gave him my word."

"Honour means nothing to the Welsh."

"It means *everything*," retorted Gervase with fierce certitude. "To him and to me. My pledge will not be broken, Ralph. If you try to lift a hand against the man, I will stop you by any means that I have. He has not hurt me and he has not hurt anyone else. All he desires is to be left alone in peace. He is a hermit."

"So why did you seek him out?"

"To ask for help."

"From some madman in a filthy sheepskin?"

"He knows, Ralph. You were right about the wolf that Hugh de Brionne caught. It did not kill the two men. The hermit knows who did."

"He told you?"

"I have not yet won his confidence."

"Leave him to me, Gervase," said Ralph. "I'll make the villain talk. If he can shed light on this business, I'll cut the truth out of him with my sword."

"Touch that man and you lose my friendship forever!"

It was such a vehement and unexpected threat that Ralph was pushed back into his seat. Gervase was never unassertive in argument, but this issue went especially deep with him. It made the older man more reflective. Ralph made an effort to understand his companion's viewpoint.

"Can you like such a monster?" he asked.

"I respect him for what he is doing."

"Living as an animal in the forest?"

"Turning his back on the world to follow his beliefs. It is no more than the monks at the abbey are doing. They have retreated into a life of self-denial in order to serve God. The hermit serves another deity and his withdrawal is more complete. He needs no brothers to share his suffering. He is a holy anchorite who chooses to worship alone."

"But the man is a heathen!" protested Ralph.

"He is not a Christian," said Gervase, "that is true. His religion goes back well before the birth of Jesus and it may seem crude and ignorant to us, but it has weathered many long centuries. Any man who can live that way for the sake of his soul must have immense strength of mind and spirit. He has not just made vows of poverty, chastity, and obedience. He has renounced *everything*. Can you not see why I am so interested in this hermit? He is a survivor from some ancient culture, Ralph. He is our guide to the past."

"All we need is a guide to that charter."

"He may help us with that search, as well."

"How?" said Ralph impatiently. "What did he tell you?"

"Enough."

Gervase was satisfied that progress had been made, but his friend wanted more positive proof of the fact. His own visit had yielded one important clue.

"Keep your gabbling Welshman," he said scornfully. "I prefer Eadmer the Moneyer. At least, he can instruct us."

"What did you learn from him?"

"This."

Ralph lifted up the large tallow candle that stood before him in its holder. Tilting it slightly, he poured hot wax onto the table, then produced a coin from his purse. He dropped the coin into the wax and banged it with his fist.

"Instead of a coin, use one of Eadmer's dies."

"When the wax hardens, the imprint would be perfect."

"*That* is what the boy stole from the mint," said Ralph. "All he had to do was to climb up that stinking hole, melt some wax and push a die into it, wait until it was ready, then clean the die and replace it exactly as it was found. Then back down the shaft with him to the boat where his

210

father was waiting. Poor little Eadmer was none the wiser." He rubbed a hand across his chin in contemplation. "I have solved the mystery of how the die was stolen, but to whom was it then given? Alric was no moneyer. Who was the miller's accomplice in this conspiracy?"

"We shall soon know."

"How? Will your Welsh hermit send us his name?"

"Do not scoff at him, Ralph."

"What can that savage offer?"

"A sharp pair of eyes in Savernake Forest."

"With a sharp set of teeth to match. You are deceived by him, Gervase. He is a wolf in sheep's clothing."

They argued on for another hour without resolution, then went off to their separate beds. Both were tired, but neither could sleep. The wine had freshened Ralph Delchard's lust and he began to muse about the beauteous Ediva once more and wish that she was beside him. She had brightened his visit to Bedwyn and offered him a refuge from the tedious litigation on which his colleagues seemed to thrive. Ediva had given him both love and priceless information. There was no more satisfying way to serve his king than between the thighs of such a woman. He was about to take her in his arms again when he at last fell into a deep slumber.

In the adjoining chamber, Gervase Bret tried to direct his imagination to Alys, but she was, for once, an inadequate occupant of his thoughts. Whenever she smiled, he saw the bearded face of the recluse; whenever she talked, he heard the rough Welsh voice in the bushes. He went through each detail of his encounter with the solitary creature in the forest and wished that he had learned enough to comprehend the man's universe. He recalled vague snatches of travellers' tales from the days when he had studied at Eltham Abbey. They talked of weird religions in distant lands and put the fear of death into his young mind as they recounted the barbaric rites that were involved.

One man had spoken of mysteries nearer home and Gervase now wished that he had paid more attention to his words. The stories were about the ancient religion of Wales when a mystic order of Druids flourished. Could the hermit of Savernake be the heir to such a culture? Had he been driven out of his native land by the spread of Christianity to seek a place where he could practice the old faith? Gervase cudgelled his brain to extract what meagre knowledge he had on the subject, but all that came was an unsatisfactory mixture of fact and conjecture. He did remember that oak trees were sacred to the Druids, and the clearing in the valley had been ringed by oaks. He also recalled the paramount importance of the sun and wondered whether the oval site had been chosen to trap its rays. But it was the most stark feature of the religion which had impressed itself upon him at the time and which now changed his whole attitude to his meeting in the forest.

Druids were said to use human sacrifices. They spilled blood in the cause of their religion. If the hermit was still practising the ancient rites with full vigour, Alric Longdon and Wulfgeat might well have been his victims. They were not attacked by any wolf. Their deaths had served a profounder purpose. Slain by the hermit, they had been necessary sacrifices on the altar of his belief. Gervase himself was lucky not to have followed them to the grave. It was not until well into the night that his demons relented and allowed his troubled mind a modicum of rest.

"Wake up, Gervase!"

"What?" He only half-heard the call.

"Come here, man. At once!"

"Why?"

"Look, Gervase! Just look."

"Do not pound my head so, Ralph."

But his friend was only banging on the door of his chamber. When Gervase forced himself to sit up and open his eyes, he saw that dawn was pushing the first spears of light in through the casement. He scrambled up and pulled back the bolt on the door before flinging it open. Ralph Delchard had been torn from his own bed, but he was in a state of great excitement. He was holding something in both hands

212

and he came in to set it down on the floor. It was a wooden chest that was ribbed with stout metal clasps.

"Where did you find it?" asked Gervase.

"Outside the front door."

"Who left it there?"

"I do not know, but one of the servants heard him. When he went to see what the noise was, he found this."

"Is it Alric's treasure chest?"

"What else could it be?"

"Have you opened the lid?"

"No, Gervase. I wanted you to be with me when I did." Ralph had brought the key which he had found in the stream near the blasted yew. "This moment belongs to both of us."

He inserted the key into the lock with anticipatory delight, but it soon became dismay. They key did not fit.

"It is the wrong chest!" he cursed.

"Or the right chest but the wrong key."

"It must fit!" insisted Ralph, trying again. "It must."

But the key still jammed in the lock. Gervase had now come fully awake. He picked up the chest and took it across to the window to get the best of the light.

"Someone has forced this chest open," he noted.

"But it is locked tight."

"The catch must have been wrenched free."

"Then the contents will have been taken."

"I think not, Ralph. This was left here by design. What value would there be in an empty chest?"

He set it down once more and removed the key, reaching instead for his dagger. Inserting it in the lock, he twisted away until there was a sharp click. One flick of its point sent the lid of the chest up and back. Ralph plunged a hand into the hoard of silver coins that lay within, but Gervase had already snatched out the most valuable item. He unrolled the parchment in the half-dark and took one glance at it.

"We have our charter," he said.

* * *

213

Leofgifu slept soundly in the house of mourning and woke to curse herself for passing the night in such comfort. It was unseemly and uncaring, yet no matter how hard she tried to find fresh tears for her father, they would not come. True sorrow had not really touched her. She had been horrified by the way he had died rather than shaken by the fact of his death. Now that she had had time to take stock, she came to see just how unhappy she had been sharing the home with him. The loss of Wulfgeat was also a gain for her. Instead of depressing her spirit, it filled her with an odd sense of freedom and it was this which activated her guilt. Leofgifu feared that she was an unnatural daughter. Wulfgeat's death meant that she was now expected to grieve for a man she had come to hate, as well as for another whom she had never managed to love. Father and husband chained her to the grave.

Activity was the best escape from brooding and she threw herself into her chores with excessive readiness. She took over duties which would normally be left to the servants and spent more time on her embroidery that morning than she had done in the previous month. Remorse still troubled her, however, and her restlessness would not be eased. It took her into the little room which her father had used for his business affairs, Leofgifu half-hoping that the sight of his ledgers and his papers might unleash a hidden spring of lamentation somewhere deep inside her and enable her to mark his passing with appropriate despair. But her heart remained cold and her mind unengaged. She sat at the table and idly reached for the first ledger.

It was over an hour before Hilda found her.

"Are you busy, Leofgifu?"

"No, no. Please come in."

"Do not let me interrupt you."

"I am glad of your company, Hilda. How are you today?"

"Do not worry about me, Leofgifu. How are *you*?"

"Still oppressed."

But she did not feel the weight of that oppression and

214

wished that she could suffer in the way that Hilda, with her shattered beauty, still plainly did. Hers was the true coinage of grief; Leofgifu was offering only counterfeit currency.

"I need your permission to go out," said Hilda.

"You may come and go as you please."

"But you might need me here."

"It is kind of you to put me first, Hilda, but I can spare you. Will you go far?"

"Only to the hunting lodge."

Leofgifu was puzzled. "Why there?"

"To speak with the young commissioner."

"Gervase Bret?"

"When he called yesterday, I was . . . too weak."

"Weak?"

"He needed help and I pulled back out of fear." Her chin lifted bravely. "But I will speak to him today and I will make sure that Cild speaks with him also."

"Cild?"

"I must be strict with him now that he is mine."

Leofgifu only partially understood what Hilda was saying, but it connected with her own inclinations. She gazed down at the ledgers she had been reading and the documents she had just leafed through, then made her election.

"You will not go to the hunting lodge, Hilda."

"Why not?"

"It is much too far to walk."

"We do not mind the journey."

"Gervase will come to the house."

"It would cause too much upset."

"Perhaps that is what I need," said Leofgifu. "Before you and Cild talk with him, I will see him myself. I may not mourn properly for my father until I fully understand the reason for his death, and Gervase may help me to do that." She kissed Hilda on the cheek. "Go back to your room. I will send a servant to fetch him at once."

The instincts of a born soldier never desert a man. After all these years, Ralph Delchard could still feel in his bones if

215

a battle ahead would go well for him. Belief in success made it virtually inevitable and he had never been robbed of a promised victory yet. As soon as he saw the chest, his hope flowered; as soon as they found the charter, it blossomed into complete confidence; and when Gervase had examined the document closely enough to proclaim its authenticity, Ralph had the surge of exhilaration that he felt always in the first cavalry charge.

Word was sent to the abbey that the commission would convene again that afternoon. A personal summons was delivered to Prior Baldwin ordering him to present himself with all of the relevant abbey charters at a given time. The morning now gave Ralph an opportunity to make some last important enquiries in the town. Gervase Bret agreed to go with him, but he was called away by a message from Leofgifu and hurried off to her house. Ralph had to pay his visit alone.

"Come in, my lord. You are most welcome."

"I am glad to see you safely returned, Saewold."

"Business detained me in Salisbury."

"How did you find Edward?"

"The earl is in fine fettle," said the reeve with an obsequious smirk. "As well as discharging his many duties as sheriff of the county, he is supervising the extensions to his castle. The building progresses."

"We saw it on our way past," said Ralph.

His eye kindled as Ediva came into the room to add her welcome and to go through the niceties. Her manner was as poised as ever, but she contrived to bestow a fleeting smile that stirred wondrous memories for her guest. Ediva called a servant and ordered refreshment, then she left the men alone for their discussion. They sat either side of a table.

"You must have missed your wife when you were away."

Saewold shrugged. "I did not have time to miss her or anyone else, my lord. Being reeve of a town like Bedwyn is not an occupation; it is a way of life and it consumes all my attention. Ediva has learned to make shift for herself."

"You are blessed in such a wife," said Ralph without irony, then he addressed himself to the matter at hand. "We have a problem, Saewold, one that must be kept hidden until we have a solution. I speak to you in strictest confidence."

"Of course, my lord. Of course."

"Do not breathe a word to anyone or the outcry will be raised and the damned miscreant will make a run for it."

"Miscreant?"

"You have a forger in the town."

Saewold was shocked. "Here in Bedwyn?"

"Eadmer confirmed it."

"When?"

"While you were away in Salisbury." He saw a means to ensure the reeve's collusion. "It is another reason why we did not disclose the crime. You would have been embarrassed in front of Edward if he had known that so much counterfeit money had been allowed to circulate within your town."

"So much?"

"We believe so."

"How long has this been going on?"

"For some time."

"It must be rooted out at once!" said Saewold. "I will not have Bedwyn tainted with false coin."

"The time to announce the deception is when it has been fully uncovered," advised Ralph. "You may gain some credit then instead of the criticism you may incur if your town is seen to be awash with counterfeit currency. You understand?"

"Yes, my lord."

"Be ruled by me."

"To the letter."

"One of the culprits has been identified, but you must help to name his accomplice. Alric Longdon was one party to this dreadful crime."

"Alric!"

His surprise was short-lived. Once he weighed up the intelligence, he saw how it explained both the miller's behaviour and his rising wealth at a time when some of his rivals

217

were struggling to make even small profits on their labour. Alric certainly had the craftiness to be involved in such a scheme, but he could never be more than the aide of a subtler mind.

"Who were his friends?" asked Ralph.

"He had none."

"Who were his relatives, his associates, his customers? Give me a list and we will scour it until we find the likeliest men. Eadmer has praised the forgery for its accuracy, so we look for very skilful hands. Who in this town could be capable of such intricate work?"

Saewold thought hard. "There are several with fingers nimble enough," he said, "but none with such diseased minds. Bedwyn has its share of poachers and thieves and drunken fools, but we do not harbour malefactors of this order. Someone who would work hand in glove with Alric? I cannot imagine such a man."

"He lives here, nevertheless," insisted Ralph, "and you must point him out to me. Fetch paper and pen to set down every name that comes to mind. Start with men in allied trades. Be quick about it, Saewold, and we may stop the rot before it spreads. Now, sir, who is your most likely moneyer? Where is your second Eadmer of the Short Stride?"

The reeve flinched as a name suddenly hit him.

"A second Eadmer," he said. "A second Eadmer."

"There is such a person?"

"Dermon—but, no, it could never be him."

"Who is this Dermon?"

"He was Eadmer's assistant at one time, but they fell out and parted. Dermon does not work in a mint anymore. He keeps accounts."

"Put his name at the top of the list," ordered Ralph. "Why did Eadmer not mention the man himself?"

"The bitterness between them was deep."

"Dermon has cause for revenge?"

"Perhaps, my lord. But cause is not means. Cause is not opportunity. Dermon is forbidden to go near the mint. He rarely comes to Bedwyn at all. I will not suspect him."

"Suspect everyone. Where does the fellow live?"

"Chisbury," said Saewold. "Dermon is now in the employ of Hugh de Brionne."

It was the third time in a row that Emma had taken her doctoring to a lowly place and been rewarded with silver. Who had left the money outside the doors of these hovels? What benefactor had taken pity on the poorest people in the area? Why had she been singled out for her share of the coins? Emma was still preoccupied with the mystery as she set off that morning to gather herbs and replenish her stocks. She skirted Bedwyn, then made her way along the river, her dog sniffing along ahead of her. When she came to Alric's mill, she stopped to throw silent imprecations at it. The beating which he had given her had scarred her soul for life. Alric might be dead, but his mill was still there to remind her of their dealings.

Emma hurried on until she reached the stream that branched off to the left. Using the cover of the wooded slope, she browsed in safety and picked herbs for her basket. The dog went on patrol. Herbs were plentiful and she threw in a scattering of wildflowers as well to decorate her home. She was bent double in the undergrowth when she heard the tell-tale growl. Her dog had scented menace. Emma rose cautiously and pricked her ears. A hissed command brought the dog to her side. The animal continued to emit a low growl, but she could neither see nor hear any movement in the forest. It was only when the growl turned to a whine of fear that she knew they had company.

"Where are you?" she called. "Show yourself."

Foresters would have come out to harry her. Poachers would have tried to scare her off. Enemies would have hurled something at her and at the dog.

"We are doing no harm."

She sensed where the danger was lurking now and turned to aim her words at the massive oak behind which it hid.

"Come no closer," she warned. "I have my dog."

But the animal was in no mood to fight on behalf of its

mistress. It was crouched at her feet in an attitude of submission, as if begging for her protection against some unseen foe. Whatever skulked behind the tree had frightened the dog into immobility. Its whine intensified.

"Leave us alone!" she called out with defiance. "I have only taken herbs to cure sickness. I am a healer."

There was a grunting noise from behind the tree that made both her and the dog back away slightly, then a large head came round the trunk to appraise her. The hermit had an unsightly face that was made even more revolting by the long, straggly hair, the thick beard, and the accumulated filth. Deep-set eyes glared from beneath shaggy brows. Now that Emma could see him, she was no longer afraid. Indeed, when he stepped out from behind the oak and stood before her, she felt a vague sensation of pity glide through her. Being the Witch of Crofton condemned her to a joyless existence, but here was someone in a far worse condition than she. His sheepskin garments were soiled and torn; his bare arms and legs were blackened and grazed. He had a powerful frame and a fierce stare, but there was no real hostility in him. Instead, Emma sensed a kinship.

"Who are you?" she asked.

He remained motionless and watched her intently.

"Where have you come from?"

The dog had lost its fear as well. It wagged its tail.

"Do you understand me?"

The great face was scrunched up with bewilderment. Emma tried to make contact another way. She reached into her basket for the wildflowers and held them out to him. He looked faintly pleased but refused with a shake of his head. Emma scooped up a handful of herbs instead, but he did not want those either. She had only one thing left to offer him and she searched in the folds of her cloak to find it. Taking a few friendly steps towards him, she offered the silver coins on her palm.

He peered at them for a second, then a craggy smile cut through the overgrown beard. There was even the ghost of a laugh. The man fished inside his own garment and brought out some matching coins to show her. With a flick of his hand, he threw them to the ground in front of her and indicated that she should have them. Comprehension dawned. Emma had met her benefactor. This strange inhabitant of Savernake Forest had distributed the money among the needy. Where it had come from, she did not know, but it was obvious that he had no need of it. There was abstract kindness in this man. He lived quite alone in self-imposed exile, but he could show care for others. His generous impulse had relieved misery in a number of distressed families.

The hermit gazed deep into her eyes and their separate worlds merged for a second to banish all contradiction. Both were lonely outcasts. Both would be spurned on sight, yet both could be forgiving to those who spurned them. Both worshipped a deity that was older than time itself and beyond the scope of common imagination. Both followed their own twisting paths to a higher state of being that could be attained only in painful isolation.

When the moment passed, the contradictions came back to push them apart forever, but the man made one last gesture of contact. Pointing up the hill, he beckoned Emma to follow, then he trudged off slowly on bare feet. She picked up the silver coins and did as he wished, keeping a few yards behind him and ordering her dog to stay at her heels. The hermit reached the blasted yew tree and gave it a rueful glance before cutting off into the undergrowth. He stopped beside a depression in the ground that was carpeted with ivy. He jabbed his finger at the spot, then raised it up to point in the direction of the town. Emma was perplexed and no wiser when the man made the identical gestures again.

The dog needed no second invitation. Its nose scented something under the ivy and it became very agitated. Emma tried to shoo it away, but its interest was too strong and it began to burrow into the ivy with its front paws. Her own curiosity was now aroused and she found a stick to slide under the covering so that she could lift it up. The hollow was deeper at the centre and she could see some sort of tarpaulin there. Her dog darted under the ivy to grab at it with his teeth, but she caught it by the collar and dragged him back. When she put her stick under the tarpaulin to raise its edge up, she was astounded by what she saw and she realised at once why the animal had been so frantic. It took all her force to subdue it and she had to use both hands to pull it away.

Emma could now interpret the hermit's gestures. He wanted her to report what she had found. Unable to do so himself, he was asking her to take the message on his behalf. He had made an important discovery that he had no means of passing on. To go to the town would be to break his own cover, and he would never do that. He belonged to Savernake now and was at one with its mysteries. She was to be his emissary. She could pass on his findings without disclosing either his existence or his whereabouts. Emma would be praised and the hermit would be safe.

She turned to thank him, but he had stolen away minutes before and run back to his clearing in the valley. While Emma waddled off with her dog and her basket, the man was sitting in the clearing with the new piece of sandstone between his knees, using primitive tools to chisel it to shape and holding it up from time to time to catch the sun. When the final stone had been properly dressed and sunk into position, his circle would be complete.

Gervase Bret flicked through the documents until he found those that had a bearing on the case. He read the Latin with consummate ease and nodded his approval. Leofgifu watched him without any regrets about what she had done. When her father was alive, she was excluded from all knowledge of his business dealings and had to pick up what she could from casual remarks and inferences. Now that she had inherited his property and his wealth, she could do as she wished with all that had been his. Wulfgeat would have been disgusted to see a member of the king's household searching freely through his papers. His Saxon blood would

222

have curdled. But Gervase was no typical Chancery clerk and his affinities with the English were just as great as his loyalties to the Normans. When Leofgifu stumbled on charters that referred to land disputes around Bedwyn, she only dimly appreciated their import, but she was happy to show them to someone who might make more profitable use of them. As he read his way avidly through the terms of a document, Gervase came to see why Wulfgeat had spoken up so bravely for the vanquished King Harold. He gathered together a small pile of charters.

"May I borrow these?" he asked.

"What are they?"

"Weapons."

"Against whom?"

"Vultures."

"Take them," she said. "I know they will be safe."

Gervase gave her a smile of gratitude. Her request had surprised but delighted him and he had rushed to the house to see her again. Pleased to find her so self-possessed once more, he was thrilled when she gave him unlimited access to her father's papers. Wulfgeat's history and motives were now much clearer in his mind.

"How else may I help?" she offered.

"By speaking to Hilda."

"She wishes to see you on her own account."

"It is the boy I need to question."

"Cild?"

"Persuade her to send him alone to me."

"Hilda will not do that."

"She may if you ask her, Leofgifu."

"The boy is her stepson. She must protect him."

"Remind her that he stole the key to the mill."

"Can she not be present while you interview him?"

"I ask you as a favour."

"What do you want from him?"

"A name."

Leofgifu nodded, then went out. He could hear her ascend the creaking stairs and enter the room above her head.

There was a discussion with Hilda that became quite heated for a while, but it produced a result. Footsteps came down the stairs and Hilda walked into the room, her hands firmly on the shoulders of Cild. She stood him in front of Gervase, then hesitated. The boy turned to plead silently with her, but she steeled herself to walk away. Gervase waited until he heard the door open and close, then he spoke.

"I will not hurt you, Cild. I am trying to find out how and why your father was killed. Will you help me?"

The boy glowered at him but said nothing.

"Let me be frank," said Gervase softly. "We have been to the mill and found your rope. We have been to the mint and found your way in. We have been to the yew tree and found your snake. We know a lot about you already, Cild."

The boy's cheeks flushed with guilt and he lowered his head. Gervase used gentle words that slashed like knives. Cild was in pain. He had thought he was safe, but Gervase Bret was dragging him back into a past that was littered with horror for him. The sight of the gory Wulfgeat came up to fill his mind and his stomach heaved.

Gervase did not browbeat. "You have done wrong," he said calmly, "but only because you were too young to know any better. You were led cruelly astray. Help yourself by telling the truth. It is the only way forward, Cild. If you lie to me, I will know. Is that clear?"

"Yes," muttered the boy.

"Did you break into the mint?" Cild shifted uneasily and Gervase applied more pressure. "Did you?"

"Yes."

"Did you take an impression of the die?"

"Yes."

"Did you give it to your father?"

"Yes."

"Did he pass it on to someone else?"

"Yes."

"What was his name?"

The boy lapsed back into a watchful silence. Gervase saw the insolence in his gaze and hardened his voice.

"We know about Wulfgeat," he stressed. "You put that snake in the sack so that it would bite him. He was your father's enemy and you wanted him dead. Murder is the most serious crime of all, even when it is only plotted. Can you hear what I am saying to you, Cild?"

"Yes."

"You must hold nothing back."

"Yes."

"Did your father have an accomplice?"

"Yes."

"Did they share the money between them?"

"They did."

"Was it someone from Bedwyn?"

"It was."

"Who?" The boy moved from foot to foot again as Gervase gave him no respite. "Who was the man, Cild? Tell me."

"I do not know."

"Who?"

"I do not know."

"Who!" demanded Gervase. "Who!"

"My father would not say!" he cried out in despair.

The boy's defences cracked and he burst into tears as the real horror of what he had done was borne in upon him. His youth was no excuse. Cild was old enough to know that theft and forgery and attempted murder were serious crimes that carried serious penalties. His father had made it seem exciting to break into the mint and he had loved the secret journeys the two of them had made to the hiding-place in the yew tree. Everything had cartwheeled out of control now. He was willing to tell Gervase Bret all he knew in the hope of gaining merciful treatment, but he could not supply a name that his father had kept from him.

Gervase saw the boy's predicament only too clearly. He was at once an accomplice and victim of his father. There was no point in questioning Cild further, because it would only sharpen his anguish. He would need to be interrogated at a later date by other authorities. The one thing Gervase

225

needed to know was the one thing that the boy had not been told. He took pity on the whimpering Cild and moved across to him, but comforting arms had already encircled the child. Hilda slipped quietly into the room to pull him to her bosom and pat him soothingly on the back.

When Gervase looked into her face, he saw the change that had taken place. Innocence had now fled. The tears that had been shed for a brutal man had now dried up. A plaintive expression had hardened into a scowl. Her voice was clipped.

"*I* can give you a name."

The shire hall was full to capacity that afternoon for the final confrontation. All four commissioners were installed behind the table. Prior Baldwin and Subprior Matthew appeared for the abbey once more and sat upright in their seats with an arrogant humility. Hugh de Brionne lounged in a chair beside them, still basking in his fame as the putative saviour of Bedwyn and confident that this would elevate him above any petty squabbles over land. Saewold's rank also entitled him to a chair and Ediva had come along with her husband as an interested observer. The rows of benches were occupied by the burgesses, Leofgifu sitting proudly among them in her father's place, with Hilda at her side. Their presence at any time in such a place would have been arresting, but during a period of mourning it was doubly startling. Minor town officials stood at the rear. Those of lesser sort found what space they could. Tall and forbidding in their chain mail, the four men-at-arms took up their positions just inside the door of the hall. There was an audible throb of expectation throughout the building.

Ralph Delchard called the assembly to order, then gave Canon Hubert his head. The commissioners' terms of reference were set out for all to hear.

"Earlier this year," recited Hubert, "our predecessors visited this county to assess the disposition of its wealth. The returns from that visit were set alongside similar details from other parts of the country so that a complete description of England could be built up. The largest holder of land in this county is—as is right and proper—King William himself, who not only took over, in 1066, the royal estates, which include the boroughs of Bedwyn, Calne, Tilshead, and Warminster, but also reserved for himself the extensive personal holdings of the families of King Edward and the usurper, Harold." There were murmurings of discontent from the benches. "The estates of King William now account for almost one-fifth of the area of this county."

The discontent became more vocal and Ralph had to curb it with his most belligerent glare before Hubert could continue. The litany rolled on.

"Next in order of wealth come four great ecclesiastical persons who built up their estates by gift and purchase well before the Conquest. They are the Bishop of Salisbury, the Bishop of Winchester, the Abbot of Glastonbury, and the Abbot of Malmesbury. Substantial holdings have also accrued to another monastic house and it is this circumstance which has brought us all here today. I speak of Bedwyn Abbey."

Prior Baldwin was unafraid. The prefatory remarks served only to inflate his confidence. Canon Hubert rumbled on with sententious fluency while Brother Simon nodded his agreement to almost every syllable that was uttered. Ralph let his colleague proceed for another five minutes before he leaned across to Gervase Bret and whispered in his ear.

"Hubert has bored them into submission. We may start."

When the speaker next paused for breath, the leader of the commissioners stepped in smartly to take over the reins.

"Thank you, Canon Hubert," he said with exaggerated graciousness. "That was a most lucid account of our presence here today. We may now move on. Like you, I will be brief."

Laughter rocked the benches at Hubert's expense. There were muted jeers from the rear of the hall. Everyone knew how rich the monastic foundations were and how pervasive their influence in the county, and they did not wish to be reminded of the power of the Church by a pompous churchman. The four ecclesiastics cited owned between them almost a quarter of all the land in Wiltshire, and there were other holy fingers in the pie. The bishops of Bayeux, Coutances, and Lisieux—all friends or relations of the king—had combined holdings of over five hundred acres and they were not the only Norman prelates who acted as absentee landlords over prime English estates. Bedwyn was a God-fearing town, but it could still resent the yoke of His ministers.

"Our enquiry," said Ralph, "related to two small hides of land. Those two quickly became four; those four multiplied still further. We were forced to broaden the scope of our investigations as the catalogue of fraud and deception grew in length." He held a long pause, then flashed a brilliant smile. "There are guilty men in this hall."

One of them was on his feet immediately.

"I will not stay and listen to these vile accusations," said Hugh de Brionne. "I have a rightful claim to all four hides but am left with two. And now you dare to try to rob me of those. It is intolerable!"

"Sit down, my lord," invited Ralph.

"Do you now know who I am—and *what* I am!"

"We certainly know what you are," said Ralph levelly. "And if you will not resume your seat and listen, the king will hear personally of your misconduct."

Hugh de Brionne issued a torrent of abuse, then sank back into his chair and smouldered. His status as the wolf-killer counted for nothing before the commissioners, who instead were treating him as a quarry to be hunted. Ralph Delchard turned to Prior Baldwin and his assistant.

"Let us start with the two hides that provoked this boundary dispute. State the abbey's position, please."

"It remains what it has been from the start," said Baldwin without bothering to rise. "We hold that land and we have a charter to enforce our claim. It was seen and ac-

228

cepted by your predecessors. The abbey has the law on its side."

"My lord?" said Ralph. "What can you add to that?"

Hugh was direct. "Only that the abbot is a grasping monster who will steal every acre of land on which he can get his fat and greedy hands!"

"Insult!" howled Baldwin.

"Truth!" yelled Hugh.

"Sacrilege!"

"Theft!"

"I demand an apology!"

"You will get it through my arse!"

The onlookers roared with amusement at the sight of two Normans shouting wildly at each other. Ralph Delchard was enjoying it all too much himself to interrupt at first, but he eventually asserted his authority and delivered a joint reprimand. Now that the two major combatants had both drawn blood, it was time to bring in Gervase Bret.

He waited for complete silence before he spoke.

"I crave your indulgence," he began. "What I have to say reaches back in time, but it has a bearing on the present and affects many of you here in this hall. There has been wilful deceit. Restitution must be made."

Gervase had the full attention of the audience. If it was a case of restitution, then someone stood to gain and someone else to lose. Gervase indicated a colleague.

"Canon Hubert has told you of the royal estates and listed all the tenants-in-chief in this part of the county. King William took that land into his possession after the Conquest in 1066, but much else was spared. He respected the dispositions made by his predecessor and ratified them at his succession." Disagreement festered in the hall, but nobody gave it voice. "That predecessor was King Edward the Confessor, a good friend to Normandy, where he spent so many years in exile. But England had another king after Edward."

There was a buzz of astonishment. The Normans had tried to obliterate the memory of King Harold from the public mind and to consign him to history as a renegade, yet here was a senior member of the king's household daring to recognise the existence of the last Saxon ruler of the island. Prior Baldwin was scandalised, Subprior Matthew was outraged, and Hugh de Brionne was seething with fury. Both Canon Hubert and Brother Simon tried to signal their disapproval and even Ralph Delchard was discomfited.

Gervase ignored the hubbub and moved steadily on.

"Grants of land under King Edward were acknowledged. I have such a document before me. Grants of land under King Harold were void. I have an example of that here as well." Gervase held up a charter in each hand. "On the right, you see a grant of land to Heregod of Longdon, father of the miller Alric. It is a royal charter issued by King Edward. On the left, you see a grant of land to Wulfgeat, lately a burgess of this town. It is a royal charter issued by King Harold. One of these charters is still valid; one is not. They are linked, however, in a more sinister way." Gervase put the charters side by side on the table. "Because of these same documents, two men died in Savernake Forest."

The ripple of noise burst into a surge of speculation and Ralph had to thump the table and yell before he brought it under control again. Gervase was brisk with detail.

"As you all know," he said, "King Edward loved hunting. While riding in the royal forest at Queenhill, in the county of Worcestershire, he was thrown from his horse and knocked senseless. They carried him to a house on the outskirts of the village of Longdon where he rested and recovered. He showed his gratitude to his host by granting him four hides of land near one of his favourite hunting lodges. It was here in Bedwyn." Gervase had learned the whole story now. "Heregod moved his family here and occupied the mill, but his charter went astray when King Edward died. There was bitter conflict over the holding. Two of those hides came into the hands of Wulfgeat by courtesy of King Harold, but they were taken away again after the Conquest. Heregod lost four hides; Wulfgeat had two of them, then lost both. Where did they go?"

He looked first at Prior Baldwin and then at Hugh de Brionne. Both began to squirm slightly. Gervase struck home.

"The abbey seized Heregod's land by means of a forged charter," he decreed. "Hugh de Brionne took the two hides of Wulfgeat with no charter at all beyond the use of force."

Uproar ensued. The accused parties jumped to their feet to plead their innocence while the rest of the hall chanted their guilt. Ralph Delchard bellowed for silence, Canon Hubert delivered an impromptu sermon on the merits of restraint, and Brother Simon waved his quill ineffectually in the air. The four men-at-arms were quite unable to stifle the chaos. It seemed as if the commission's business would have to be suspended. Then the pandemonium ceased abruptly. Nobody seemed to know why at first and they stared at each other open-mouthed. Then they realised what had altered the whole atmosphere inside the hall. Abbot Serlo had entered.

He stood in the doorway with quiet dignity and waited while a path hastily cleared itself in front of him. Then he made a stately progress towards the table and held out a magisterial hand. Gervase gave him the charter which had come from the miller's chest and the abbot studied it with glaucous eyes. Prescience had brought him to the hall and conscience made him ready to face his accusers. Only he could truly speak for his abbey. In delegating the task to his subordinates, he was shirking a sacred duty. It was still not too late to make amends. He could not tarnish his hopes of sainthood at the eleventh hour. Abbot Serlo finished reading the document, then turned to address the hushed gathering. There was no hint of complaint, self-pity, or evasion.

"We have sinned," he said honestly. "For almost twenty years, the abbey has taken rent from land that belongs by right to the heirs of Heregod of Longdon. We have sinned against them and we will pay full recompense. Bedwyn Abbey will restore those two hides to its lawful holder and repay every penny that was harvested from them."

The simplicity of his public confession added to its force. He swung round to face the four commissioners.

"Bear with me," he requested. "How this has come about, I do not yet know, but I have my suspicions. Let me enquire further into the matter. You have uncovered one forgery. There may be others. I will work swiftly to rid my abbey of every whisper of evil."

One baleful stare was enough to jerk Baldwin and Matthew to their feet. Abbot Serlo left with the same ethereal tread with which he had entered, but his two companions crept out apprehensively behind him. There would be long and painful discussions within the abbey confines and further tremors would shake its ordered calm.

There was a general murmur of admiration for Abbot Serlo's performance and even the mocking Hugh de Brionne was for once impressed. The prelate had been dignified in defeat. He had also set a precedent, and Gervase Bret was quick to seize on it.

"The abbey has admitted its error and offered to pay for it in full," he said to Hugh. "Will you follow where they lead? Will you restore those two hides and offer recompense to the injured party?"

Hugh snarled and looked for a way out of his plight, but Ralph Delchard cut off his retreat. He threw a smile of gratitude to Ediva before he rounded on his opponent.

"If you wish to contest the matter," he threatened, "we will have to call witnesses. The town reeve will be first. He knows better than anyone how that land was obtained."

Hugh and Saewold coloured as they traded a look. A partnership which had brought mutual benefit to them over two decades had just fallen apart. Ralph somehow knew about the acquisition of two hides from Wulfgeat and he would prosecute his case vigorously. In admitting one abuse of property rights, Hugh might be able to conceal all the others. He stretched himself to his full height and strove for a gallantry that rang quite hollow.

"There is error on our side, too," he conceded, "and we

offer the most humble apologies for the oversight. I give my word as a soldier that it will be put right at once."

The commissioners were satisfied. Details had yet to be worked out and new documents drawn up, but that could wait. They had carried the day. When Ralph Delchard dismissed the assembly, he was actually given a cheer. Feared and resented when they came to Bedwyn, they had won a better opinion from the town. It would be a happier place for their visit. Hugh de Brionne made straight for Saewold and dragged him out. Ediva lingered to steal a last glance from Ralph. Canon Hubert congratulated himself on his crucial role in the afternoon's proceedings and Brother Simon reinforced that illusion by his unctuous flattery.

Leofgifu and Hilda descended on Gervase. They were both overwhelmed by the turn of events. Hilda sobbed with joy.

"It is all mine?" she said in disbelief.

"Yes," he promised. "You inherit from your husband."

"Four hides of land?"

"With all the arrears due to you, Hilda. Bedwyn Abbey and the lord of the manor of Chisbury will make you a rich woman between them."

"What will I do with such wealth?" she wondered.

"Enjoy it," said Leofgifu. "You deserve it."

Hilda took her hands and squeezed them hard.

"We will share this good fortune together."

Before Leofgifu could protest, there was a disturbance at the rear of the hall as someone tried to push in past the guards. Hot words were exchanged and a dog barked. Ralph saw the newcomer and snapped a command.

"Let her pass!"

Emma was released by two of the men-at-arms and she curled her lip at them before proceeding down the hall. Ralph knew that she would venture into the town only on an errand of the greatest importance and so he took her aside at once.

"How is your arm?" he asked considerately.

"It is better, my lord."

233

"No more threats from the town bullies?"

"They leave me alone now."

"Yes," said Ralph. "They needed a killer and Hugh de Brionne gave them one. That lifted suspicion from you. They no longer believe that your dog was the wolf of Savernake."

"He is not, my lord. The wolf is still in the forest."

"You have seen him?"

"I have come to take you to the place."

Bedwyn Abbey felt the chill wind of ignominy blowing through its cloisters. Abbot Serlo was closeted in his lodging with Prior Baldwin and Subprior Matthew as he tried to assess the extent of their perfidy. The absence of all three from Vespers made the singing flat and the obedientiaries dispirited. When their saint was angry, they all felt the weight of his displeasure. Brother Thaddeus was anxious.

"What has happened, Peter?" he asked.

"We will know in good time."

"Father Abbot went into the town with good humour and came back in disarray. What can have upset him?"

"He will tell us when he chooses."

"Someone will pay for this," said Thaddeus, spying a personal angle in it. "Should I lay in a supply of fresh birch twigs, do you think?"

"It will not be necessary."

"Father Abbot relies on my arm."

"Save it to guide the plough," said Peter.

They were walking across the cloister garth and talking in muted tones. Thaddeus wanted to probe deeper into the mystery of the abbot's wrath, but Peter saw something which made him excuse himself and hurry away. Brother Luke was in conversation with Gervase Bret.

"You work in the bakehouse, I believe," said Gervase.

"I learned the trade from my father."

"Where does the abbey get its grain?"

"It used to come from the mill of Alric Longdon."

Gervase heard what he expected, then turned to welcome

Peter as the sacristan came up with an enquiring smile. Brother Luke was now in the presence of the two men he respected most in the world, but they pulled him in opposite directions. He could not choose between them.

"Have no fear," said Gervase. "I have not come to seduce Luke away from the order. I merely require his assistance for a short while."

"My assistance?" said Luke.

"Leofgifu suffers greatly over the death of her father. I have tried to counsel against it because it may only increase her woe, but she insists on going there."

"Going where?" asked Peter.

"To the spot where he died."

"In the forest?"

"Yes, Peter," said Gervase with a sigh. "It was a grim place when Alric Longdon lay there, but now it has seen two hideous deaths. I hate to conduct her there."

"Nor shall you," said Peter firmly. "Leofgifu must not go. Her father is dead and she must mourn for him in the privacy of her house. Stifle these wild thoughts of hers."

"I have tried in vain."

"Let me speak to her."

"She refuses to see anyone else," said Gervase. "I have to humour this madness and that is why I come to you. It was Luke who guided us to that dreadful part of the forest and we need his help once more."

Luke was eager. "I will gladly give it, Gervase."

"No," said Peter, "you must stay here. Father Abbot would never give permission for you to leave."

"How, then, will we find the place?" asked Gervase. "I must take Leofgifu there this evening. She will give me no rest until I do. And she can find no peace herself until she knows the worst about her poor father."

"Let me go, Peter," said Luke. "Please let me go."

"Brother Thaddeus will teach them the way."

"But I know it as well as he."

Peter was adamant. "I will decide," he said.

The novice was abashed. A last chance to spend more

235

time with Gervase had just been crushed before his eyes. A final opportunity to seek advice from his new friend about the decision that confronted him had gone. He was forced to stay within the enclave. It made the pull of the outside world and its untold wonders even stronger. Obedience was a virtue, but it was one that was starting to suffocate him. Did Brother Luke really want to spend the rest of his days in such a way?

It was a warm evening and the insects still droned. The river curled on down to the town and some wildfowl wheeled and dipped above it. A light breeze fingered the leaves. It was a time for lovers to walk hand in hand beside the forest, but Gervase Bret found himself in another station. Led by the plodding Brother Thaddeus, he and Leofgifu went slowly along the river-bank and past Alric's mill. She was still in evident distress and had pulled her hood down to cover her face. Gervase offered his arm to support her.

Thaddeus made a few blundering attempts to comfort her, then fell into silence, striding out ahead of them and keeping an eye peeled for any suitable birch trees along the way. Peter had given him specific instructions and he did not deviate from them. When they reached the fork where the stream diverged from the river, their guide stopped and pointed.

"Climb up and follow the water."

"Will you not take us?" said Leofgifu.

"I would be in your way, dear lady. This is between you and your father, and I would not intrude. I will stay here."

"We will find it," said Gervase.

They went into the trees and began the ascent. Gervase waited until they were out of sight of Thaddeus, then he smiled at her in gratitude. Leofgifu was showing bravery and composure. She was unaware of the real danger that lurked, because she could not be told. She was simply doing what had been asked of her. Gervase knew the best route up the hill, but her slowness held him back. It took some time before they reached the point where the stream issued from the chalk. He drew her well back from the yew tree and indicated the patch of ground which had been churned up.

"Your father died here, Leofgifu," he said.

"Where was he standing?"

"Right on this spot."

Gervase Bret faced the bramble bushes as both Alric and Wulfgeat had done, but he was forewarned and forearmed in a way that they had not been. There was a hungry growl, then the head of a wolf came hurtling straight at him through the bushes. Leofgifu screamed in alarm, but Gervase was ready for his assailant. Flicking his head to avoid the snapping teeth, he grabbed at the body and got a firm hold. They fell to the ground and grappled madly. The teeth went for his throat, but he pushed the head aside with an arm. The struggle intensified. Gervase was no miller with his mind on his money. Nor was he a burgess with thoughts only of a charter. He was a strong young man with a dagger in his hand. When his first lunge drew blood, there was a yell of pain from a human mouth.

The wolf was driven to a frenzy and made one last effort to bite at his face. Gervase lay on his back, the animal astride him, holding it off with one hand while trying to stab it with the other. But the beast had a surge of manic power and the weapon was struck from Gervase's hand. The great ugly head rose up to strike and the silver teeth opened wide in a smile of triumph.

But the attack never came. Before the animal could move an inch, a sword whistled through the air and its head was sliced off. It spun through the air and rolled to a halt in the bushes. Ralph Delchard stood over the fallen body and kicked it aside. Gervase was panting too heavily to speak, but he gave a smile of thanks as his friend helped him up.

Leofgifu had been terrified by the suddenness of it all and had not dared to look at the fierce struggle. When Gervase put a consoling arm around her, she opened an eye to peep at the dead carcass and saw that it belonged to a man. The wolf of Savernake was no more than the head, skin, and paws of a real animal. A cunning craftsman had used his skill to construct a set of vicious silver teeth which were fitted into the mouth and which operated on a spring. The hands which had made an exquisite silver box in which to store frankincense could also produce this lethal device. A trusted sacristan with access to all the robes and vestments in the abbey had sewn the pelt of the wolf onto some rough dark cloth so that it formed a complete disguise for the wearer. He had even fixed silver spurs to the creature's claws so that it could tear its prey more readily. Designed and made in the abbey, the death garb was hidden near the place where it would be needed. When it was put on, it turned a thwarted lover into a wild animal.

Alric Longdon and Wulfgeat had indeed been savaged by the wolf of Savernake, but he was known by another name. The only person who could have lured him to that same part of the forest again was Leofgifu, and Gervase had used her quite deliberately for that purpose. Ralph had been stationed nearby to lend his help, but that did not lessen the horror of it all for Leofgifu. She was petrified. Clinging to Gervase, she stared down in disbelief at the face of the man she had once loved and whom her father had forced her to abandon. The person who had wanted to be her husband had degenerated into a manic killer. Murder had come full circle. Brother Peter now lay on the very spot where his victims had perished. The wolf of Savernake was slain.

Epilogue

IT WAS THE SECOND FUNERAL IN A WEEK TO BE HELD IN THE parish church at Bedwyn, but it was very different from the first ceremony. Alric Longdon had been buried as the prey of a wolf and sent into his grave by a handful of mourners. Wulfgeat had been buried as a murder victim and dispatched by half the town. The old Saxon priest had read the service over the proud Saxon burgess before commending him to his Maker. The coffin had then taken its grisly secret six feet down into the earth. Sorrow and revulsion had jostled those who watched.

Leofgifu was now truly in mourning. Her father had been killed by the man he had forbidden her to marry. Robbed of his happiness and forced to watch his beloved take another man as her husband, the silversmith had sought refuge behind the cowl, but it had not stilled his rage. His hatred of Wulfgeat had grown with the passing years and it had been expressed in the most appalling way in Savernake Forest. Leofgifu felt that she had to take some responsibility for the tragedy. As she wept over her father's corpse, she was steadied by the hand of Hilda. They were united in misery now. Their lives would henceforth be shared and the boy who had been corrupted by a malignant father would be redeemed by two loving mothers.

Brother Luke watched it all from the corner of the churchyard. The revelations about Brother Peter had been a shattering blow to him and he had prayed for guidance in his travail. When the funeral party began to disperse,

239

Gervase Bret walked across to the novice for a parting word.

"Forgive him, Luke," he counselled. "Brother Peter was sick in his mind. He is to be pitied as well as reviled."

"My pity goes to Alric the Miller and to Wulfgeat."

"One was his friend and one was his enemy. He worked with Alric to produce those counterfeit coins and he put his share into the abbey coffers. It was a heinous crime, but Brother Peter was using foul means for a fair purpose."

"Why did he murder his accomplice?" said Luke.

"Because of the charter. Because Alric's money was used to purchase something which could threaten the abbey. That charter was bought with false coin. Peter was unwittingly helping to undermine the house which had taken him in and saved him from despair."

"So Alric betrayed him."

"Yes, Luke. That is why he was killed." Gervase glanced over at Hilda. "And maybe there was another reason."

"What was it?"

"Jealousy."

"How could Peter be jealous of a man like Alric?"

"Because of a woman like Hilda. When they devised their scheme to make counterfeit money, Peter saw it as a way to help the abbey. Not only did Alric spend his share on that troublesome charter; he used it to buy a beautiful wife."

Brother Luke understood. His erstwhile friend had fled into monastic life when the woman he loved was wrested away from him. Peter then had the galling experience of seeing an ugly and unprepossessing miller find himself an attractive young wife to share his bed. The worm of jealousy inside him grew into a writhing serpent and devoured all his scruples and restraints. Brother Peter struck out with envious brutality at another man's happiness.

Luke now realised something else as well. He saw that in asking him about the grain supply at the abbey, Gervase had been trying to establish a link between Alric and the sacristan. A miller with a reason to pay regular visits to the house could easily contrive meetings with his partner. Counterfeit coin could be hidden in an empty flour sack that was taken back to the mill. The accomplices had planned their villainy with care, but they were operating from different motives. That was what finally sundered them.

The novice's fresh face was crumpled with grief and disgust, but some good had come out of the hideous evil.

"I have made my decision," he announced.

"To leave the order?"

"To remain within it, Gervase."

"But why?"

"I take my example from Peter."

Gervase was stunned. "You admire a murderer?"

"No," said Luke, "but I seek to fathom the darkness of his mind. Inside the abbey, he was my dearest friend and the kindest soul in the world; outside it, he was a vicious fiend with a taste for blood." He looked up at Gervase. "Can you hear what I am saying?"

"Very clearly."

"Goodness lives within the order."

"Step outside it and terrible things may happen."

"It is the same with me, Gervase. I am a weak vessel. This cowl gives me strength and offers me a purpose that is worthy of me. If I forsook it, I would be led astray into all manner of transgression. I will stay where I am safe."

The clack of horses' hooves made Gervase look over his shoulder. His colleagues had come to collect him and had brought his mount with them. It was time to leave. Gervase turned back to the novice.

"I must be on my way, Luke," he said with reluctance. "You have chosen well and for the right reason. If I pass this way again, I will visit you at the abbey."

"You will always be welcome."

"And forgive Brother Peter in the fullness of time."

"I will try," said Luke. "His favourite quotation will serve to help me."

"What is it?"

" *'Cum dilectione hominum et odio vitiorum . . .'* "

"St. Augustine," said Gervase nostalgically.

" 'With love for mankind and hatred of sin.' "

"There is another translation, Luke, and it fits Peter's case more neatly: 'Love the sinner but hate the sin.' "

They embraced, then parted. Gervase crossed to the waiting horse and hauled himself up into the saddle. After a wave to Brother Luke, he set off with his companions on the road out of Bedwyn. They collected half-smiles and nods of gratitude as they went. The town would never love them, but it had learned to respect them. Injustice had been righted. They had confronted the might of an abbey and exposed wickedness at its very heart. Servants of a Norman king, they had not been afraid to denounce a Norman lord.

Ralph Delchard rode beside Gervase and boasted of their other successes in the town.

"We solved two murders and unmasked forgery," he said with a chuckle. "And all because I saved poor Emma from being torn apart by that mob."

"Come, Ralph," argued Gervase, clicking his tongue. "It was not as simple as that. My visit to the hermit turned our fortunes. It was he who took the chest from the yew tree and distributed the coins among the poor of the town. It was he who found that charter locked away with the money. Because I dragged that piece of sandstone to him, he gave us both chest and charter."

"Emma showed us where the wolf-skin was hidden."

"But who showed Emma?"

"My witch deserves all the credit."

"My hermit was the true hero."

"A Welshman would never aid a Norman!"

"This one did."

"Only because Emma put a spell on him."

They bickered happily for a mile, then agreed to see the whole visit to Bedwyn as a collective triumph.

"Everyone helped," said Gervase. "Brother Luke helped by telling me about the abbey; Brother John helped by talk-

242

ing of his days as a rent-collector; Leofgifu helped by letting me see her father's papers."

"I, too, was helped," Ralph pointed out. "Saewold helped by going away to Salisbury and Ediva by staying at home. It was she who brought down Hugh de Brionne."

"Do not forget Hilda."

"It was she who gave us the name of Brother Peter."

"Only because Leofgifu had confided in her the details of her broken romance." Gervase grew sad again. "Now I see why Leofgifu pressed me so closely about life in an abbey. That was where her lover had been driven by desperation and she wanted to know exactly the kind of life that he had been leading since their enforced separation."

Ralph looked at him. "Do *you* still want to be a monk?"

"No, Ralph."

"Do you not pine for the celibate life?" he teased.

"No, Ralph."

"Would you not like to be another Abbot Serlo? There is a golden halo waiting for such a man." Ralph grinned and nudged him. "Be honest with me, Gervase. Do you not harbour a secret desire to emulate him? Would you not love to be revered by all as a saint?"

"Indeed, I would," confessed Gervase.

Then he remembered that Alys awaited him in Winchester.

"But not yet. . . ."

Edward Marston

Published by Fawcett Books.
Available in your local bookstore.